"Tell me, Abigail, why it is you don't subscribe to the belief of romantic love between marriage partners."

She blinked and cut a glance at John. "What?"

"I'm curious to know if you are one of those women looking for all-consuming passion in a marriage partner."

"I shall never marry."

He laughed, assuming she was joking. But when she simply stared at him, his amusement faded. "You cannot be serious."

She shrugged. "Who would marry me?" A faint smile traced her lips. "According to Dr. Pitcock, my head is too big."

"No—what he said is that you are surprisingly normal for such a bright woman. I suppose you think there isn't a man capable of keeping up with you."

Books by Elizabeth White

Love Inspired Historical

Redeeming Gabriel
Crescent City Courtship

Love Inspired Suspense

Under Cover of Darkness
Sounds of Silence
On Wings of Deliverance

ELIZABETH WHITE

As a teenager growing up in north Mississippi, Elizabeth White often relieved the tedium of history and science classes by losing herself in a romance novel hidden behind a textbook. Inevitably she began to write stories of her own. Torn between her two loves—music and literature—she chose to pursue a career as a piano and voice teacher.

Along the way Beth married her own Prince Charming and followed him through seminary into church ministry. During a season of staying home with two babies, she rediscovered her love for writing romantic stories with a Christian worldview. A previously unmined streak of God-given determination carried her through the process of learning how to turn funny, mushy stuff into a publishable novel. Her first novella saw print in the banner year 2000.

Beth now lives on the Alabama Gulf Coast with her husband, two high-maintenance teenagers and a Boston terrier named Angel. She plays flute and pennywhistle in church orchestra, teaches second-grade Sunday school, paints portraits in chalk pastel and—of course—reads everything she can get her hands on. Creating stories of faith, where two people fall in love with each other and Jesus, is her passion and source of personal spiritual growth. She is always thrilled to hear from readers c/o Steeple Hill Books, 233 Broadway, Suite 1001, New York, NY 10279, or visit her on the Web at www.elizabethwhite.net.

ELIZABETH WHITE

Crescent City Courtship

Steeple
Hill®

Published by Steeple Hill Books™

STEEPLE HILL BOOKS

Steeple
Hill®

Recycling programs
for this product may
not exist in your area.

ISBN-13: 978-0-373-82814-2

CRESCENT CITY COURTSHIP

www.SteepleHill.com

Printed in U.S.A.

While Jesus was having dinner at Levi's house, many tax collectors and sinners were eating with him and his disciples, for there were many who followed him. When the teachers of the law who were Pharisees saw him eating with the sinners and tax collectors, they asked his disciples: "Why does he eat with tax collectors and sinners?" On hearing this, Jesus said to them, "It is not the healthy who need a doctor, but the sick. I have not come to call the righteous, but sinners."

—*Mark* 2:15–17

To Emma—because she loves historicals
and because she prays.

Chapter One

New Orleans, November 1879

Gasping for breath, Abigail Neal pounded on Charity Hospital's enormous oak front door, bruising her fist and driving a splinter into the heel of her hand. She'd covered the six blocks from the District at a flat-out run, but no one had offered to pick her up and take her to her destination. Not that she'd expected it.

"Come on, come on," she muttered. "Someone answer the door." She pounded again, this time with the flat of both hands. The sound echoed off the tall columns and wooden floor of the porch and reverberated through the hallway inside.

Where was everyone? Yanking the splinter out of her hand and sucking away a welling drop of blood, she peered through the little pane of glass in the door. Why lock the door of a hospital? To defend against marauding sick people?

Tess wasn't going to make it if a doctor didn't come soon.

Abigail was about to bang again when a pair of filmy,

protruding eyes met hers on the other side of the window. The latch scraped back and the door opened, revealing a short, barrel-chested man with a pockmarked face. "You'll have to go to the back door," he said, squinting up at her. "Nurses are all in evening prayers."

"I don't need a nurse. I want a doctor." Abigail forced herself to stand still, clutching her fingers together to keep from wringing her hands. People often wouldn't help a person who seemed desperate.

The man scratched his head, disturbing the few wisps of gray hair clinging to his shining scalp. "Ain't no doctors here to the front. That's why I says go to the back and wait—that's where the clinic is." He looked her up and down. "You don't look sick, no ways."

"I'm not sick," Abigail said, striving for patience. "I want you to fetch a doctor so that I can take him back to the—I want him to come with me."

"Ain't none here right now," the guard repeated stubbornly. "Doc Laniere's teaching a surgery lesson—"

"Doctor Laniere?" Abigail grabbed the man's arm. "He's the one I want. Someone told me he's very kind and he's the best doctor in the city."

"He's the best all right. But he's busy, and—"

"Take me to him immediately." Abigail straightened, well aware of the intimidating effect of her full height. "What is your name?"

"They call me Crutch." The man glanced uneasily over his shoulder. "Mayhap I could see if Nurse Charlemagne—"

"I told you I don't want a nurse. I want the doctor." Abigail found herself on the verge of frustrated tears. Every moment of delay endangered not only Tess's life but that of the baby. Pride hadn't done a bit of good so far. "Please, Mr.

Crutch. My friend is having her baby—she's been laboring all day and most of last night. She's getting weak, I don't have a way to get her here and I don't know what to do."

An enormous sigh was followed by a clicking of tongue against teeth. "He's gonna squash me like a mosquito," Crutch muttered, then to Abigail's relief, disappeared through a white pedimented doorway beyond the staircase.

Even though Crutch left the door standing wide, allowing an unobstructed view of the unadorned entryway, Abigail remained on the enormous two-story porch, unwilling to risk expulsion. She stood watching horse-drawn carriages rattle down Common Street. Some turned on Baronne before reaching the hospital, some continued to Philippa, where they rounded the corner of the beautiful green sward of grass which gave Common Street its name, then disappeared beyond tall rows of businesses. The scene was infinitely refined and orderly.

And she was going to bring the great doctor back with her to a tenement in the District. Well, he would just have to take her and Tess as he found them. She sat down on the broad top step of the porch and linked her fingers across her knees.

An interminable time later, Abigail heard the clatter of footsteps on the stairs behind her. She jumped to her feet and turned, expecting to see Crutch returning with the doctor. Instead she found a young man striding toward her with a black leather case in one hand and a fine felt hat in the other.

"I'm John Braddock," he said with curt nod. "I understand you need a doctor."

"Yes, but—" Wide-eyed, she stared at him. That name. What an odd coincidence. She blinked. "Mr. Crutch went for Dr. Laniere. He should be right back."

"I sent him to bring the mule cart around for us."

"But—I wanted the house surgeon. Where is he?"

Braddock frowned. "Dr. Laniere is conducting a surgery. Do you or do you not need a doctor?"

"I do, but—"

"Then we'd best hurry. Here's Crutch with the cart." He ran down the steps to the drive path, where the messenger was alighting from a small wagon pulled by a lop-eared mule.

Abigail picked up her skirts and followed. "But are you a doctor?" He was very young, perhaps in his mid-twenties.

Braddock vaulted onto the seat of the cart and took the reins from Crutch. "This is a medical college," he said, reaching a hand down to Abigail. "I'm a second-year student, top of my class. Professor Laniere wouldn't have sent me if he didn't think I could deliver a baby. Come on, get in."

Abigail stared up at him. A *student?* But Dr. Laniere was in surgery and Tess needed help now. She allowed young Braddock to pull her up onto the narrow seat, settling as far away from him as she dared without pitching herself onto the pavement.

"Where is the patient?" he asked, glancing at her.

"Tchapitoulas Street."

"That's a long street. Which part?"

"The District," she managed, burning with humiliation. "We're next to the saloon on the corner of Poydras."

"I might have known." He flapped the reins to set the cart into motion.

Abigail refused to look at him again, although the jostling of the cart forced her elbow to brush his again and again. She gritted her teeth. By the time they traversed the short distance to the tenement room she shared with Tess, her nerves were a raw jangle of anxiety, fear and resentment.

The young doctor spoke not another word to her until

he stopped the cart in front of the saloon and lightly jumped down to tie the mule to a hitching post. He reached for his bag, then offered a hand to Abigail. "Perhaps you could tell me what the trouble is and who I'm to treat."

Disdaining his hand, Abigail got down from the cart on her own. "My friend Tess has been laboring to deliver her baby all day and most of last night. She was so weak and frightened…I didn't know what to do."

"When did contractions start?"

Abigail hurried for the door of the tenement. "About this time yesterday."

Braddock grabbed her arm. "She's been in labor for twenty-four hours and you're just now asking for help?"

"I've delivered babies before." She jerked away from him. "It's just that I've never encountered this difficulty." Not for the first time she wished she'd had the opportunity for training this rich boy had. Then she'd have known what to do without incurring his disdain.

"Never mind. Which room?" They were in the tiny ground-floor entryway. Narrow unpainted doors opened to the right and left and the treads of a rickety staircase wobbled straight ahead.

"This way." Abigail turned to the door on the right and lifted the door latch. There was no key because there was no lock. "Tess?" She entered the dark, shabby little room, frightened by the silence. She could sense the silent young doctor behind her.

A soft moan came from the shadows where Tess's pallet lay against the wall.

Relieved, Abigail hurried over. "Tess, I've brought a doctor. He's going to help us bring the baby out."

"I can't…I'm too tired, Abby." Tess's voice was a thread.

Abigail fell to her knees and laid a gentle hand on Tess's distended belly. "Yes, you can. Dr. Braddock is going to help you." She looked over her shoulder to find him setting his bag on the table.

He looked up. "We'll need all the extra linens you have. You've a way to boil water?"

Abigail swallowed. "Of course."

"Abigail? Abby?" Tess's voice sounded terrified. "It's starting again. The pain—" A scream interrupted her words, ripping from the center of her being.

Torn between compassion and the practical need to attend to the doctor's wishes, Abigail hurried to find the pile of clean rags she'd been collecting against Tess's lying-in. As she mended the fire she'd left burning low in the tiny cookstove that squatted against the only exterior wall of the room, she was conscious of Tess's inhuman, wailing accompaniment to Braddock's rather jerky movements.

He laid out a collection of shining instruments on one of the rags, arranging them with fastidious neatness. He seemed slow, reluctant.

She watched him with resentment. *She* should be the doctor, not him.

By the time she had a tin pot of water boiling to her satisfaction on the stovetop, Tess's screams had subsided to whimpers. Abigail gestured for Braddock's attention. "Now what?"

He got to his feet. "We need to let the water cool a few minutes. I want to wash my hands and instruments. Do you have lye soap?"

She frowned. "We need to hurry. She's not going to be able to stand another contraction like that."

Braddock scowled. "I'll remind you that you came to me for help. Professor always washes everything."

Abigail stared at him. If she argued with him, he would stand there until Kingdom Come, and Tess would die. Tight-lipped, she found him the soap, then knelt beside Tess to bathe her head with a cool cloth. "Hold on," she murmured. "Just a few more minutes."

Behind her John Braddock doused his instruments one by one in the boiling water, then returned them to the clean cloth. After removing the pot from the stove, he stood waiting for it to cool, hands in the pockets of his trousers, staring at nothing.

Abigail watched him. His body was tall and strongly built inside those fashionable clothes. He'd laid the beautiful hat on the shaky pine table, revealing a headful of wavy golden brown hair. She supposed one could call him good-looking, although her perspective on handsome men was admittedly skewed. She had yet to see him smile, but his nose was firmly arched, with fine nostrils, and the eyes wide-set and intelligent.

His brain was the most important part of his body as far as she was concerned.

Finally, just as Tess started screaming again, he decided the water was cool enough to the touch and proceeded to thoroughly soap and rinse his hands. Catching Abigail staring as he dried them, he gave her a mocking bow.

"Now, your ladyship, I'm ready."

Chapter Two

John knelt beside his moaning patient and stared at the baby in his hands. For the first time in his life he uttered the name of God in prayer. He'd never lost a life before— at least not on his own.

He laid the stillborn infant on a ragged towel, then turned to the woman who had been quietly hovering behind him for the past two hours. He held out a shaking hand. "Give me that needle and suture."

She handed him the implements he required, watching his every movement with vigilant, protective eyes.

He began the job of sewing up the woman's torn body. "Here, hold this sponge."

His provisional nurse knelt and followed his gestured instructions. "What about the baby?"

"You can bury it later. It's more important to take care of your friend."

Abigail gasped, dropping the sponge. "The baby's dead? How could you let it die?" She picked up the infant and cradled it against her bodice. Her face twisted and silent sobs began to shake her thin body.

John swallowed against a surge of sympathy but kept stitching. Crying wasn't going to bring the baby back to life. He finished the sutures, efficiently mopped the wound and sat back on his heels. He studied his patient's chalky face. At least she was still breathing, harsh painful gasps between bloodless lips. Her eyes squeezed shut as he drew her dress down over her knees. She would live.

"Where's her husband?" He got up to rinse his hands in a bowl of sterilized water, wiped them on the last clean towel, then opened his bag to stow his instruments.

"I'm not married." The gritty whisper came from his patient. Grunting, she tried to sit up. "Abigail, let me see the baby."

"Here, lie down or you'll start the bleeding again." John knelt to put a hand to her shoulder, which was almost as thin as the skeleton that sat in a spare chair in his boarding house bedroom.

The patient speared him with pain-clouded eyes. "I have to see him."

"It's—it was a girl," John stammered. "She didn't make it."

"A girl. Please, let me hold her just a minute."

John met Abigail's eyes for an agonized moment. She looked away.

"Give it to her," he managed.

His patient took the infant's naked, messy little body against her own, cuddling it as if it were alive and ready to suckle.

What was a fellow supposed to do? He was no minister capable of dealing with these depths of grief. Inarticulate anger seized him as he took a deliberate look around. The tiny, shabby tenement room was scrupulously clean—apparently the lye soap had been put to use—but the odor of mildew and age infused every breath he took. This was no place for two young women to live alone, no matter what their morals.

Dr. Laniere would have known exactly how to deal with the situation. But back at the hospital, Crutch had interrupted the professor demonstrating the amputation of an infected finger for a ring of medical students. The professor had sent John, assuring him he was perfectly capable of delivering a baby.

Eagerly he'd accepted the assignment. John had always assumed he could do anything he set his mind to. But his confidence had diminished as he realized the breech presentation had left the baby in the birth canal too long.

Capable. A crack of despairing laughter escaped him. Lesson learned.

Unfortunately, there was nothing more he could do here. Snapping the latch of his bag, he turned toward the door.

He'd taken no more than a couple of steps when he found himself deluged from behind by lukewarm water. It streamed down the back of his neck, plastered his hair to his forehead and nearly strangled him as he took a startled breath.

With a choked exclamation, he turned to find Abigail glaring at him, the cracked pottery bowl held in her hands like a battle mace.

"Where do you think you're going?" she demanded, looking as if she might fling the bowl at his head, too.

Speechless, John dropped his bag and swiped water out of his eyes with his sleeve. Intent on getting to the patient, he hadn't properly looked at the woman who had summoned him. For the first time it dawned on him that the woman's few words had been spoken in cultured tones, rather than the typical Creole waterfront accent. And although she was dressed in a ratty brown skirt and blouse, she had the tall, sturdy build of a warrior princess. Nobody would call this woman beautiful, but it was a face a man couldn't forget once he'd seen it.

A furious face. Light green eyes glittered with the flame of peridots set in gold.

John found his voice. "How dare you."

It wasn't a question. It was his equivalent of a bowl of water dumped over the head, uttered in a drawl cultured by a lifetime spent in the elite drawing rooms of New Orleans.

"How dare I?" She bared a set of lovely white teeth, but it was not a smile. She clonked the bowl down on the table and stalked up to him. He was a tall man and her eyes were on a level with his lips. "I'll tell you how I dare. I prayed for you. Not for Tess and the baby, but for *you!* I could tell you were scared spitless, you stuck-up beast." She sucked in a breath. "You *laughed.*"

Stung to the heart, John sucked in a breath. Of course he hadn't been laughing at her or Tess, but at the irony of his own impotence.

"What do you want me to do?" he said through stiff lips. He could hardly let her see his humiliation, but perhaps he could redeem himself somewhat.

The girl studied him, taken aback, as though she'd expected him to either hit her or leave without a word. "You could at least help me bury the baby."

"I'm a doctor, not a grave digger."

"You're not much of a doctor, either."

John flinched at this brutal truth. "Is there a…grave-yard nearby?"

The girl shook her head. "We're nearly underwater here. The charity burial grounds is on the north side of the city."

Tess began to cry, clutching the child closer.

John didn't know what to do with this slide into help-lessness. Despite her derisive words, Abigail looked at him as if she expected him to do something heroic. Clearly he had a maudlin trollop, a corpse and an angry Amazon to deal with before he could go home and go to bed. And he'd been up since before dawn.

With a sigh he walked toward a rusty sink in the corner of the room and activated the pump. He stuck his head under the anemic stream of murky water, rubbed hard, and came up dripping. His coat was ruined, but that was the least of his worries at the moment. Slicking his hair back with both hands, he turned. "Abigail, wash the baby and wrap her in a blanket. We'll take Tess to Dr. Laniere. Then I'll send someone from the hospital to take care of the burial."

Abigail nodded, a rather contemptuous jerk of her severely coifed brown head, but moved to obey.

John knelt beside his patient. "Where are your clean clothes?" He touched her shoulder again, aware of the awkwardness of the gesture.

Her anxious dark eyes followed Abigail's ministrations to the child. She shook her head. "I don't have any."

John sat back on his heels and looked around. Other than the cookstove, a shaky three-legged table shoved next to the far wall and the two straw-filled cots, there wasn't a stick of furniture in the room.

His sister, Lisette, had two armoires stuffed with more dresses than she could wear in a year. Her shoes lined a dressing room shelf that ran the entire length of her bedroom.

The abject poverty of these women filled him with guilt.

Releasing a breath, he gathered Tess up in his arms, ignoring the blood on her skirt that soaked through his sleeve and the shabby shoes tied to her feet by bits of rope. He concentrated on rising without disturbing her sutures.

The girl let out a gasp of pain and clutched his neck.

"It's all right, you're all right," he muttered.

"Be careful!" Abigail turned, clutching the blanket-wrapped bundle close. "Should I go look for help?"

The last of John's patience fled. "Just open the door," he said through his teeth.

Those light eyes narrowed. She gave John a mocking curtsy as he passed with Tess in his arms. "Your lordship."

He was grateful to find the cart still tied in front of the building. Equipages had been known to disappear during calls in this part of the city, especially after dark. Thank God he had decided at the last minute to bring it. Riding would have been faster, but one never knew when a patient would have to be hauled to hospital.

Hitching her skirt nearly to mid-calf, Abigail climbed into the back of the cart with a lithe motion that gave John an unobstructed view of trim ankles and a pair of down-at-the-heels black-buttoned boots. She sank cross-legged onto the clean straw and opened her arms. "Here, lay her head in my lap."

Swallowing a time-wasting retort, John complied. Later he would impress upon her who was in charge.

Abigail stroked Tess's damp reddish hair off her forehead, a tender gesture at odds with her brisk, no-nonsense manner. She looked up at John, brows raised. "Let's go."

Scowling at her presumption, John climbed onto the narrow bench at the front of the cart and flapped the reins.

With a snort the mule jerked into motion. As the cart bumped over the uneven bricks of Tchapitoulas Street, John could hear an occasional groan from his patient, accompanied by hisses of sympathy from Abigail.

"Can't you be more careful?" she shouted over the clop of the mule's hooves and the rattle of the cart.

He stopped, letting another wagon and several pedestrians pass, and stared at her over his shoulder. "Would you care to drive, Miss—?"

"Neal." Darkness had nearly overtaken the waterfront, but John detected a hint of amusement in her tone. "My papa often asked my mother the same thing when I was a little girl." All traces of levity vanished as she sighed. "Forgive me. I know we have to hurry."

"Yes. We do." Surprised by the apology and puzzled by an occasional odd, sing-song lilt in the girl's cultured voice, John stared a moment longer, then turned and clicked his tongue at the mule. He would question Abigail later—after the baby was buried.

A grueling ten minutes later, the cart turned a corner onto St. Joseph Street, leaving behind the waterfront's crowded rail depots, dilapidated shanties, cotton presses and towering warehouses. Inside the business district, two- and three-story brick buildings hovered on either side of the narrow street like overprotective mammies. Streams of green-slimed water, the result of a recent rain, rushed in the open gutters beside the undulating sidewalks. Businessmen intent on getting home after the day's work hurried along, ignoring the stench of decayed vegetation, sewage and shellfish that permeated everything.

John frowned, unable to overlook the city squalor. He had tried to convince his father that a platform of sanitation reform would solidify his mayoral campaign. The senior Braddock preferred more socially palatable topics of debate. If all went well, John's father would be elected in November.

If all did not go well, the pressure would be on John to quit medical school, go into the family shipping business and try for political office himself. Phillip Braddock often opined that power was a tool for good; he meant to grab as much as possible, even if it had to come through his son.

Because John had no intention of becoming anyone's puppet, he was concentrating on getting his medical diploma and staying out of the old man's way. As much as John admired him, his father had a great deal in common with the new steam-powered road rollers.

As he guided the cart onto Rue Baronne, he wondered what his father would have to say about these two passengers. Probably shake his leonine head and expound at length on the wages of sin.

He glanced over his shoulder again. Abigail had rested her elbow on the side of the cart and propped her head against her hand. She seemed, incredibly, to be asleep, with Tess dozing in her lap.

What set of circumstances had brought the two of them to such a pass? He saw women like them often, when he and his friends did rounds in the waterfront, but he'd never before had such a personal confrontation with a patient. Or a patient's caregiver.

"You just passed the hospital," Abigail said suddenly.

"I thought you were asleep." Annoyed to have been caught daydreaming, John flipped the reins to make the mule pick up his pace. "We're not stopping at the hospital.

Dr. Laniere has a clinic and a few beds at his home. Tess will be better cared for there."

"I see." Abigail was quiet for the remainder of the trip.

The professor's residence on Rue Gironde was a lovely three-story brick Greek revival, with soaring columns supporting a balcony and flanking a grand front entrance at the head of a flight of six broad, shallow brick steps. Wrought iron graced the balcony and the steps, lending a charming whimsy to the formal design of the house.

John bypassed the curve of the drive circling in front of the house and took a narrower path that passed alongside and led around to the back entrance into the kitchen and clinic. The house and grounds were as familiar to him as the home he'd grown up in. The Braddocks and the Lanieres had maintained social ties since John was a boy, despite the fact that the Lanieres' loyalties to the Confederacy during the "late upheaval" had been in serious doubt. It was even rumored that Gabriel Laniere had been a Union spy and had fled prosecution as a traitor, leaving Mobile with his wife and a couple of body servants in tow. Phillip Braddock chose to discount such nonsense; ten years ago he had been appointed to the board of directors of the medical college, and remained one of its main financial contributors and fund-raisers.

John drew up under a white-painted portico designed more for function than elegance, which opened into a tiny waiting room off the clinic. He got out and tied the mule, then went around to reach for Tess and the baby. As he slid his arms under her back and knees, Abigail stopped him with a hand on his shoulder. An oil lantern hanging beside the door illuminated a surprising sprinkle of freckles across her formidable nose.

"Thank you for bringing us here," she said. "You didn't have to."

And why had he? John studied the anxious pucker between her level brows. He frowned and straightened. "Hope Willie's still here," he muttered to himself. "We'll need to send the baby to the hospital for burial preparation while we get Tess settled." He shifted his burden and stepped back. "She needs a clean gown and I want to check her sutures after that ride."

Abigail struggled to her feet, apparently numb from having sat in one position so long. "Who's Willie?"

"House servant. Butler, coachman, a bit of everything." John moved aside as Abigail swung over the side of the cart to the ground. When she appeared to be steady on her feet, he jerked his chin at the door. "Ring the bell and somebody will let us in."

Abigail pulled the tasseled bell cord and moments later the door opened with a jerk.

"Winona." For the hundredth time John shook his head at the waste of such exotic loveliness cooped up in a kitchen and doctor's clinic. "Is there an empty bed in the ward?"

The Lanieres' young housekeeper's smooth dark brow folded in instant lines of concern. "Mr. John! What you doin' here so late?" Clucking her tongue, Winona moved back to let him enter with his slight burden. "Of course there's a bed. Nobody else here, in fact. Who's this poor lady?"

She led the way out of the waiting room into the well-stocked dispensary, then into a third room. She lit a gas lamp on a plain side table. Bathed as it was in quiet shadows and antiseptic odors, the room looked inviting enough. John was glad he'd elected to come here, rather than the hospital.

"A maternity call I made late this afternoon. Breech

delivery." As Winona turned down one of the four beds with movements unhurried but efficient, John kept an eye on Abigail. She stood just inside the room, hands clenched in the folds of her skirt. She looked more than out of place. She kept looking out the window as if expecting to be followed. "This is Abigail Neal," he said.

Winona, in her unassuming way, exchanged nods with the other woman.

"We lost the baby," John said as he laid his burden on the smooth, clean sheet.

"Bless her heart," Winona breathed, touching Tess's wan face and pulling up the top sheet.

"She'll be fine, but we need to arrange a burial in the morning." John took the baby out of Tess's arms. "Where's Dr. Laniere?"

"Gone to deliver another baby."

John winced. "Gone how long?"

"Maybe an hour. He'd just come back from the hospital and sat down to supper. Miss Camilla's upstairs puttin' the children to bed."

"All right. I'll stay until he comes back." John glanced at Abigail, who looked like she might topple over, if not for the wall behind her. "Winona, could you fix Miss Neal a cup of tea and a biscuit or two? Maybe find her a clean dress and a nightgown for the patient?"

Winona nodded. "Was just goin' to suggest that. Be back in a bit." She paused in the kitchen doorway and gave Abigail a kind glance over her shoulder. "Ma'am, there's a chair over there in the corner if you want to sit down."

"Thank you—" But Winona had already disappeared. "What a lovely young woman." Abigail moved the wooden straight chair close to the bed.

"Yes, and she's a wonderful cook, too." John had been moving about the room, but when the silence became prolonged, he looked around to find Abigail, head bent, folding pleats in her ugly skirt. "What's the matter?"

"Nothing."

John shrugged and moved to the window, where he stared at his reflection in the dark window. He hoped the professor would be back soon.

Chapter Three

Abigail straightened the lye-scented sheet across Tess's shoulders and brushed the lank hair away from her face. The chair beside the cot had become most uncomfortable in the last hour, despite the pleasure of the tea and biscuits Winona had provided.

Tess, now clothed in a plain white nightgown Winona pulled from a supply closet, was finally asleep. Abigail herself had been given a faded dark blue cotton dress with elegant jet buttons marching up the front and ending at a neat white stand-up collar. She couldn't remember ever having worn such a lovely garment.

She looked up at John Braddock. He had ceased prowling the room and now towered at the foot of the bed, holding Tess's nameless little one close to his sharp-planed face. He had not put the baby down once since he'd picked her up. Expression somber, he brushed the waxen cheek with his knuckle, then examined her minute fingers one by one.

Abigail wondered what drove the emotions that crossed his expressive face. Was it remorse for the loss of his little patient? Did he regret his earlier condescension?

She could hardly believe some of the things she'd done and said to him in the past few hours. Up to this point, her anger at him and fear for Tess had given Abigail strength beyond herself, but something about the young doctor's tearless grief flayed her emotions. She bent to lay her forehead beside Tess's shoulder and let hot tears soak the sheet. She was empty. She didn't know what to do, where to turn.

"Birth and death, all at once."

Abigail turned her head. "What?"

"I never realized how closely tied they are. Some of us get a lot of time and some get none at all." John lifted his gaze from the baby's face and Abigail saw stark confusion in the heavy-lidded hazel eyes. "Do you think it's all predetermined? Am I wasting my time?"

"I don't know." She sat up and scrubbed away her tears with both hands. "The baby might have been dead before you got there." It was hard to admit that. "Tess would've died, too, if you hadn't come. I was thinking—I'm not sure I could've carried on if she had."

John's face was a study in consternation. "Is she your sister?"

"No." Abigail adjusted the sheet again and checked to make sure Tess's breathing was still regular. "Six months ago I arrived in New Orleans with nowhere to go, no family and no friends. Tess took me in and helped me find a job."

He stared at her and she felt her face heat. What must she look like to this educated, expensively dressed young high-brow? Even in stained and wrinkled clothing, with his thick hair falling into his eyes from a deep widow's peak, he looked like he belonged in somebody's parlor.

"Where did you come from?" His elegantly marked

brows drew together. "You don't look like the usual fare from the District."

Abigail came out of her chair. "Give me that baby right now—" she tugged at the infant corpse—"and get out of here." When he resisted, looking down at her as if she were crazy, she glared up into his multicolored eyes. "If you don't like the way I look, go put on your smoking jacket and settle down for a beer with the fellows. Then you can laugh over us slum wenches to your heart's content and not think about us one more second."

The fellow refused to behave in any predictable way. He hooked his free arm around Abigail's shoulders and yanked her close, the baby between them. "Abigail, I'm sorry." His voice was husky, almost inaudible.

Abigail stood with her face buried in the fine, still-damp wool of John's coat, the soft, bulky shell of a baby pressing against her bosom. Her world shifted.

How long? How long since she'd been held in the hard strength of a man's embrace? Not since she was a small girl, before her mother left and her father became the Voice of God.

She ought to pull away from this improper embrace. Humiliating to need it so much. No more crying, though. She stood stiff, wondering what he was thinking.

"Braddock, what's going on here?" The deep, resonant voice came from the doorway.

John Braddock let Abigail go and stepped back. "S-Sir! I'm so sorry, but I didn't know what else to do."

"Looked to me like you knew exactly what you were doing."

Abigail turned, straightening her hair and smoothing her skirt in the presence of the tall, distinguished man who strode into the clinic carrying a black medical bag. His thick black hair, gray-shot on the sides, and the lines fanning out from intelligent black eyes put his age somewhere in the mid-forties, but the trim, athletic figure would have rivaled many a younger man.

Abigail glanced at John, waiting for an introduction. The younger doctor seemed to be struck dumb with mortification. She dropped a curtsy toward the professor, whose mouth had quirked with disarming humor. "Thank you for coming, Dr. Laniere. I'm Abigail Neal. I'm the one who came for you on behalf of my friend Tess."

"Ah, yes." Dr. Laniere's expression sobered. "The difficult labor." He approached Tess and bent to lay a gentle hand against her forehead, then lifted her wrist to check her pulse.

Abigail met John's gaze. She started to speak, but he shook his head once, hard, his lips clamped together. "Prof, the baby didn't make it." At the professor's inquiring look John continued doggedly. "Breech presentation kept the baby too long without oxygen. The mother was losing blood quickly, so I made the decision to save her." His tone was firm, almost clinical, but Abigail heard the note of distress in the elegant drawl.

The young doctor's contained anguish inexplicably drew Abigail's sympathy. She had a crazy urge to comfort him.

Dr. Laniere steepled his fingers together, propping his forehead against their tips. For a moment the only sound in the room was Tess's harsh breathing, then the professor dropped his hands and looked up with a sigh. He approached John to clasp his shoulder. "We'll talk about your procedures later, Braddock." He laid his other hand on the baby's head, as if in benediction. "Why did you bring him here?"

Although he'd missed his guess at the swaddled

infant's sex, Abigail noted with gratitude that he didn't call the baby "it."

"They wanted a burial and didn't have any place to go," said John. "I told them you'd help us find a minister and a gravesite."

"Did you?" Dr. Laniere sounded amused.

"Please, sir," Abigail intervened before John's defensiveness could spoil their advantage. "We'd be grateful if you could help us. All we can afford is the charity catacombs and I just can't see that poor little one abandoned there."

Dr. Laniere stood with his hand resting on Braddock's shoulder, but he fixed Abigail with a look so full of compassion that she nearly broke down in tears again. "I understand your distress. But you know the baby is in the arms of the Father now." He smiled slightly. "Perhaps, of all of us, the *least* abandoned."

Abigail wished she could believe that.

Hope lifted the discouraged droop of John Braddock's mouth. "That's so, isn't it, sir?"

"As I live and breathe in Christ." Dr. Laniere squeezed his student's shoulder. "Now let's see what we can do to make your patient more comfortable and take care of the baby's resting place."

"You will not give her that beastly powder." Abigail stood in the kitchen doorway, effectively preventing John's entrance into the clinic. The professor had gone to take care of the burial arrangements, leaving the two of them to watch over Tess. "I've known women who never rid themselves of the craving, once they taste it."

John showed her the harmless-looking brown bottle of morphine. "But it would ease her pain and help her sleep."

"Yes, but if you slow her heart enough, she may not wake up at all."

"What do you know about it?" John stiffened. "We'll ask Dr. Laniere."

She'd studied on her own, but hadn't known enough to help her mother. "I know what I've seen—"

"John, at the risk of sounding uncivil, what are you doing here so late?"

Abigail turned.

A pretty, curly-haired young matron entered the clinic with a baby of about six months propped on her hip. She tipped her head to smile at Abigail around John's shoulder. "I'm Camilla Laniere. Meggins, say 'How do you do.'" She picked up the baby's hand to wave.

John looked guilty. "I'm sorry if we disturbed you."

"Nonsense. I was just surprised to see anyone here, that's all."

When the baby stuck her chubby fist in her mouth, Abigail smiled. "How do *you* do, young lady?"

"Afflicted by swollen gums, I'm afraid," said Mrs. Laniere, brushing her knuckles gently across the baby's flushed cheek. "We came down for a sliver of ice." She paused, a question in her soft voice. "I didn't know we had a patient in the clinic."

Abigail brushed past John. "I'm not the patient, ma'am. My name is Abigail Neal, and my friend Tess is in the ward here. Your husband sent Mr. Braddock to us. He brought us here when—" She faltered. "Tess is very ill. She lost her baby."

"I'm so very sorry." Mrs. Laniere reached to clasp Abigail's hand. She glanced at John, heading off his clear intention to continue the opium debate. "You did well to bring them here, John. What have you done with my husband?"

John blinked, reverting to some instinctive standard of manners. "He's taking care of laying out the—the body. He sent Willie to find a couple of grave diggers."

"Ah. Then I assume we'll have the burial in the morning."

"Yes, ma'am, before church." He hesitated. "Because the professor will be back soon, I believe I'll leave the patient in his hands. She's resting fairly comfortably now. I've a pharmacy test to study for." He pressed the vial of morphine into Abigail's hand. "You can trust Dr. Laniere to do the right thing."

"I'm sure I can." Pocketing the opiate, Abigail gave him a dismissive nod. "Good evening, Mr. Braddock."

"Good evening, Miss Neal."

When he closed the door behind him with a distinct thump, Meg flinched and snuggled her face into her mother's neck.

Shaking her head, Mrs. Laniere hugged the baby. "Please overlook John's abruptness. He's…a bit tense these days."

"I suppose I should have thanked him." Abigail leaned against the table, rubbing her aching temple. "Does he think he knows *everything?*"

"I'm afraid it's rather characteristic of the *genus homo.*" Mrs. Laniere smiled. "But John in particular, being considered brilliant in his field, tends to be a bit…insistent in expressing his opinions."

Abigail laughed. "That's one way to put it."

"You must be worried about your friend." Mrs. Laniere hesitated, swaying with the baby. "My dear, would you care to sit down with me for a cup of tea?"

"I couldn't impose. Tess—"

"—is resting. We'll be near enough to hear her if she

calls. And I'd like a bit of intelligent female conversation while I nurse the baby."

Abigail studied Camilla Laniere's frank, friendly face. There seemed to be no ulterior motive. She smiled faintly. "I'd adore a cup of tea, Mrs. Laniere."

"Please. Camilla. I'm not *that* much older than you."

The doctor's wife led the way into the kitchen, then unceremoniously handed the baby over to Abigail and began tea preparations. Despite her itchy gums, Meg seemed remarkably placid. Giving a contented sigh, she popped her thumb in her mouth and laid her head on Abigail's shoulder.

After a startled downward glance, Abigail smiled and patted her charge's cushioned bottom. Leaning against the dough box, she watched Camilla's familiar movements around the roomy, well-equipped kitchen. "Where did the servants go?"

"Winona and Willie are our only house servants." Camilla measured tea into a lovely floral china teapot. "They both go home on Saturday evenings to be with their families on the Lord's Day."

"I suppose we interrupted your family time tonight, but I was so grateful when your husband arrived—"

"My dear, you mustn't apologize." Camilla set the kettle on the stove to boil and smiled over her shoulder. "Gabriel is always glad to be of service. I would have been down here myself if I hadn't been putting the children to bed."

As Abigail stared into Camilla's golden-brown eyes, something flashed between them—an intuition of friendship, an offer of human connection. Abigail looked away, hardly able to bear this sudden kindness.

After a moment Camilla quietly took the baby, leaving Abigail empty-handed and feeling foolish. "I think you need a place to stay tonight. To be with your friend." She laughed as Abigail shook her head. "I'm being utterly selfish, you know. Winona and Willie won't be back until tomorrow evening. If our patient needs something, you'd be here for her."

"All right." Abigail returned the smile. "I'll stay. And of course you must call me Abigail. 'Miss Neal' ran away many years ago and hasn't been heard from since." Touching the baby's pink foot, she looked up from under her lashes. "Besides, I have to make sure the Barbarian doesn't try to feed opium to Tess."

Feeling a soft little hand patting her cheek, Abigail struggled out of deep sleep into utter darkness.

"Winona! Winona, wake up, I'm thirsty!" lisped the small, invisible person behind the hand. "It's hot and Mama's rocking the baby and I can't sleep."

Abigail suddenly remembered where she was. Winona's little room off the clinic, just a few steps from Tess's bed in the ward. This must be one of the Laniere children.

She sat up. "I'm not Winona, I'm Abigail. But I'll get you a drink of water—just a minute, let me light a candle."

"Ooh! Just like Goldilocks! What're you doing in Winona's bed?"

Abigail laughed. "Winona will be back tomorrow." Swinging her legs off the side of the bed, she lit the candle and held it up so she could see the wide, bespectacled eyes of a little boy who looked like his mother—probably around seven years old, judging by the missing front teeth. His hair curled in every direction but down and his night-gown was buttoned two buttons off, so that the hem hitched crookedly around his knees.

He poked his spectacles up on his button nose with one finger. "You ain't Goldilocks. Your hair's brown."

Abigail tugged the braid hanging over her shoulder, wishing for a proper nightcap. "It is indeed. What's your name?"

"Diron. Are you gonna get me a drink or not?"

Since Camilla had thoughtfully provided a pitcher of clean water and a cup for her guest before retiring, Abigail smiled and poured a drink for the boy. Diron downed it quickly and held out the cup for more. It was then that she noted the small red blister on the child's forehead.

"Just a minute." She reached out to push back the bright curls. His forehead was warm.

Enduring her touch with a long-suffering frown, Diron scratched his stomach.

"How long have you been itching?" she asked.

"I dunno. I must've got a bunch of mosquito bites. Can I *please* have some more water?"

"Certainly. But I want to see your tummy."

She poured the water, then while he drank it, matter-of-factly unbuttoned his nightgown. His chest and upper abdomen were covered with the tiny red blisters. Chicken pox.

No wonder the poor child was so hot and thirsty. Camilla was busy with the baby, but she would want to know.

When Diron finished his water, Abigail took him by the hand and led him into the clinic and through the kitchen. The sound of both of their bare feet slapping against the wooden floors tickled her sense of humor and she enjoyed the feel of his small warm hand in hers. He was a trusting little fellow.

In the carpeted hallway she saw the stairs to the upper

floors. It was a large, airy house, bigger than anything Abigail had been inside before, with lots of screened windows and light, gauzy curtains stirred by a cool night-time breeze.

On the first landing she felt Diron tug her hand. "Miss Lady. I'm tired." He gave an enormous yawn.

"Would you like a piggy-back ride?" He nodded and she walked down a few steps to let him climb on. "Goodness, you're a big boy." She grunted as he clutched her around the neck and waist. "Hold tight now."

As Abigail trudged up the remaining steps to the first floor, Diron leaned around. "Where'd you get that funny accent?"

"China," she replied without thinking.

"Oh, pooh. I didn't believe you was Goldilocks, neither."

Chapter Four

A chill had sneaked across the river during the night, sending fog drifting across the graveyard, twining through Abigail's hair and muting her and Dr. Laniere's footsteps. The ground was soft, even on this elevated patch a mile or so away from the river, and she had to step over puddles of water in the shallow hollows of sunken graves.

Abigail carried the baby, dressed in a tiny white gown worn by Meg just a few months ago. Camilla would have attended the funeral service, but she'd had to remain with the feverish and itchy Diron. Tess was induced to remain in bed only by Abigail's promise of writing down exactly what was said at her baby's interment.

They were to call her Caroline.

"Here we are," said Dr. Laniere, halting beside a tiny fresh grave, barely three feet long and a couple of feet wide. He opened the lid of the small wooden casket he'd carried from the house and looked across the top of it at Abigail. "It's time to put her in the casket." His deep-set dark eyes were somber, filled with sympathy. "Remember—"

"I know. She's with the Father." Abigail closed her mind against the instinct to pray. She'd been brought up to talk to God at every turn and the habit kicked in at moments of stress. But it was difficult to believe God was really interested in either her or this small wasted life.

Placing the baby in the box, she arranged the lacy white skirts in graceful folds. She was glad Tess couldn't see this. She could remember Caroline cuddled in her arms like a white-capped doll.

Dr. Laniere placed the lid on the box and was about to lower it into the grave when pounding footsteps approached.

"Wait!" John Braddock ran out of the mist, panting. In one hand he carried his black medical bag. "Professor, I want to see her again before you bury her."

Dr. Laniere straightened.

Abigail hadn't expected the young doctor to actually come for the burial. She was even more surprised that he'd apparently already been on a medical call. "What are you doing here?" she blurted, sounding perhaps more defensive than she'd intended.

"I've a right to be here," he said breathlessly. "I delivered this baby, and—" He swallowed. "Let me see her, please."

When the professor opened the box, Braddock removed his hat, clutching it as he stared at the baby. "I'm so sorry," he muttered. "I promise I'll learn to do better."

Abigail's throat closed. She didn't want to like this privileged rich boy. Pressing her lips together, she looked away.

She heard the lid go back on the box and then the gritty sound of wood landing on sand and clay. The two men picked up the shovels left by the grave diggers and began to fill in the small hole in the ground.

The job took less than a minute. She made herself look

at the mound of fresh dirt, the only visible trace of Tess's baby—except the scars on her friend's body. She thought of her father's pontifications on Scripture. Ashes to ashes, dust to dust. The Lord cherishing the death of his beloved.

She couldn't find anything particularly precious about this stark moment.

"Oh, God, we know you're here." Dr. Laniere lifted his resonant voice. "We know you give and you take away and you are sovereign. We pray you'll remind us of your presence even in the darkness of grief. We pray you'll be ever near to Tess as she recovers. Please champion these young women and help them find real help as they seek you. Please use Camilla and the children and me to meet their needs. And I pray you'll hear and meet young Braddock's desire to be a healer, even as you heal his heart."

What about my *desire to be a healer?* Abigail thought as the professor paused. *What about* my *wounded heart?* She opened her eyes and looked up just as a ray of sunshine broke through the patchy fog. An enormous rainbow soared from one end of the graveyard to the other. She caught her breath.

"In the name of our Lord, who takes our ashes and turns them to joy…Amen."

The professor and John replaced their hats. Abigail, shivering in the cool morning dampness, hurried toward the cemetery entrance. She wanted to get back to Tess, to write down the words of the service before she forgot them. *Ashes to joy…*

"Wait, Abigail." Shifting his medical bag to the other hand, John caught up with her, took her hand and pulled it through his elbow. "I thought you should know I went back to the District last night."

"Did you?" Stumbling on the soggy, uneven ground, she

reluctantly accepted the support of his arm. "Needed a bit of alcoholic sustenance?"

"No, I—" He gave her an exasperated look. "Must you assume the worst?"

She shrugged. "I don't know many men who lead me to expect anything else."

"Well, in this case you're wrong. I went back there because I'd heard a child coughing in the apartment next to yours. The walls are so thin—"

"Yes, they are." She didn't need to be reminded. "That would be the McLachlin baby. He has chronic croup. I've tried to get Rose to move him out of that mildewy apartment, but she can't afford anything better."

"Well, I went back to see about him. Stupid woman wouldn't let me in, even though I *told* her I was a doctor."

Abigail looked up at him. "To the contrary. For once she was using her head, not letting a strange man into her apartment."

There was a brief silence. "I see your point." John opened the graveyard gate and held it as Abigail passed through. "Then perhaps you'd agree to return with me this afternoon and persuade her of my good intentions. I'd like to look at the baby to see if anything can be done about that cough."

Abigail hesitated. "She can't afford to pay you."

"I know that." He let out an exasperated sigh. "Prof encourages us to see charity cases when we have time. It's good practice."

"Oh, well, then. For the sake of your education, I suppose I'd best come with you."

He stiffened. "Miss Neal—"

"Mr. Braddock." She squeezed his elbow. "I was only tweaking you."

He looked at her for a moment before a slow grin curled his mouth. "Were you, indeed? Then for the sake of *your* education, I'll allow you to observe a man who practices medicine for more than money. Perhaps you might learn something."

His eyes held hers. Something shifted between them. Abigail looked over her shoulder to find the professor's re-assuring presence several paces back.

John followed her gaze. "Prof, I'm going back to Tchapitoulas Street with Miss Neal to look after a sick little boy."

"Fine. Just bring her back before noon and you may stay for dinner, too." Dr. Laniere waved them on and turned off toward Daubigny Street, where his family attended church.

For the next couple of blocks, Abigail maintained a tense silence. In the distance church bells began to ring. "Are you a church-going man, Mr. Braddock? Perhaps your family will wonder where you are."

"My family would be quite astonished to see me at all on Sunday before late afternoon," he said easily. "I don't live at home."

"Oh." When he didn't elaborate, she looked at him. "Then a wife or—or sweetheart?"

"I assure you I am quite unattached at the moment. Are you trying to get rid of me?"

"Of course not." Abigail looked away, blushing, as they turned the corner at the saloon. "I agreed to come with you to check on the baby." Her relief that he was unattached was absurd. There was nothing personal whatsoever in his escort.

"Yes, you did. And here we are." He stood back as Abigail opened the outer front door and knocked on the door across the entryway from her old apartment with Tess.

She could hear the baby crying inside, Rose's anxious voice, the other two children giggling and shrieking. "Rose?" She knocked again. "It's Abigail."

The door jerked open and Rose appeared with the baby on her hip. A little girl and a little boy of about four and five clung to her skirts, one on each side. "Abigail—what are you doing here? Is something wrong?"

Abigail glanced at John over her shoulder. "I brought Dr. Braddock with me. He wants to look at Paddy."

Rose's big blue eyes widened. "Paddy's fine."

Abigail laid a hand on the baby's back and felt the rattle of his lungs as he breathed. He'd tucked his face into Rose's shoulder, but Abigail could just see the curve of a feverish cheek. "Rose. Please let us in. Denying trouble never made it go away."

Rose stared at John, one hand clasping the baby, the other protectively on her daughter's head. Abigail knew she must be thinking of the drunken husband who had brought her and the children over from Ireland and abandoned them two months ago. As she'd told John earlier, Abigail herself had little reason to rely on any man's trustworthiness. But some tiny part of her insisted on giving this one a chance to prove himself.

John seemed to realize he was here on sufferance. "Mrs. McLachlin, I think I know what's causing Paddy's cough. If you'll just let me look at him for a minute, I can give him some medicine and he'll feel much better tonight." His tone was, if not exactly humble, moderate enough to reassure.

Baby Paddy suddenly erupted in one of his fits of croupy coughing. Rose took a flustered step back. "All right. Come in, both of you, but don't look at the mess. The children have been playing all morning."

Abigail would not have increased Rose's embarrassment for the world, but she couldn't help marveling that the young Irishwoman had survived this long on a laundress's wage with three small children. Clearly she was in dire straights. Except for two dolls made from bits of yarn and a pile of rusty tin cans the children had been playing with in the center of the room, there was little difference between this apartment and the one Abigail had shared with Tess. Poverty had a way of leveling the ground.

To her surprise, as she and Rose seated themselves on the two wooden chairs, John took off his hat, sat down cross-legged on the floor and opened his bag. He produced a couple of splinters of peppermint candy wrapped in waxed paper and smiled at the two older children, who stared at him from behind Rose's chair. "Look what I've got here, widgets. I'll give it to you, but you have to open your mouths wide and let me see if there's room for it to go in."

The little girl, Stella, glanced at her brother. "It's candy," she whispered.

"I want it," he whispered back. The first to conquer his shyness, he edged toward John, who held the candy just out of reach. Apparently seduced by the twinkle in John's eyes, he dropped his jaw and stuck out his tongue. "'ee? 'ere's 'oom."

John laughed and deftly plied a tongue depressor as he peered down the little boy's throat. "There is, indeed. Here you go." He laid the candy on the boy's tongue. "What's your name?"

"Sean." The boy danced backward, eliminating any chance of the candy being snatched away. His eyes closed in ecstasy. "Marmee, I like this."

"Me! Me!" Stella gaped wide as she crowded close to

John, gagging slightly as he depressed her tongue. But she patiently held still to let him look at her throat. When she received her candy, she sucked on it furiously, gazing at John with adoration. "Can Paddy have some too?"

John shook his head. "Paddy's too little. But maybe he'd let me look at his throat anyway?"

By this time, Rose was thoroughly disarmed and handed over the baby without further protest. John took him with a gentle competence that reminded Abigail of the way he'd held poor little Caroline that morning. Her throat closed as Paddy blinked up at the doctor's handsome young face.

John examined the baby thoroughly, laying his ear against Paddy's chest and back to listen, gently moving his arms and legs, palpating the glands beneath the soft little chin. He tracked the movement of Paddy's eyes by moving his finger back and forth, grinning when the baby grabbed it and tried to suck on it. "No, no, boo. Dirty." He looked at Rose as he lifted Paddy onto his shoulder and patted his back. "Definitely teething, which causes fever. But the cough worries me. It means there's mucus draining into his stomach, maybe collecting fluid in his lungs. You'll need to suction out as much of it as you can, keep him at a comfortable temperature, wash everything that goes in his mouth. Keep him fed—which means taking care of yourself." His eyes softened as he looked around at the bare room. "Do you get enough to eat?"

Distress took over Rose's worn young face. "I do the best I can, but there aren't many vegetables available this time of year, and meat…" She swallowed. "I can't afford—"

"Fish," Abigail blurted. "Tess and I used to go to the docks early in the morning and ask for whatever wasn't quite good enough to send to the market. You can make stews and gumbo, rich in good stuff."

Rose blinked back tears. "Maybe I could ask Tess to bring back extra…in return for laundry service."

Abigail exchanged a smile with John. "I'm sure she'd be happy to when she's back on her feet."

John handed the baby back to his mother and began to repack his bag. "Yes, that's a good idea. And meantime, wrapping the baby up and taking him outside for cool night air will ease his breathing and help him sleep. Just be sure he doesn't get too cold."

Rose stood up and swayed with Paddy clasped to her bosom. "Dr. Braddock, thank you for coming back. I shouldn't have been rude to you last night." She hesitated as John rose and dusted the seat of his trousers. "I'm sorry I can't…I don't have the money to pay you for your trouble."

He stared at her, a hint of the old arrogance drawing his brows together. Or perhaps, Abigail thought, it was simple embarrassment. "I don't need your money," he said.

"Then perhaps you'd care to bring your laundry by." Rose's soft chin went up. "I'm considered the best in the neighborhood."

Catching Abigail's warning look, John shrugged. "I've no doubt you are. We'll see. But I promised to return Miss Neal to the clinic before noon, so we'd best hurry. I or one of the other fellows will stop by here tomorrow to check on Paddy. I'll send some bleach to wipe down the floors and ceiling. Some say that keeps down the spread of croup." He gave Rose a quick nod and offered his hand to little Sean. "Help your marmee out by playing quietly when the baby's asleep, won't you, old man?"

Sean nudged his sister. "Would you bring more candy when you come back?"

John winked. "I'll see what I can do."

"Goodbye, Rose." Abigail smiled at her neighbor as she followed John out to the entryway. "Don't forget about the fish."

"Thank you, Abigail." Rose's expression was considerably less troubled than when they'd first arrived. "I don't know what else to—just thank you." She shut the door hurriedly.

As they began the long walk back to the Lanieres', Abigail took John's proffered arm and sighed. "She'll listen to you, I think." She glanced at him. "You were very sweet to the children."

She knew she'd used the wrong word when his fine eyes narrowed. "Perhaps you'd expected me to growl at them."

Smiling, she shrugged. "You did surprise me a bit. I confess your motivations confuse me, John. People like Rose—and Tess and me, for that matter—cannot pay you in coin, and you seem to have a rather contemptuous attitude toward our entire class. Why do you want to be a doctor? Is it simple scientific hunger?"

He didn't immediately answer. "Imperfections bother me," he said slowly. "I suppose that could be considered a character flaw. But I see no reason for those little ones to suffer from hunger and disease if there's anything I can do about it." He glanced at her, cheeks reddened, she thought not entirely from the wind whipping off the river. "I don't mean to be arrogant."

An inappropriate urge to giggle made Abigail look down, pretending to watch her step. "Because imperfections annoy me as well, I'll take it upon myself to correct you as needed." She gave him a mischievous glance from under her lashes.

To his credit, John laughed. "Magnanimous of you, Miss Abigail. You'll give me lessons in social intercourse, and I'll keep your considerable predisposition for interference well occupied. We should get along famously."

Almost lightheaded with the unexpected pleasure of intelligent repartee with an attractive—if slightly prickly—male, Abigail turned the conversation to his background with the Laniere family. John Braddock was like no man she'd met in her admittedly abnormal life. Perhaps she had more to learn than she'd thought.

"It's got to be here somewhere," John muttered to himself that evening as he skimmed through the last of six pharmaceutical books he'd borrowed from Marcus Girard. He sat on his unmade bed, his back propped against the wall, a cup of stout Creole coffee wobbling atop the tomes stacked at his elbow.

The cramped and exceedingly messy fifteen-by-fifteen-foot room on the second level of Mrs. Hanley's Boarding House for Gentlemen was one of John's greatest sources of personal satisfaction. It hadn't been easy to endure his mother's tearful accusations of ingratitude nor his father's blustering threats of disinheritance. But in the end, John's determination to live on his own had worn them both down. Two years ago, on his twenty-third birthday, he had packed his clothes and books into four sturdy trunks and had them carted to the boarding house. He then rode his black mare, Belladonna, to the livery stable around the corner on Rue St. John—another serendipitous circumstance which afforded him no end of amusement.

Mrs. Clementine Hanley insisted on absolute moral purity in her lodgers—the enforcing of which she took quite seriously and personally. She also set a fine table and could be counted upon to provide fresh linens daily.

Unfortunately, she was not so dependable in the matter of functioning locks.

John looked up in irritation when the doorknob rattled. The key worked its way loose and hit the floor with a clank. "Girard, if you come in here again, I'm going to souse every pair of drawers you own in kerosene and set them on fire."

The door opened anyway and Marcus's ingenuous, square-cut face insinuated itself in the opening.

John glared. "Go away!"

Marcus leaned over to pick up the fallen key and tossed it at John. The key plunked into the half-full coffee cup. "Oops." He gave John an unrepentant grin. "A little iron supplement for your diet, old man."

Snarling under his breath, John used his pillow case to mop up the sloshed coffee. "You'd better have a good reason for interrupting me again." He fished the key out of his cup.

Marcus swaggered into the room with his usual banty-rooster strut, hands thrust into the enormous pockets of a peacock-blue satin dressing gown. He paused in front of the skeleton spraddled in a straight chair under the room's tiny, solitary window.

"Hank, old bean." Marcus bowed, sketching a salute. "I trust this evening finds you hale and hearty."

John resisted the urge to laugh. Encouraged, Marcus could go on for hours in that oily false-British accent. He closed the book on his finger. "What do you want, Girard?"

"Stuck-up rotter, ain't you?" Giving the skeleton a thump on the cranium, Marcus hopped onto the window sill and folded his arms across his barrel chest. "Came to rescue you."

"Rescue me? The only way you can rescue me is to find me another pharmacy book."

"Braddock, I've lifted every book m'father has on the subject. If what you're looking for ain't there, it just—ain't there. Come on, I know you've memorized the lists for the test. Let's toddle over to the District and slum a little."

The notorious red light district was located a few blocks from the medical college and Mrs. Hanley's Boarding House. It also happened to be where John had encountered Tess and Abigail. Yesterday's experience had destroyed whatever appeal the District once had. And going back with Abigail this morning to visit the McLachlin family had turned it rather into a source of conscience.

John opened the book again. "I'm busy. And if you had even half as many brains as Hank, you'd take one of these books down to your room and have a look yourself."

Marcus gave John a puzzled look. "What's got into you today? You didn't go to church this morning, did you?"

John gave a bark of laughter. "Not exactly. I attended a funeral."

Marcus sat up straight, his thin, sandy hair all but on end. "I'm sorry, Braddock! Who died?"

"Nobody you know." John had no intention of exposing the life-changing experiences of the last two days to Marcus's inanities. "I'm just—not in the mood. *Comprendez-vous?*"

Marcus pursed his lips. It was common knowledge that John's family ties took him in directions that less well-connected students could only dream of. "Certainly. I understand. Death and all that." He slid off the window seat and sidled toward the door. "You were my first choice of companion, but I guess I'll head down to Weichmann's room to see if he'd care to get his head out of the books for a bit." He paused with his hand on the doorknob. "If Clem asks, tell her we've gone on a call."

Mrs. Hanley would certainly ask, should John be so foolish as to stick his nose outside the room. He gave Marcus an absent wave as the brilliantly hued dressing gown disappeared into the hallway. There had better be no emergency calls tonight.

He took a sip of the stone-cold coffee, then propped the cup on his chest, dropping the book onto the floor. He'd been studying the composition and medicinal uses of opium for hours and there was still no conclusive evidence that Abigail Neal was wrong. It was true that opium and all its derivatives—including morphine and laudanum—could be addictive when consumed even once. Certainly the substance was effective as a painkiller, but were the side effects worth it?

John didn't know. He was discovering there were a lot of things he didn't know. The more he studied medicine, the more he realized its practice was largely in the realm of guesswork, intuition and trial and error. Frequently even mysticism. Even Dr. Laniere, his favorite professor and mentor, sometimes made fatal judgments. He had as good a record of success as any physician John had yet to meet, but…people did die under his care.

Why didn't God just tell people how to go on? Why did they get ill and injured in the first place? If he could heal at all, why didn't he heal everybody?

Irritated at the intrusion of such unscientific thoughts, John slung his coffee cup onto the bedside table and got up off the bed. He took a deep breath and bent to touch his toes a few times.

He'd been entertaining a lot of God-related meanderings ever since the delivery of that stillborn baby. All day he'd had a sense of someone looking into his mind, prodding his thoughts and feelings. One of the main reasons he'd taken Abigail back to visit that croupy baby was to escape the strong urge to go to church.

Just a bit spooked, he turned a full circle, taking in his familiar surroundings. Nothing out of order. The narrow, tumbled bed with the coffee stain on the pillow. The square table holding a pile of anatomy textbooks and the Tiffany lamp his mother had given him on his twenty-first birthday. Sepia-toned photographs of his parents and her sister Lisette on the mantel above the tiny fireplace. Hank holding court in the chair under the window. The plain mahogany chifforobe with its mirror reflecting his confusion back at him.

John thrust both hands through his hair and stared at his own reddened eyes. Not enough sleep lately. That was all it was.

Then he looked at his hands. They shook. The nails were immaculate, the signet ring on his left little finger dull gold with a garnet set into the family crest. Rich man's hands? Healer's hands?

He hurried to the window, leaned out and sucked in a draft of thick, clammy, November air. He'd lived in New Orleans all his life and the humidity had never bothered him before, but he found himself struggling for a breath. No wonder little Paddy McLachlin was so sick.

John looked down, watching passersby fading in and out of the pools of gaslight spotting the sidewalks. When had it gotten dark out? Maybe he should try to catch up to Girard and Weichmann after all.

He pulled his head back inside the room, banged down the window sash and yanked the curtain closed. He sat down to tug on his boots, decided against a coat and tore out of the room, slamming the door behind him. He pounded down the stairs, shoving the useless key into his pocket.

God couldn't influence his thoughts if he wasn't there.

Chapter Five

The next morning John slumped at a table in a nearly empty classroom, listening to the heavy marching of the clock on the wall behind him. Traffic clamored from the street outside the open window to his left.

He stared at the test in front of him and wondered which of the medicines he'd just listed would be the quickest remedy for acute hangover. Maybe he should go straight for the arsenic. Quelling a strong desire to hang his head out the window and heave, he contemplated the top of Dr. Girard's bald head, visible behind the Monday morning *Daily Picayune*.

Marcus's father was a cold-hearted old goat, a brilliant lecturer whose written tests had been known to reduce grown men to tears. He sat at the front of the lecture hall, behind a bare table which exposed his short legs, stretched out and crossed at the ankle. His scarlet-and-lemon-striped waistcoat, half-inch-thick watch chain and green paisley ascot revealed the source of Marcus's love for sartorial splendor.

John wished the professor had his son's amiable temperament.

He was one of only two students left in the room. Everyone else, including Marcus himself, had either completed the test or given up in despair. He glanced across the room at Tanner Weichmann. Weichmann had not indulged in spirits last night, but had come along more or less to keep Marcus out of trouble. In fact, it had been he who put both Marcus and John to bed, after paying for a hack home and supporting the two of them up the narrow stairs. Good thing Clem slept like the dead or they might all have been out on the street tonight.

John supposed he should be grateful not to have awoken in a gutter somewhere, robbed of his clothes and money. Weichmann was a serious pain, but he was dependable. Perhaps not as gifted a scientist as John, not nearly as much fun as Marcus, but methodical to the point of insanity. John was certain he'd finished the test long ago, but Weichmann would check his answers to make sure every word was spelled correctly and all sentences complete.

Weichmann suddenly looked up, his dark eyes probing John's. He wiggled heavy black brows and elaborately pulled out his watch.

John couldn't resist looking over his shoulder at the clock. Nearly noon. Time was almost up. He suppressed a groan, bent over his paper again and dredged up the therapeutic and alterative uses of mercury. By the time he finished his answer, Dr. Girard had folded his paper in a neat square and waited, stubby fingers linked and his brow creased in impatient lines. John looked around. Weichmann had disappeared.

"Braddock, you seem determined to make me miss my noon meal," growled Dr. Girard. "Are you quite finished?"

"Yes, sir. Sorry, sir." John rose and clattered down the steps of the amphitheater, sticking his pencil stub behind his ear. He reluctantly handed over his paper. "When will you have them graded?" If he failed this test he would have to repeat the course. Pharmaceuticals tended to be his downfall because of the spellings.

Without looking at him, the professor stuffed John's test into a leather portfolio. "You'll know soon enough." He rolled out of the room without a backward glance.

John ran a hand around the back of his neck, popping the joints to relieve tension. At least it was over. Pass or fail, there was nothing he could do about it now. He needed to go lie down.

He headed for the door and nearly jumped out of his skin when someone grabbed his arm as he passed into the hallway.

"How did you do, Braddock?"

John wheeled. "Careful, Weichmann, or you'll be cleaning your shoes. I'm still a bit unsteady this morning."

Weichmann gave an evil chuckle. "Speaking of morning, you missed rounds. Prof wasn't happy."

Dr. Laniere wasn't the only professor, of course, but every med student distinguished him with the title. No one wanted to disappoint Professor Laniere.

John lifted a shoulder and continued down the hall toward the stairs. "Couldn't be helped. What did you tell him?"

"Told him you had a previous engagement."

"You did not."

"No. But I should have. Braddock, you never drink. What's gotten into you, old man?"

Since the words were almost a direct quote of Marcus's the day before, John hurried down the marble stairs without replying. He wasn't going to admit that a prostitute's dead baby had resulted in his hearing from God.

Weichmann's long, skinny legs had no trouble keeping

up. "There's a few minutes for lunch before anatomy lab. Want to go for a beignet and coffee?"

John's stomach revolted. "No!"

"Oh, sorry…Didn't think."

John sat down and planted his elbows on his knees, laying his pounding head in his palms. He could feel Weichmann hovering behind him on the stairs, his breath wheezing and whistling. It took little to get the young Jew's asthma kicked up.

"No, *I'm* sorry. I don't know what's wrong with me." John stared at the gray squiggles in the white marble between his feet. "Weichmann, has God ever communicated with you? You know, like Moses and the burning bush?"

Weichmann didn't answer for a long moment. John could hear the clatter of students changing classes down in the east wing and, through the open windows, the rattle of carriages passing in the street. The heavy odors of mildew and chalk and the stench of the dissection lab drifted from two floors up. He looked over his shoulder and found Weichmann staring at him as if he'd lost his mind.

"Maybe you'd better go home and go to bed," suggested Weichmann.

John's head fell back against the wrought-iron spindles of the stair rail. "I was planning to." He got to his feet and descended the remainder of the stairs. At the bottom, he turned to Weichmann, who followed tsking like an agitated squirrel. "Don't tell anyone I asked that, would you?"

Weichmann shook his curly head. "Nobody would believe me if I did."

The haunting strains of a hymn sung in a rich, throbbing contralto drifted through the kitchen and clinic/dispensary to the ward, where Abigail was feeding Tess her evening meal of barley soup. In the daylight, Abigail had discovered the ward to be a large, airy room with doors opening into the kitchen on one side and the clinic on the other. The three long, curtainless windows of the third wall looked out on the garden, where even in late fall birds sang in tall flowering shrubs and fruit trees gave off an intoxicating scent. Lined up on the interior wall of the room were four narrow cots, each with its own bedside table holding a small basin-and-pitcher set, with a chamber pot underneath the bed.

"I know not what the future hath of marvel or surprise," sang the unseen singer, "assured alone that life and death His mercy underlies."

Sighing, Abigail spooned soup into Tess's mouth. The song brought to mind a vivid image of her mother, singing over her fine embroidery, dressed in the traditional Chinese wide-sleeved, knee-length cotton overshirt and loose trousers. Darling, vulnerable Mama, trying to fit in despite her "devilish" blue eyes, red hair, and normal-sized feet. Papa had thought to have Abigail's feet bound, but Mama managed to convince him that, at the age of five, too much growth had already taken place.

The Chinese women had been repelled by such foreign females. Abigail, always tall for her age, got into the habit of slumping. Only since returning to America had she trained herself to stand upright.

The words of the hymn seemed a symbol of all Abigail had run away from, a mockery of the dire circumstances of her life.

Tess had awakened off and on all day, slowly gaining strength. Still, Abigail couldn't help worrying. She had been much safer in the relative anonymity of the District.

Besides, if she and Tess didn't report for work tomorrow, they might return to find that they had been replaced. Their miserable jobs in the sail loft were all that stood between them and starvation—or prostitution. The Lanieres seemed to be kindhearted folk, but there was a limit to most people's charity, as she knew only too well.

"Who is that singing?" whispered Tess, pushing away the spoon. "Thank you, but I don't want any more."

Abigail set the bowl on the floor, leaning over to lay her head on the sheet beside Tess. She was so tired. She'd been up until dawn this morning, giving cornstarch baths to Diron and his ten-year-old sister Lythie, also discovered to be stricken with chicken pox. Camilla had been occupied with the fussy and equally poxy baby Meg. After Abigail snatched a few hours of sleep, Tess had wakened and called for her. She'd sat trying to stay awake in this uncomfortable wooden chair all day.

Winona came back yesterday afternoon to take over the household duties, but Abigail had seen little of her, other than at mealtimes.

Abigail yawned. "Sounds like an opera singer. Do you suppose the Lanieres hired someone to entertain us?"

Tess giggled, gladdening Abigail's heart. It had been a long time since Tess had anything to laugh about. "Go and see, Abby. I want to meet her."

"All right." With mental reservations that any guest of the Lanieres would care to meet two women from the District, be they ever so inwardly genteel, Abigail picked up the half-empty bowl and pushed to her feet.

She found Winona straining cooked pears into an enormous pot on the kitchen stove. All Abigail could see of her was the mane of inky curls cascading down her slender back, a pair of café-au-lait-colored arms, bare beneath the rolled-up sleeves of a coarsely woven blue-and-white-checked blouse, and a plain brown gathered skirt.

But the voice. Abigail marveled as it poured from the woman's tiny body like the throaty eulogy of a dove: "I know not where his islands lift their fronded palms in air; I only know I cannot drift beyond his love and care."

Abigail wanted to weep at the beauty and hope of the words and melody.

Winona turned around to dump the pear pulp into a bowl next to her elbow. When she saw Abigail, a smile lit her face, turning the dark eyes to black gemstones. Her features had an exotic sort of elegance, more interesting than any pale perfection. "Ooh, you startled me!" She laughed, giving the sieve a good shake with competent, blunt-fingered hands, then set it down to wipe her fingers on a towel tucked into the waistband of her apron.

"I heard you singing." Odd to hear such a glorious sound from a servant. On the other hand, who was she to look down her nose at anyone?

"Pshhh, I'm sorry. Miss Camilla said not to disturb you, if you and the lady patient was asleep." Winona gave a rueful shrug. "I get carried away."

"Oh, no, it was lovely." Abigail smiled. "We—Tess and I—thought it was an opera singer."

Winona went off into gales of throaty laughter. "Me? Oh, help us, that's a good one!"

Abigail found herself joining in. "Your voice is finer than a woman I know who once sang on the stage in Paris." Amusement died as Abigail pictured poor Delphine's perpetual drug-induced stupor. These days her voice was rarely lifted in anything other than black despair.

"I wish I could learn from a real teacher." Winona turned as an insistent knock sounded at the kitchen door. "That would be Mr. John. He's the only one of Dr. Gabriel's students who comes direct to the kitchen. Can't nobody talk him into coming to the front door." She went to open the door.

Abigail found her heart clanging around in her chest like the Vespers bell in the tower of St. Stephen's. She'd wondered when Braddock would deign to bestow his presence upon them again.

"Afternoon, Mr. John." Winona moved to let him in.

He came in, hatless and stock askew, his coat shockingly draped over his arm. His tall form was backlit by the late afternoon sun that streamed across the kitchen courtyard and gilded the top of his head. He stopped and stared at Abigail for a long moment.

She touched her hair, then cursed herself for such a ridiculous, feminine instinct. She snatched her hand behind her back.

He shifted his attention to Winona, who had gone back to her preserves. "How is Tess?"

Winona looked around, amusement curving her lips. "I don't know, Mr. John. You better ask Miss Abigail here. I been so busy helping Miss Camilla with the children and tending to the laundry, I ain't had time to even look in on her. Miss Camilla say the lady's been in good hands." She smiled at Abigail.

"Tess is a little stronger." Warmed at Winona's praise, Abigail lifted her chin. "Even without the opium, she slept well last night and most of today."

"I'm glad to hear it." He gave her a curt nod and stalked off toward the clinic.

Abigail gave Winona a wry glance. "Is he always this charming?"

An inscrutable smile played around Winona's full mouth. "He can turn it on when he wants to."

Abigail didn't want to know what that meant. "When will Dr. Laniere be home?"

"Oh, right about—" The kitchen door rattled and opened—"now." The doctor came in whistling, with his hat under his arm, and Winona reached to take it from him. "Miss Camilla said to tell you she's up in the nursery when you get home. The two older boys're down with the pox now. It's a mess for sure."

The doctor's cheerful expression fell. "All five of them? Poor Camilla." He sighed. "All right. I'll just check on Miss Montgomery, then I'll see about the children. I'm sure Camilla's got things under control."

Abigail followed him into the clinic, where she was just in time to witness the unhorsing of Sir John the Terrible, who had leaned over to grasp Tess's wrist between thumb and two fingers.

Abigail slipped past Dr. Laniere when he halted just inside the ward, holding his hat behind his back with both hands. He rocked on his heels, watching his student with a sardonic expression that Abigail found impossible to interpret.

"Well, Mr. Braddock." Dr. Laniere's dry tone conveyed not a trace of the tenderness he'd shown in his ministrations to Tess. "I see that having skipped early rounds, you decided to compensate with a late-evening tour of duty. I trust you've recovered your customary blooming health."

Braddock dropped Tess's hand with a start and backed up a step. "Professor! I was just—"

"No, no, carry on, Braddock. You were doing quite well. Would you like to borrow my stethoscope?"

Braddock recovered his aplomb. "No, sir." He discreetly pulled back the sheet to examine Tess, who turned her head away, enduring the humiliation with her eyes closed.

Abigail anxiously watched her friend's face. She'd give anything to be a doctor herself, able to spare women the degradation of being handled familiarly by male strangers. It wasn't the first time she'd entertained this utterly hopeless dream. She clenched her hands, silently, fiercely repeating it, almost a prayer. All she wanted was a chance to study, to learn the things John Braddock took for granted.

Resentment gave her boldness. "I'll take Mr. Braddock's rounds tomorrow morning if he doesn't want to go."

John Braddock snorted. "Very funny." Straightening, he dropped the sheet back into place and folded his arms across his chest.

Abigail's bravado disappeared when Dr. Laniere turned. "What did you say?"

"I s-said I would like to assist you as nurse. I've quite a bit of experience." Abigail found her knees shaking. She put a hand against the wall behind her.

"I don't believe that's exactly what you said." Dr. Laniere tapped his lower lip with a finger. "But if you'd like to assist, you may meet me in the carriage house at seven in the morning. We'll see what you can do. So I suppose you should stay another night or two. Camilla could use an extra pair of hands, if you don't mind pitching in."

Abigail felt the blood rush from her head. "S-Sir! Do you mean it?"

"Professor!" Braddock's hazel eyes all but popped out of his head. "This woman is no nurse! She's a prostitute!"

Abigail came away from the wall, indignation overpowering her sense of unworthiness. "Tess and I are both respectable women who have fallen on difficult times. We are not prostitutes. Do not compound your idiocy by spouting such utter claptrap!"

"My *idiocy*—"

Dr. Laniere raised a hand. "The two of you may continue this discussion outside, if you please. I wish to examine my patient in peace and quiet." When Braddock looked about to argue, the professor's brow knit. "Now."

Braddock clamped his lips together and stalked toward the doorway into the kitchen. He paused beside Abigail and bowed with elaborate exaggeration. "After you, ma'am." He waited for her to precede him out of the ward.

She grasped her skirts as daintily as if they were finest silk and gave him the curtsy her mother had made her practice before a mirror when she was a little girl. Rising with gratifying grace, she turned to Dr. Laniere. "I shall meet you in the carriage house in the morning, sir." She smiled at her unexpected champion. "Thank you, sir."

Braddock followed her outside into the shadow-dappled courtyard, shutting the door sharply behind him. "What do you think you're up to?"

She whirled to face him. "Accepting an invitation."

"You invited yourself. What possible help do you think you'll be—you'll only get in the way of those of us who have paid tuition and earned a spot at the professor's side."

"What difference does it make to you whether I'm there or not? Do you think my brain will absorb all the information in the room, leaving you without any?" Closing her eyes, she placed her thumbs at her temples in imitation of a French Quarter spiritist. "Ooh, I think you're right. I definitely sense your intellect dissipating by the second." She looked at him in mock sympathy. "No wonder you seem so monumentally stupid."

"Don't be absurd." His mouth quirked a little in spite of the heavy frown. "It's a matter of what's fair."

"Fair?" She could feel her fingers curling into her skirt. "How does Dr. Laniere's generosity remove your benefit? Besides, even if I had the wherewithal to pay tuition, I wouldn't be allowed to take classes with you. So don't prate to me of fairness, Mr. Braddock."

His mouth opened, but he couldn't seem to articulate whatever was boiling behind those hot multihued eyes. "It's just not right," he finally muttered. "We keep women out of medicine to protect them."

"Well, I've been protected right out of my homeland and my family, thank you very much," she said. "Now that I've landed on my feet here, you're not going to convince me to go back."

"Miss Neal—Abigail," his voice softened, "I wouldn't send you back to the District. I merely want you to consider carefully before you force your way into a place where you won't be accepted, much less welcomed. The other fellows will be brutal if you show up tomorrow morning."

Abigail stared at him, chin raised. "Your warning is well taken. And I shall prepare myself accordingly." She dipped him another curtsy and turned for the door. "Good afternoon, Mr. Braddock."

She forced herself not to look over her shoulder as she reentered the kitchen, leaving her adversary fuming on the other side of the door. John Braddock had a thing or two to learn about women if he imagined he'd thwarted her desire to follow rounds in the morning.

Chapter Six

"Girard, if you want someone to crack your knuckles, I'll be happy to do it for you." John continued his circular route around the Charity Hospital entryway, almost hoping for an excuse to vent some of his pent-up restlessness.

John and Marcus, trailed by Weichmann, had arrived at Charity Hospital thirty minutes earlier than the time appointed for rounds with Dr. Laniere. None of them wanted to be accused of slacking, and John was determined to be the epitome of punctuality and dependability for the rest of his life.

Miss Charlemagne had let them in, her garments pristine as always, though John had noted a streak that looked suspiciously like a pillow crease on the elderly woman's round cheek. No one had ever seen her so much as yawn. She was the first person he saw in the morning and always seemed to be available for nighttime emergencies. He could only suppose she slept with her eyes open. She was not a nurse, but her genius for administration made her more valuable to the doctors who attended from the medical college than a hundred nurses.

After pocketing the brass key suspended from her belt with a copper chain, she had cautioned the three young men to be quiet, then whisked herself into the chapel to pray. John had considered asking her to pray for him, but the memory of Weichmann's response to yesterday's mention of God and burning bushes dissuaded him.

Weichmann, seated beside Marcus on the next-to-lowest step of the central staircase, pulled out an enormous pocket watch that he claimed had been given to him by an uncle descended from German royalty. "Braddock, there's probably time to send Crutch out for breakfast. I wish you wouldn't be so stubborn."

John took another turn across the tiled foyer. "If you'd seen Prof's face last night—"

"We *did* see it, when you didn't appear yesterday morning." Marcus grimaced. "If you have a death wish, Braddock, there are less painful ways to go about it. I had more to drink than you did and I still managed to get up on time."

Weichmann put away his watch. "Are the tests graded yet?"

Marcus avoided John's eyes. "I don't know."

John pounced. "You've seen the grades. Did I pass?"

"I told you I don't—" Marcus tried to pull John's hands away from his cravat. "Let go, you Neanderthal. I saw mine, but Pa caught me before I got any farther."

Releasing his friend, who indignantly tried to restore order to his mangled neck cloth, John shoved his hands into his trouser pockets. "So what was your score?"

"Let's just say I won't be starting my own pharmacy anytime soon. And don't say you told me so. I studied in my own way, it just didn't stick. All that Latin. Gads! Why can't we speak English?"

At that moment the front door opened, admitting Dr. Laniere, followed by a troop of medical students and a beautiful young woman.

John did a double take. He'd never imagined Abigail Neal would have the brass to show up this morning. She wore a different dress than the ugly black one she'd had on yesterday, this one a high-necked affair that quite incidentally duplicated the new-leaf color of her eyes. It was a bit short-waisted, and…his gaze traveled to the hem, which, judging by the deeper hue of the fabric, had been recently let out. He frowned, shaken by this reminder of Abigail's poverty.

"Mr. Braddock, if your breakfast disagreed with you this morning, I shall be happy to excuse you to return to your bed."

John looked up to find Dr. Laniere and the other students eyeing him with varying degrees of amusement, sympathy and gleeful malice. Abigail herself gazed over his shoulder, an expression of supreme indifference on her serene face. Except for the slight quirk at the corner of her mouth.

"Gads!" repeated Marcus. "You ain't bringing a *woman* into the hospital, are you, Prof?"

"Ah, I neglected to introduce Miss Neal, didn't I?" Dr. Laniere turned to smile at Abigail, sweeping an ironic hand toward John and his cohorts. "Miss Neal, I present to you Marcus Girard and Tanner Weichmann, both second-year students. Mr. Braddock you've already met, of course."

"Already *met* her?" blurted Marcus. "Is this your Amazon?"

John sent a scalding look over his shoulder, ignoring the guffaws of his fellow students. He regretted the pink that stained Abigail's sharp cheekbones.

Her lips tightened, but she looked down at Marcus as if he were a particularly nasty species of cockroach. "And you would be his…" She hesitated. "Harlequin?"

Marcus, red-faced and speechless, tugged the carnelian-and-saffron diamond-patterned waistcoat down over his trim stomach.

Laughter erupted among the other fellows and John struggled not to join them. She'd pegged Girard to the penny. Time to flank his troops and reconnoiter. "Nurse told us a new gall bladder case arrived last night, Professor. Second ward."

"Excellent," said Dr. Laniere, "but first I wish to make one thing clear to you gentlemen." The doctor's deep-set eyes bored directly into John's. "Miss Neal is here at my express invitation and I expect her to be treated with the utmost respect and courtesy." Prof tented his long, elegant fingers beneath his chin and scanned the faces of his students one by one. "Am I understood?"

Silence fell as everyone else looked at John. He swallowed hard. He had nothing against the woman, really. In fact, there had been a moment of connection at the baby's funeral—a connection he was at a loss to explain. Although she was odd as a three-legged duck, he had no objection to handing off nursing duties to her, as long as she kept her mouth shut and didn't challenge him at every—

Her lashes lifted; the magnificent green eyes slammed into his and he suddenly realized Abigail Neal's presence was going to be a very dangerous thing, indeed. This was no off-limits matron with a pillow crease on her cheek. Intelligence and humor and mockery and all sorts of mysterious elements were buried in those eyes. He was going to have to be very careful not to get left behind in his chosen profession—especially if Professor Laniere decided to take Abigail Neal under his wing.

Abigail lifted her chin and John bowed with as much irony as he could muster. "Quite," he said. Which didn't really answer the question, but seemed to satisfy Dr. Laniere.

Prof led the way up the stairs to ward two, John on his heels, with Weichmann and Marcus and the other students trailing.

John was acutely aware of Abigail Neal's quiet presence just to his left. She glided along, turning to look into the open door of the first ward as they passed. The moans of the patients within drifted toward them, creating a music John found soothing in a bizarre kind of way.

He was looking forward to the gall bladder examination. Taking tests on medicines was all well and good, but a fellow learned best by doing.

Professor Laniere breezed into the ward, a broad open room smelling of carbolic acid. Through a bank of four un-curtained windows, evenly spaced along the west wall, weak sunlight splashed across the bare plank floor and six white-painted iron beds.

A nurse was feeding something soupy to a patient in the middle bed. She looked up and smiled at the professor. "Dr. Laniere, you'll be happy to know Mrs. Catchot is feeling like eating her grits this morning."

"Capital." The professor approached the bed, inserting the earpieces of his binaural stethoscope into his ears.

Some time ago, John and the other students had been allowed to examine the auscultation instrument. He'd found it much more efficient and precise for diagnosing lung ab-errations than those favored by older physicians. Dr. Girard, for example, still carried a short, tubular monaural steth carved out of ivory. The instrument had no earpiece at all, just a flat plate that allowed sound to dissipate into the air. John had been angling for his father to cave in and buy him a stethoscope like Professor Laniere's for his birthday.

Prof moved the bodice of the woman's gown aside and set the stainless steel listening bell against her chest.

She gasped. "That's cold!"

The doctor spared her a sympathetic glance, but held the trumpet of the stethoscope firmly in place. After a moment, he gestured for Abigail to approach. "What do you hear?"

She hesitated, then accepted the instrument from his hand. Brushing back wisps of hair escaped from the knot at the back of her head, she inserted the two rubber earpieces into her dainty ears. Ignoring the patient's objection, Abigail listened, eyes widening. She looked up at the professor with a grin. "That's amazing!"

He nodded. "Indeed. Now what do you *hear?*"

Abigail sobered, concentrating her gaze inward. "It's… off," she said slowly. "There's a sort of…bump, I don't know how to say it."

"Yes. Arrhythmia." Dr. Laniere gave her an approving glance. "We can tell a lot about a patient's body by listening. Remind me to loan you my extra stethoscope. You may get a sense of what a healthy body should sound like by practicing on any willing party." He looked down at the woman on the bed. "But I believe you came in complaining of abdominal pain?"

"No, sir." The patient's voice trembled. "My belly hurts. Especially right after I eat."

The professor nodded, a twinkle in his eyes. "I beg your pardon. Your belly, of course." He chose Weichmann to quiz. "Diagnosis and scientific name?"

"Cholecystitis, sir. Inflammation of the gallbladder."

"Correct." Another approving nod. "Show Miss Neal the correct procedure for palpation, Weichmann."

Weichmann's lips tightened. John knew the young Jew desperately wanted to be a doctor, though he was perhaps the least gifted in the class. The small Orthodox community from which he'd come provided little in the way of modern medical care and his mother's slow, painful death from a corrosive brain disease was a powerful impetus for Weichmann's educational pursuit.

He also detested being the center of attention.

But he straightened his shoulders and drew the sheet down, exposing the body with relative modesty from lower sternum to groin. He bent to observe the contour of the abdomen at eye level. "Breathe normally," he instructed the patient. After a moment he straightened. "Please cough."

John felt a light hand on his arm. He looked down to find Abigail intently watching the examination. "What's he looking for?" she whispered.

"He's observing the movement along the inguinal canal." John couldn't help feeling superior. She wouldn't know what the inguinal canal was.

"Ah. The Latin is *inguinalis,* which is the groin." She chewed the inside of her cheek. "So we want to see if there are abnormalities there?"

John stared at her. "That's right."

Weichmann laid his flattened palm against the patient's abdomen. The woman craned her head to see the professor. "Does everybody have to stare at me?"

Dr. Laniere's smile was kind. "Mrs. Catchot, this is a teaching hospital. My students can't learn if they don't watch."

"I know, but what is that *girl* doing here?" The woman's voice was petulant.

"Miss Neal is studying nursing. She may be the one to care for you later. The more she knows, the better she'll be able to attend you." Dr. Laniere gestured for Weichmann to continue the examination. "You should start light palpation farther away from the most tender point."

"She could flex her knees a bit to make that easier," Abigail murmured.

John glanced at her, annoyed at the distraction.

Dr. Laniere cleared his throat. "Weichmann. You're forgetting something else."

Weichmann reddened. "Mrs. Catchot, let's pull your knees up slightly to relax your abdominal muscles."

Groaning, the patient complied as John intercepted a triumphant look from Abigail. "How did you *know* that?" he demanded in an undertone.

She smiled. "Simple physics."

Dr. Laniere snapped his fingers. "Braddock, pay attention. You'll be next."

"Yes, sir." He scowled at Abigail, then turned his focus back to the examination.

Again laying his hand on the woman's belly, Weichmann gently flexed his fingers, progressing toward the spot where she'd reacted earlier. She began to whimper in pain and poor Weichmann looked like he wanted to run from the room. "Mrs. Catchot, I need you to relax. Can you take some deep breaths?"

The patient lifted her head. "It hurts. I'm going to die."

"I don't think so," said Weichmann. "It's just a—"

"You're doing a fine job," interrupted the professor, laying a hand on Weichmann's shoulder, "but I'll take over from here." He moved to the patient's right side and slid one hand behind her ribs, then placed the other flat on her anterior abdominal wall. "A deep breath through your mouth, please."

As John watched the firm, sure pressure of Dr. Laniere's hands, the woman's inspiration turned into a gasp of agony. "Students, note that when Weichmann released the pressure of his fingers, the pain increased. Rebound tenderness is an indication of organ infection. Deep palpation confirms the diagnosis. I want each of you to copy my movements and see if you can feel the sharp, smooth, flexible edge of the liver—which is normal—and the enlarged gallbladder. Mrs. Catchot, please bear with us. We are going to make you feel better soon."

One at a time the six students placed their hands on the patient's midsection. When John's turn came and the shape of the organs slid under his hand, the power of knowledge rushed through his entire body. The woman gasped as he pressed the infected gallbladder and he resisted the urge to flinch in sympathy. A physician must remain in control.

"My turn," said Abigail boldly.

John looked up frowning, but she stared him down. He grudgingly moved aside, giving her room. She had been standing with her arms crossed, fingers tucked under her armpits. Dropping them, she leaned over the patient, placing her hands in the correct position.

"Your hands are warm," mumbled Mrs. Catchot, visibly relaxing.

Abigail began the examination, her movements becoming more deft until she found the tender spot. "Hold on. Oh, I feel it." She looked down into the patient's eyes. "I'm so sorry. You must be in a lot of pain." She glanced at the professor. "Will you remove the infected organ?"

He'd been observing the procedure with a finger to his lips. "What do you know about surgery?"

She looked frightened. "Nothing." She backed toward the wall, head tucked against her chest.

"Humph." Professor Laniere, frowning, returned to the patient's side and replaced the woman's gown and bedclothes.

John took his life in his hands and stepped close. "Will you, sir? May we watch you take it out?"

The professor glanced at him, but addressed his patient. "Mrs. Catchot, your pain is caused by an inflammation of a tiny sac attached to your small intestine and liver. If we remove it, you'll have a good chance of recovering with no residual effects."

The woman's eyes widened. "*Remove* it? You're going to cut out part of my stomach?"

"Mr. Braddock, please give Mrs. Catchot a brief summary of what is involved in cholecystostomy." The professor's black eyes narrowed. "Gently."

John blinked, snatching for last week's lecture during dissection laboratory. "The surgeon—Dr. Laniere—will administer ether anesthesia. Then he'll make a small incision in your lower abdomen. The gallbladder will be removed with a quick cut and the intestine tightly sutured back together. A few stitches will repair the abdominal incision."

"But—if you cut it out, won't I die? The Good Lord put it in there for a reason!"

"This surgery has been successfully performed for about ten years now," John assured her. "You'll recover in about six weeks and never miss that little piece of flesh."

"Thank you, Mr. Braddock, that's quite enough," said Dr. Laniere drily. "I assure you, Mrs. Catchot, that if you *don't* have the surgery, you'll continue to experience excruciating pain, and the infection could poison your entire system, leading to an early demise." He patted the woman's rigid shoulder. "Try to rest. I'll send someone in to prepare you for surgery. Come with me, gentlemen."

The whole troupe hustled to keep up as the professor exited the room. John, the tallest, managed to edge out everyone except Abigail.

Dr. Laniere spoke without looking over his shoulder. "Girard, you will give Miss Neal the history of the cholecystostomy."

"Yes, sir!" Marcus all but ran to catch up with Abigail's long, gliding steps. "Dr. John Stough Bobbs from Indianapolis, Indiana, was operating on what he thought was an ovarian cyst and rather accidentally found some stones in an inflamed gallbladder. He took them out, stitched up the gallbladder and left it in the abdomen. But here's the funny part—" Marcus burst out laughing. "The patient recovered and outlived Dr. Bobbs!"

A wicked glint of humor lit Abigail's eyes. She looked at Marcus, eyebrows up. "Just think how many of your patients will outlive you and your drinking partners." She slid a glance at John.

The woman had a tongue sharper than any scalpel. "Alcohol is a fine preservative," he said, annoyed. "Girard didn't finish. Just last year, Marion Simms designed and performed the first cholecystostomy on a forty-five-year-old woman with obstructive jaundice. Unfortunately, she lasted only a few days because of internal hemorrhaging. But Dr. Laniere has been to Berlin to observe Carl Langenbuch, who perfected the procedure." He looked at his teacher. "Langenbuch is only twenty-seven years old and he's already director of Lazarus Hospital. Prof says we'll see astonishing things in our lifetime."

Abigail looked away. "I'm sure you will."

The history lesson was aborted as the class approached another ward. As they examined a young man whose foot had been amputated at Antietam, John made a deliberate effort to ignore Abigail's distracting presence. Before he knew it, they'd finished rounds and were given half an hour to themselves before afternoon lectures.

John met Marcus and Weichmann in front of the hospital for their daily run to the French Quarter for gumbo. He didn't care what happened to Abigail Neal. Weichmann caught him looking over his shoulder as the three of them dodged through the midday traffic on Rue Baronne.

"She stayed to talk to Professor." Weichmann grinned.

"Who?" John quickened his pace.

"The girl. The *pretty* girl. You'd better guard your spot as the favorite."

Marcus snorted. "Prof ain't the susceptible sort." He dug his elbow into John's ribs. "Unlike some people."

"Shut up, Girard," John muttered automatically. He glanced at Weichmann. "I've got more important things to worry about than a street tart with a penchant for voyeurism."

Weichmann shook his head. "Smartest street tart *I've* ever run across."

"Citing your broad experience," John said with a quelling frown. "Let's talk about something more interesting—ingrown toenails, for example."

Girard exchanged delighted glances with Weichmann. "Braddock's got his drawers in a twist because the lady's got better hands than he has. Fifty says she'll give him a private lesson in deep palpation before the end of the term."

John grabbed Marcus by the shoulder and whirled him around, heedless of the milling crowd on the street corner. "If I hear you speak of her that way again," he said through his teeth, "I'll take your head off."

Girard's mouth fell open. "You called her a street tart!"

"I was mistaken."

Girard swallowed. "Weichmann, Braddock just admitted he was wrong. Look for the four horses of the Apocalypse."

Suddenly aware of just how foolish he had made himself, John laughed and let go of Girard's shoulder. "Best hope not. By all accounts, I doubt any of the three of us are ready."

Chapter Seven

After the hospital rounds, Abigail was not allowed to accompany the men to the medical college for lectures; she was not a tuition-paying student, of course, and even if she were, women were not allowed into the hallowed halls of the medical college.

The decision to stay created complications. The fear of being found out never left for one moment, and of course she would be giving up the job in the sail loft. Although she would eventually have to go back for her few belongings, the opportunity to learn medicine under the tutelage of a man of Dr. Laniere's stature was too good to pass up.

So she agreed and presented herself to Camilla Laniere, who found other chores requiring Abigail's attention: trapping and disposing of a mouse determined to build a nest in the clinic medicine chest, folding piles of linens and alphabetically organizing the contents of the pharmacy. Every so often she would run upstairs or return to the clinic to check on her patients.

But by mid-afternoon, Tess, far from lying in bed where

she should be, insisted she was well enough to go home and back to work.

"You aren't well enough to go back." Abigail held Tess by the shoulders to keep her in her chair, looking to Camilla for support. "Besides, we need you here in the clinic."

"I'm glad you're feeling well enough to be up and around a bit." Camilla stood in the clinic doorway with Meg in her arms. "But I wish you wouldn't try to do too much too soon. Your fever only began to come down last night."

Tess looked down, pleating the black skirt Winona had lent her. "It's too hard. I can't watch the children…"

Abigail knelt and took her friend's restless hands. "Tess—"

"And I'm no good with nursing. Sewing is all I know how to do."

With a smile, Camilla glanced at the pile of darning in her workbasket on the table. "There's plenty of that around here. I could truly use your help."

Tess got up and moved to the window. Pressing her hands against the glass, she watched a fine carriage rattle down the brick side street. "You're very kind, Mrs. Laniere, but I simply don't belong here." She turned her head and met Abigail's eyes. "You don't either. You should go back with me."

Stung, Abigail got to her feet. "If you insist on leaving, I can't stop you, but I'm going to stay here as long as they'll let me. I'll go back to the District when I've learned enough to make a difference—"

"Make a difference?" Tess turned her back on the sunny window. "People are going to do what they're going to do. So what if you save a few lives? Save them for what? More poverty and prejudice and hopelessness?"

Camilla took a step toward her. "My dear—"

"And you—with your beautiful dresses and fine house and handsome husband. What do you know about where we came from? What do you care?" Tess's face was white. "I used to be just like you—" She pressed her fingers to her lips.

This was more than Abigail had learned about Tess in the six months she'd known her. She reached for her friend.

Tess shook her head hard. "Let me go, Abby." She looked at Camilla. "I'm sorry to have insulted you, ma'am. You didn't make my choices for me. But you can't undo the consequences, either." A small, bitter smile curved her lips. "There's much truth in what the Bible says about that."

"There's *all* truth in the Bible, although you're missing the healing parts." Camilla's deep sigh blew Meg's fine curls. "As Abigail said, we can't hold you here. But remember, you're always welcome to come back."

"Thank you, ma'am." Tess hesitated, then rushed to kiss Abigail's cheek. "Goodbye, Abigail. You've been a good friend."

Before Abigail could blink, Tess was gone. She stood there, tears escaping in a messy flood. Helplessly she looked at Camilla. "What can I do?"

Camilla's soft, heart-shaped face was tight with emotion. "Pray that God will deal with her."

"You heard what she said! God doesn't help those who don't believe in Him."

"Is that what you think?" Camilla's smile suddenly lit her face. "Oh, my dear. You do indeed have a lot to learn."

Later that night Abigail turned the page of the textbook she'd been studying, setting the candle flame aflutter. Camilla had firmly adjured her to get a good night's sleep, placed the candle in her hand, and sent her up to her new attic bedroom.

After Tess's departure, the day had been a long one. To keep her mind off worrying about her stubborn friend, she'd catalogued in her neat script the clinic's medicines in a book Camilla gave her, separately noting all the names she didn't recognize. After supper she presented the list to Dr. Laniere, who smiled and went to his library for the book now lying across her lap.

Resisting the urge to rub her stinging eyes, she adjusted the pillow behind her back. Sleep beckoned, but she had to know about the anesthesia to be used on that poor woman in the hospital. Maybe, armed with information, Abigail could return in the morning before the surgery and allay some of the woman's fear.

Here it was. Ether, a flammable gas with a distinctive, sticky-sweet odor. Side effects could include postanesthetic headaches, nausea and vomiting. But it had been found to be more effective than chloroform as an anesthetic during surgery.

Abigail frowned. The side effects sounded almost as unpleasant as the disease. She set the book aside, blew out the candle and settled under the fresh sheet with which she'd made up her bed. The Chinese women she'd tended who had died of internal infections—some of which she suspected were gallbladder related—could undoubtedly have been saved if this relatively simple surgery had been performed. If only she'd known how. If only she could watch and learn.

She pictured John Braddock's face that morning as he'd realized she could perform an examination every bit as thorough and skillful as he could. Smiling, she fell asleep.

Miss Charlemagne let John in without a cross word about the earliness of the hour and he took off his hat and stared at her in surprise. He'd left his curtain open so the rising sun would wake him early. Filching a biscuit from Clem's gigantic bread box, he'd let himself out, saddled Belladonna and made it to the hospital before the church bells chimed six.

Faintly smiling, Miss Charlemagne gestured toward the spartan little room off the entryway, furnished for the use of doctors in consultation with patients' families. "Miss Neal struck up a conversation with Crutch, so I sent them into the parlor to keep the noise down."

"Miss Neal?" He frowned. "She's here already?"

The smile slid perilously close to a smirk as she patted his arm. "You've quite the task to keep up, don't you? Call me if you need me."

Juggling a confusing mixture of irritation and anticipation, John headed for the parlor. He stopped in the doorway, trying to decide whether to laugh or call the watch.

Abigail and the hospital handyman faced each other in the two wing chairs, knee to knee. Crutch had removed his jacket and sat in his shirtsleeves, still and rapt, as Abigail listened to his chest with Professor Laniere's spare stethoscope.

John folded his arms and leaned against the doorframe. "How industrious of you, Miss Neal, I must say."

Abigail jumped, dropping the bell of the stethoscope, and turned. "John—Mr. Braddock! You frightened me."

"My sincere apologies." He bowed. "Perhaps in future I should announce my presence with a ram's horn."

"A simple knock on the door would suffice." Her hand fluttered to her hair as she removed the stethoscope from her ears, a self-conscious little gesture that softened his inclination to tweak her. "I thought I'd have time to look around and talk to any of the patients who might be awake."

She hesitated. "Everyone's asleep, so I persuaded Mr. Crutch to let me practice auscultation upon him."

"I trust you found nothing out of order." John nodded at Crutch. He was a good man, if a bit simple.

The elderly handyman jumped to his feet, proudly thumping his chest. "Lady says I'm right healthy. The old ticker's strong as a mule."

"I'm very happy to hear that."

Abigail rose, clutching the bell of the stethoscope in one hand, her skirt in the other. "Mr. Crutch, I apologize for interrupting your morning routine," she said evenly. "Thank you for your assistance."

"Don't mention it, miss." Crutch shuffled into the entryway and looked over his shoulder at Abigail. "Mayhap you'll want to check the young doc here's chest. There's some say he ain't got no ticker at all." With a sly grin he disappeared in the direction of the kitchen.

Resisting the urge to protest such nonsense, John turned the ladder-backed desk chair around and straddled it, folding his arms along its back. Abigail's patent discomfort at being alone in the small room with him was almost comical. She edged behind the wing chair she'd vacated, as if to place as much distance between them as possible.

He rested his chin on his forearms and looked up at her in amusement. "What do you think, Miss Neal? Is there a hole in my barbarian chest cavity?" When she gasped, he laughed. "Camilla told me what you said. Although how you can equate the desire to ease a patient's pain with lack of civilizing manners is beyond my understanding."

She fingered the modest frill of lace at her collar. "Of course there's nothing wrong with anesthetizing before surgery. I studied everything I could find on the subject last night."

He studied the purple shadows beneath her fine green eyes. "Perhaps *all* night?"

She moistened her lips. "I got plenty of rest, though I thank you for your concern."

He *was* concerned, although it galled him to admit it even to himself. "You must have arrived before the sun rose. Did you walk all the way here by yourself? Next time, let me know and I'll come round to get you."

"Thank you, but…as it happens, I rode in to the hospital this morning with Dr. Laniere."

"Where is Prof?" John looked over his shoulder. Wouldn't do to get caught sitting idle.

"He's upstairs with paperwork." There was a long moment's silence during which Abigail avoided John's gaze. Finally she huffed a little sigh. "Why are *you* here so early, Mr. Braddock? Making sure you don't fall out of favor again?"

"As a matter of fact, yes. But my rotation is with Dr. Girard today."

"Dr. Girard?"

"Marcus's father. Chemistry and clinical medicine. He's less exacting than Prof in some ways, but considerably more volatile of temperament."

"Indeed." Abigail grinned. "I should think that would make you friends."

He frowned. "I'm not volatile."

She tipped her head.

"I'm not. In fact, I'm going to be magnanimous to the point of offering my body on the altar of science." He thought of Marcus's remarks about palpation and felt his cheeks heat. "I mean, perhaps you'd like to listen to my chest and lungs to see if there's indeed anything missing."

"I'm not sure that's a good idea." She stayed behind the wing chair, looking as if she didn't quite trust him.

He could hardly blame her. But he shrugged out of his jacket and began to unbutton his vest. "Come, Abigail, missishness will get you nowhere in our profession." He leaned forward across the back of his chair. "You start by telling me to take a deep breath."

She glanced at the open doorway, biting her lips together. Then, squaring her shoulders, she put the stethoscope's earpieces in her ears and approached him. She hovered beside him, a foot or so away. Finally she laid her hand on his shoulder and pressed the steth bell between his shoulder blades. "Take a deep breath."

Involuntarily he sucked in a breath, jerking at her touch, modest and impersonal but warm through the linen of his shirt.

"Thank you. Now out."

He forced himself to release his breath slowly. There was a very good reason women should not be allowed to treat men. She moved the bell to a position just above his left kidney. He breathed again, in and out.

"Your lungs are quite healthy," she said. "But I'm detecting an alarming acceleration of the pulse."

John looked up at her and found the green eyes brimming with laughter. He sat up straight as she stepped back, removing that warm hand from his shoulder. "Perhaps you'd like to listen to my chest."

"Some other time, Mr. Braddock. Your fellow students will arrive soon and I wouldn't want you to risk a reprimand from your irascible professor."

He regarded her narrowly as he reached for his outer clothing. "Will you be joining us for rounds?"

"I'm afraid not. Dr. Laniere wants others to train me in some of the less complicated nursing duties this morning. But he says I may watch the gallbladder surgery. So I'll see you in the operating theater at nine."

"Very well." He rose, buttoning his vest. "I wish you a successful morning, then. Until we meet again." He bowed and exited the room, resisting the urge to see if she followed. Abigail Neal was proving to be a most unsettling addition to the hospital staff. In the presence of such a lovely, off-limits young woman, no wonder his pulse rate refused to remain normal.

Even for such a relatively simple procedure as the removal of a gallbladder, the surgical amphitheater was crowded with students, doctors and interested citizenry—all men. Dr. Laniere had planted Abigail in a corner seat—she could still hardly comprehend his courtesy and generosity—and repaired to a scrub room to prepare himself for the operation. As the room filled, loud male conversation echoed off the vaulted ceiling and marble panels set between the huge windows, but the seat beside her remained empty. Apparently no one wanted to contaminate himself by proximity to the brazen hussy in the ugly dress.

Which was just as well. She wanted to observe without having to make conversation. It was a good thing God had seen fit to bless her with keen eyesight. She was so far up in the tiers of seats she was likely to suffer a nosebleed from the height. But no complaining. She was here. She was unmolested. The Toad would never think to look for her here.

Still, she couldn't help examining the backs of all those

heads below her and to the right. None of them, thank God, had the lumpy, flattened shape she'd trained herself to watch for and run from.

"I'm going out on a limb to assume that the seat isn't taken. May I?"

Abigail looked up to find John Braddock, hat in hand, at the far end of the aisle. To reach the empty seat beside her, he would have to step over several gentlemen, all of whom were looking at her with various levels of curiosity and disdain.

She sighed. There went her solitary enjoyment of the experience. "I suppose."

"Pardon me. I beg your pardon," John repeated as he made his way down the aisle toward her. When he finally reached her, he sprawled in the seat, dropping his hat onto his knee. "Whew. That was a job." He looked at her. "It took me a few minutes to find you, stuck way up here in this treetop. I usually only sit here when I have a test to study for."

"I imagine Dr. Laniere was hoping to keep me from attracting too much attention. Which, thanks to you, seems to be a lost cause." Still, she couldn't help a surge of pleasure that he had sought her out. She folded her arms. "How were your rounds with the dyspeptic Dr. Girard?"

"As usual, he singled me out for acerbic asides about illiterate rich boys. As if he hasn't raised three of those himself. But, fortunately, I maintain perspective. The more he growls, the happier he is." He sent her a wry smile. "And what about you? Did you learn anything today?"

"Yes." Abigail nodded. "I was taught the proper way to lift a patient from one bed to another, and the science of bedpans."

A stir at the front of the theater caught Abigail's attention. A couple of orderlies trundled in a cart with the patient, lying on her back with her hands folded across her stomach. She seemed to be asleep.

As a hush fell across the observing audience, John sat forward. "I watched them put her under anesthesia," he whispered to Abigail. "She fought the ether like a wild woman."

"She must have been frightened to death." Busy with the nurses that morning, Abigail had not been allowed to see the patient as she'd hoped to do. She studied John's face and was relieved to find sympathy rather than the avid excitement she'd expected. "How would you do it differently?"

He frowned. "I'm not sure. I wonder if there's a way to prepare the patient—"

"Shh!" someone hissed from the other end of the row.

Abigail jerked her attention back to the operating theater. Dr. Laniere, assisted by a couple of students Abigail remembered from yesterday's rounds, was adjusting a row of gleaming instruments laid out on a nearby table. An older gentleman in beard and spectacles, whom she assumed to be another surgeon, busied himself with the lights and then stationed himself at the foot of the patient's bed. Abigail could hear the men murmuring to one another, and she'd have given anything to know what they said.

As if he'd read her mind, Dr. Laniere lifted a hand and addressed the audience. "Gentlemen, we are about to begin the procedure to remove an infected gallbladder, commonly referred to as cholecystostomy. Symptoms that indicate acute sepsis include enlarged gallbladder, persistent pain in the abdomen and a slight jaundice of the skin. Please observe that the patient is completely under the influence of ether-based anesthesia and will neither feel nor remember the incisions."

Absorbed in the surgeon's deft movements and clinical explanations, Abigail sat forward, clasping her fingers around her knees. The operation proceeded almost to the letter as Marcus Girard had described it yesterday. There was blood, yes, but far from swooning in disgust, Abigail found herself awed and fascinated that such a drastic action as invasion of the body with a knife could result in healing.

Incision. Removal of infected tissue. Suturing. Scarring. Regeneration.

As she watched, Abigail ran the words through her mind. Spiritual implications nudged her heart, but she pushed them away until later. Right now she needed to learn what she could from the physical experience.

She'd almost forgotten John's vital presence to her right when he drew in a sharp breath. "She's hemorrhaging."

The action on the theater floor suddenly quickened as sponges, clamps and needles flew, and every person in the audience leaned forward. Then, as quickly as it began, it was over. Dr. Laniere gained control, sutured the patient's internal incision and moved back to let one of his students close.

"You may relax now, Abigail—the danger is past." John's amused baritone broke into Abigail's concentration.

She looked down to find, to her utter horror, that she'd been clutching his hand. Releasing him, she brushed her palms together as if washing them. "I'm so sorry—"

"Never mind, I understand," he said with a surprising absence of teasing. "Prof is a dynamic surgeon, but I admire him most because he makes it look so easy." He looked around and lowered his voice. "Some of the surgeons with a deal less skill are much more apt to play up the theatrics of a situation. Flourishes, raised voices, all that nonsense. Prof teaches us to take care of business with thoroughness and precision."

Abigail nodded, distracted by the lingering sensation of John's large, fine-boned hand wrapped around hers. Helplessly she remembered the feeling of his broad shoulder under her hand as she'd stood in the hospital parlor, listening to him breathe. Strong, vital, male. Oh my, she was undone. "Will Mrs. Catchot recover now?" she said rather at random.

"Undoubtedly." John rose as the gentlemen around them began to stir, discussing the operation they'd collectively witnessed. He offered Abigail a friendly hand to assist her to her feet.

She stared at it for half a second, then jumped up on her own. "Oh, dear, it's nearly noon. I promised Camilla I'd come back to help—please excuse me, Mr. Braddock."

He stared at her, nonplussed, but moved to the end of the row and waited for her to hurry past. "Would you like to join me and the fellows for—"

"No, thank you, I really have to go." Dipping a curtsy, she fled down the theater steps, dodging doctors and laymen lingering in conversation.

Only when she was safely on her way back to Rue Gironde on foot did she realize what a ninny she'd been, allowing her ridiculous, unwanted interest in John Braddock to keep her from learning what she could.

Taking a breath and releasing it, she slowed her steps. She looked up at the sky, where weak sunlight filtered through a bank of soft gray clouds. Control had brought her this far. Persistence and willingness to face her fears. She'd finally maneuvered her way to safety and a possible means of attaining her desire to become a doctor. If she could only stay the course, who knew what she might accomplish?

Besides, she wasn't afraid of John Braddock. What nonsense.

Chapter Eight

The midweek French market was a jumbled discord of music, laughter and multiple languages, a gumbo of color, odor and movement. Inured to the crowd and noise, John effectively blocked out everything but his single-minded quest for the perfect orange. He was crouching to poke through a pile of fruit in a vendor's basket when a hand touched his shoulder.

He looked up to find Abigail Neal standing over him.

"Behold, the vassal on his knees." Eyebrows quirked in amusement, she swept a dramatic hand through the air.

"Abigail!" He lunged to his feet. "I thought you were going back to the Lanieres'."

"I did." She gestured vaguely in the direction of Rue Gironde, setting the empty canvas bag in her hand flapping. "Camilla sent me to buy a chicken for the evening meal and I saw you over here." She plucked the orange out of his hand. "I thought you medical people never stopped to eat."

"Citrus helps ward off colds and influenza."

"Indeed." She examined the orange as if she'd never seen one before. Perhaps she hadn't.

John chose another one and called to a dark-skinned woman seated on a three-legged stool at the booth's entrance. "I'll take both of these. How much?"

The woman, dressed in a multilayered gown and head rag, answered in the Acadian French mumble of the Quarter; John drew a penny from his pocket and tossed it to her. He looked at Abigail and jerked a thumb in the direction of a jambalaya vendor's stall. "Come on, I'll buy the rest of your dinner."

She hesitated, looking over her shoulder at a poultry farmer's noisy stall.

He handed her one of the oranges. "Camilla won't expect you back right away. I daresay she won't even know you're gone." He didn't know why he was insisting when she'd made it clear she didn't want his company. But then he'd never been able to resist a challenge. Smiling with gentle mockery, he backed toward the stall from which the aroma of crawfish, onions, peppers and tomatoes drifted like a siren song. "Come on, Abigail. You know you're hungry."

She looked down at the sack dangling from her wrist. "I suppose I could stay Chanticleer's execution for another hour." Tossing the orange over her shoulder and catching it behind her back, she picked up her skirts. "All right, then."

He glanced at her as they approached the jambalaya booth. "You've read Chaucer?"

She shrugged. "Where I grew up, there wasn't much to do but read."

"Considering your vocabulary, that doesn't surprise me. But *Canterbury Tales* is a fairly bawdy choice."

She slid him a sidelong look. "Make up your mind, John. Either I'm a lady or I'm not."

The conundrum had entered his mind more than once

since her abrupt departure from the operating theater. Sometimes it seemed she understood the rules of society and other times she appeared to delight in flouting them. He stared for a moment without answering, then turned to the aged mulatto stirring a pot of something fragrant over an open cookfire. "Two bowls of jambalaya, if you please."

A few minutes later they were seated side-by-side on a low brick wall opposite the market, watching the foot traffic pass by as they ate. Abigail had already finished her orange, dropping the fragrant rind onto the ground for the seagulls, and was engaged in scooping jambalaya into her mouth with an oyster shell provided by the vendor. A cluster of dark-skinned women swayed past, one of them winking over her shoulder at John.

Abigail glanced at him. "Do you ever wonder where all these people come from? Where they live and what sorts of occupations they have?"

"I'm fairly certain what those particular women do," John said drily.

"You thought the same about me, but you were absolutely, unequivocally wrong."

"Unequivocally?" He'd have to admit he'd never met a prostitute with quite the vocabulary Abigail flaunted. "I stand corrected. Perhaps you could redirect my ignorance as to how you and Tess *did* manage to support yourselves in that squalid little room I found you in."

"We worked in the sail loft on Julia Street. I waxed twine and Tess hand-stitched grommets."

He gave her a skeptical look. "Where did you learn to do that?"

"Tess taught me. She was working there—she's quite a seamstress, you know—and put in a good word for me. The work isn't difficult to learn, just tiring and a bit hard on the hands." She rubbed her fingers together and he could hear the swishing of callus against callus. "Some days I thought my back would break from sitting in one place for ten or twelve hours straight."

John frowned. "That's inhumane."

Abigail looked down at the oyster shell in her empty bowl. "It kept us out of the brothels." Brushing off further questions with a wave of her hand, she smiled at him. "Thank you for my dinner. I was actually looking for you because I wanted to ask you something."

Wary, he searched her face. Her sharp cheekbones had filled out over the last few days, turning her from a gaunt Amazon into quite a striking young woman. Her hair glowed with healthy streaks of umber and gold and, loosened a bit from its severe brown bun, revealed a distinct wave. The green eyes, bright and rested, regarded him with frightening intelligence.

"You may ask," he said, "but I make no promises."

"I would expect no less from you, Mr. Braddock" she said tartly. "Yesterday I heard Professor Laniere reading a piece from a medical journal to Camilla. The subject was autopsy. The author seemed to think the practice a bit of, shall we say, overkill." Her lips twitched.

John chuckled. "The medical profession is divided over the issue, but Prof advocates autopsy as a method of preventing disease. The more one knows about what causes death, the better the chances of heading it off the next go-round."

"I gathered that." Abigail tipped her head. "Which is why I want you to teach me what you know about it."

John stared at her. "You can't be serious."

"Why not?" She set her bowl down on the wall. "I know the professor makes you fellows cut up and examine every charity case that comes through the hospital morgue. Surely you're capable of demonstrating the rudiments."

"Of course I'm *capable*." John scowled at her. "But you'd not be allowed into the morgue. And—and even if you were, where would we get the body to examine? And why do you *want* to do this?" The idea of a woman willing to watch a human body cut from stem to stern, the organs lifted out, weighed and measured, prodded and poked…

Preposterous.

Abigail leaned forward. "The body is a mystery I've longed for some time to unlock. Tess, for example. I'd no idea how to help her baby get out safely because I didn't know the arrangement of the parts inside."

"I know the arrangement of parts, but that didn't help me," John pointed out. "Besides, I can draw that for you with pencil and paper. Any good anatomy textbook will show—"

"I've seen the textbooks. I want to examine the organs' texture and color, compare the sizes of male and female, see the physical arrangement inside the body. And I want to see anomalies. John, you of all people must understand this…this craving I have to know." Her eyes burned into his.

John had never met a woman like this one. His mother and sister swooned at the sight of blood—or at least pretended to. Camilla Laniere, somewhat more down-to-earth, never shied away from her husband's work or her children's needs. But John had never heard her express a desire to observe an autopsy, much less participate in one.

"I'll ask the professor," he said reluctantly. Prof would put the hammer down on the idea.

"I already asked him. He said he didn't have time to spare from his family and his students—"

"Then there you have it." John shrugged. "It's out of the question—"

"—but he said if one of his students wanted extra practice and was willing to go in after hours, he'd approve the release of the body."

John set down his bowl with a clatter. "I can't believe that!"

"It's true. Ask him."

"Why didn't you ask one of the other chaps? Weichmann or Girard would jump at the chance to show off."

"Because I want the best. If I can't have Dr. Laniere, I want you."

John resisted her blatant flattery. "You don't know what you're asking. Have you ever seen an adult cadaver?"

She nodded. "I assure you I can tolerate more than you think. Look, I'll make it worth your while. I was going to propose a trade."

"A trade?" Startled, he laughed, taking in her shabby dress and broken shoes. "What could you possibly have that I would want?"

For a moment she regarded him with cold fury. "I was going to offer to tutor you in Latin and Greek—which I happen to be very good at."

Somehow he knew she wasn't making false claims. "What makes you think I need help with Latin and Greek?"

She reached into his jacket and plucked out his dictionary. Her thumb fanned the pages. "I saw you sneaking glances yesterday as we made rounds. And this morning in the surgery theater. You're afraid Girard will outgun you."

"Girard? You're mad. He can barely speak English."

"Then it's Weichmann. You're terrified of losing first place in the class." Her eyes dared him to deny it.

Pressing his lips together, he stared across the street, where the new Courtyard Hotel was undergoing construction, the masons calling to one another, singing over the slap of brick and mortar, scrape of trowel. Abigail had somehow hit on his Achilles' heel. Although he was acknowledged to be brilliant in maths and sciences, reading had never come easily, and Latin declensions gave him migraines.

But as she said, if he could somehow turn his problem around, his place would be secured. The professor had given him another chance to prove himself. Supervising an autopsy, even for the benefit of a woman, was a privilege.

"All right. I'll do it." He frowned at Abigail to squelch her obvious triumph. "But you'll do exactly as I say and don't tell any of the other fellows about it."

"But you said—"

"I don't want them to get any ideas. Are we agreed on the terms?"

She looked at him silently, then nodded, a brief jerk of her head. "Agreed. Can we begin tonight?"

"If there's a body available."

Her smile was grim. "In this city, right here by the waterfront, there's always a body available. Where and when shall I meet you?"

"You've no business walking anywhere alone after dark. I'll come for you at eleven." He thought for a moment. "I'll have to let Miss Charlemagne in on it, get the key from her. She won't tell anyone."

Abigail's smile broadened to a grin. *"Mors gaudet succurrere vitae."*

"You might start your tuition by translating that."

"Death rejoices to help those who live."

Abigail waited for John that evening in the clinic entryway. Winona had just gone to bed, leaving a small oil lamp on the table to spread orangey shadows into the kitchen.

The young housekeeper had stood in the doorway of her room, shaking her head over Abigail's insane desire to cut open dead bodies in the middle of the night. "It's all well and good for Mr. John and the other students hacking people apart, but you're a lady." When Abigail just shrugged, Winona snorted and disappeared, taking her disapproval with her.

Abigail slid back the small window panel in the door and peered out into the dense darkness. She wiped her sweaty palms down the sides of her skirt. She wasn't ready for this as she'd pretended. An adventure that had seemed like a good idea in the bright noonday sun of the French Quarter now loomed with nightmarish grimness.

She took a hard look at herself. Leaning against the door, she looked down at her hands. The nails had been trimmed to the quick, the cuticles and fingertips cracked from exposure to lye cleansers. Not the hands of a lady. But what had the title ever given her or any other woman she'd known? Protection? She pictured her mother, imprisoned in a Chinese missionary compound, unprepared for any work except maintaining her white skin and corresponding with herself in a journal.

There had to be more. Abigail would *make* more, gladly forfeiting her right to be called anything except a useful human being.

At a soft rap on the door at her back, she turned and released the latch. John Braddock stood there, shifting from one foot to the other. Dressed simply in white cotton shirt, loose breeches and boots, he held a lamp in one hand and the handle of a large wooden case in the other.

He moved back to allow her to pass. "Are you ready? I had trouble getting out of the house, so we're a bit late."

"I'm ready." She stepped into the carriageway and kept pace with him until they reached the street. The residential area was quiet at this time of night; only the sound of water dripping from leaves after a late-afternoon rain shower accompanied their footsteps. The scent of frangipani from someone's garden drifted on a sultry breeze. They'd walked two blocks before she broke the silence. "Why would you have trouble leaving the house?"

He glanced at her, lips curved. "My landlady's a bit of a dragon."

Abigail smiled. "Why don't you live at home? Winona says your family is wealthy and well-connected."

"I prefer that my mother not be aware of all my comings and goings."

She could understand that. "You're fortunate to have choices."

He looked down at her again, a gleam of curiosity in his eyes. "Do you not have a family who wonders where you are?"

"My mother left before I did."

"Left where?"

"The mission compound." There could be no harm in telling him that much.

"Your father is a missionary? I've been trying to place your accent. Where is he?"

Abigail knew she'd said enough. "In a sensitive area. It's best that I not divulge his location."

John swung the lamp high, throwing light across Abigail's face. She shielded her eyes.

"Who are you?" he demanded. "You speak like a lady, but comport yourself like...like no other woman I know."

"Perhaps your circle of acquaintance isn't as large as you seem to think." She walked on.

He quickly caught up to her, but maintained a stubborn silence until they reached the hospital entrance. The building loomed, white stucco gleaming in the light of the stars.

"John." Abigail touched his forearm: hard, corded sinew and muscle, live and real. She needed the grounding of his company.

He kept walking, heading for the rear of the hospital. "What is it, Abigail?"

She trotted after him. "I'm sorry I keep offending you. Truly I know what a favor you're doing by bringing me here, especially because you probably need to study." She hesitated. "Can you accept that there are things I can't tell you without putting myself in danger?"

He wheeled. "There's a reason you're so determined to learn how to keep people alive. Who did you kill, Abigail? Was it your husband? This father of yours in the mission compound? Did he beat you? It happens all the time." He lowered his voice. "Who was it?"

After a stunned moment Abigail got her voice back. "You think I *killed* someone?" A hysterical giggle escaped. "You're willing to give a murderess an autopsy knife?"

He swung the lamp wildly, slashing light across the drive path. "What am I supposed to think? A handsome, educated young woman like you—living in a tenement, versant with medical terminology—refusing to talk about your family? It doesn't make one bit of sense!"

Abigail smothered her laughter. "I assure you my father is alive and well. And I've never been married."

"Then what? What are you running from?" John steadied the lamp, his expression troubled, but for once, not particularly threatening.

Abigail bit her lip and stared at the strong, tanned throat rising like a Greek column from the open collar of his shirt. For reasons she couldn't immediately put her finger on, she was reluctant to lie to him.

"Myself, I suppose," she murmured. "I didn't want to be that girl anymore. The one who did what they said, who watched bad things happen." She met his stormy hazel eyes. "My mother escaped and I knew I could, too. It just took some planning."

"And this is worth it?" He glanced around, slopping oily light onto the hospital's mildewed walls. "You're better off here?"

"As long as…" She folded her lips. "Yes. It's better. Now let's go inside. I want to know what you know."

He stared at her a moment longer, sighed, then turned to rap on the door.

It opened to reveal Miss Charlemagne, bearing a small lamp like a gnome in a children's picture book. She nodded as if she welcomed visitors into the morgue at midnight on a regular basis. "Come in, children. I've made tea if anyone cares for refreshment."

Shoving away the discomfort of John's questions, Abigail smiled at the woman as she stepped inside the shadowy anteroom. "Thank you, but we don't have much time. We won't keep you, if you have other duties."

The older woman gave John an uncertain look, as if confirming his authority.

He sighed, visibly restraining impatience. "Dr. Laniere instructed me to make sure we finish well before dawn."

"Then come with me. I've had Crutch move the body onto the table for you." She turned, skirts swishing, and led the way through an open doorway to the left, through which Abigail could see lights burning.

As they entered the room, the odor of formaldehyde bombarded her senses, watering her eyes and stinging her nose.

"This is most extraordinary," said the woman, turning up several lamps in wall sconces to illuminate a white-shrouded body lying on a slanted marble table. The sides of the table were raised, portals in the lower corners providing drainage into a couple of metal buckets. "I've never heard of an autopsy at night."

"There's a lot about this that isn't normal." Gesturing for Abigail to stand beside him, John inclined his head to Miss Charlemagne. "We'll call you when we're finished."

Miss Charlemagne glanced at a bell pull suspended from the ceiling and stretching through an aperture in one wall. "Ring for me, then. I'll be in the kitchen, preparing for morning meals."

"She likes you," Abigail observed as John reached into his pocket for a pair of kid gloves.

"It's mutual." He handed them to her and produced a second pair for himself. "Put those on."

She slipped on the gloves, marveling at their tight fit. "Where did you get these?"

"Begged them from my sister's maid. She'll never miss them." He took a deep breath. "Are you ready?"

Abigail nodded, mentally bracing herself. "Is it a man or a woman?"

"Female." He stripped back the shroud, exposing dark hair and the gray, still face of a young woman.

Abigail swallowed. At least the eyes were closed. The cheeks were puffy, the mouth slack. She fought a feeling of invasion, as if she were the second-in-command of a conquering army. The upper torso came into view. "Stop," she blurted. Blushing, she looked up at John, but found only sober and respectful interest in his expression as he continued to remove the shroud.

His eyes flicked to her face as he folded it and laid it on a nearby table. "There's no embarrassment in death, Abigail," he said with a certain amount of sympathy for her discomfort.

The embarrassment was that hundreds of women died daily in the tenements around the hospital, alone and unwanted by their families, abandoned to the indignities of the surgeon's knife. She could learn from this one.

She braced herself as John opened his case of implements. Out of their velvet bed they came, one at a time, shining sharp steel. He explained their uses as he laid them on the table.

Skull chisel. Rib cutters, looking like a small pair of pruning shears. Scalpel. Suture needles that reminded her of her job in the sail loft. Toothed forceps. Bone saw.

Abigail watched and listened, wholly absorbed. She was going to make a difference. Armed with knowledge, she *would* make a difference.

Chapter Nine

"*Mortui vivos docent*," Abigail murmured, staring down at the red-brown liver in her hands.

"The dead teach the living." John nodded at the stainless steel scales. "Lay it down there. We're going to weigh it first."

Abigail glanced at him as she laid the spongy organ in the scale. "You *can* translate when you try."

"I can do a lot of things when I try."

"What does that mean?"

His gaze dropped to her mouth. "Nothing."

She looked momentarily disconcerted, then shrugged and adjusted the balance weight. "Two and three-quarter pounds. That's light."

"Yes." He studied her a moment, puzzled by her reaction. Had she really not understood the subtext of his comment? "You've read Morgangni's pathology text?"

"Professor Laniere let me borrow it yesterday."

John grunted. She'd probably read the whole thing in a couple of hours. "You don't know how privileged you are, having access to that library." He moved back to the table. "All right. Now put the liver on the table and we'll dissect it." He handed her a scalpel. "Short incisions across each lobe, spaced one inch apart."

She bit her lip as she obeyed. "Like this?"

"That's it." He watched her competent movements. "Stop. What do you see inside the cuts?"

"Lobules. Veins." She bent to peer at the liver. "The color doesn't look right."

"How do you know?"

"The drawings from the textbook…" She hesitated. "The texture is brittle. It's supposed to be dense."

"That's right." He gently inserted his thumbs into a cut to spread it open. "Do you know what the liver does?"

"It's a…filter of sorts. Aids in digestion. A toxin would do this kind of damage, wouldn't it?" Abigail looked up at him, her green eyes intent.

He nodded. "This is similar to cirrhosis—diffuse fibrous content. Typical of patients from the District."

"Alcohol abuse," Abigail said sadly. "Or maybe opium."

John lifted his shoulders. "This woman was a prostitute, a known opium eater." He nodded at the clock on the wall. "We won't be able to stay much longer. Quickly, show me the left hepatic duct, the inferior vena cava and the hepatic artery."

As she did so, she explained the etymology of each word. John listened, absorbed, repeating back what she'd taught him. She was a good teacher, patient and thorough.

They finished with the liver, then removed and examined the reproductive organs. The uterus was scarred, indicative of multiple abortions. Abigail's eyes went glassy when dissection revealed a tiny embryo imbedded in its lining, but she blinked and correctly named the parts as John touched them.

He returned all the dissected organs carefully to the body's cavity. "Look in the case for my needle and sutures. We'll sew her up and be out of here."

Without speaking, Abigail complied with jerky movements.

John held the body together and watched her neat, evenly spaced stitches. "Very good."

She looked up at him briefly. "I worked in a sail shop for six months."

"So you've never...sold yourself in the District?" He couldn't contain his curiosity about this odd, brilliant, self-contained young woman. In his wildest imaginings he wouldn't have conjured a gently bred woman possessing the brass to enter a hospital morgue in the dead of night for the purpose of cutting open and examining a naked dead body.

Tugging on the final stitch, she fashioned a neat knot and clipped the thread. She backed away, her body taut, trembling, her eyes narrowed. "I'm going to tell you this one more time," she said, voice low and fierce, "and if you ask me again, I will happily demonstrate my finesse with a scalpel. I haven't to this point been forced to sell my body to survive, although I have lived among women who have. There's a thriving trade in this city of which you may not be aware—it is a vile form of slavery and it is to these women I wish to minister." She stepped closer to John then, fisting her gloved hands at her sides. "And *that* wish makes it possible for me to endure your insults to learn what you know."

Odd she might be, John thought, and decidedly prickly, but she had a very fine pair of eyes and her refusal to buckle under his questions made him smile. He took her hand and gently pried her fingers apart, removing the needle and returning it to its case. "All right, Abigail," he said mildly. "Objection noted." He reached up to pull the bell cord. "Crutch will be here shortly, to dispose of the body. We'd best wash our hands." He gestured toward the basin and ewer sitting on a table across the room. "You first."

"Thank you." Abigail stalked around the table and lifted the ewer to splash water into the basin.

Watching her stiff back, John shook his head. "I truly meant no insult. I only wondered."

She looked over her shoulder. "Is that an apology?"

He considered for a moment. "Yes, I think it was."

"All right, then. You are forgiven. But the subject is closed." She moved aside to allow him access to the ewer.

As he washed, he studied Abigail from the corner of his eye. She stood head bowed beside the shroud-covered figure on the table, almost as if she were praying. An intriguing woman, perhaps more attractive than any lady he knew. His mother would be horrified at his assessment.

He smiled.

Abigail trailed behind as John supervised Crutch in the removal of the body.

"Careful, Crutch," said John, steadying the horse-drawn wagon waiting in an alley behind the hospital. "The poor woman led a hard enough life. Let's don't add to her embarrassments by dropping her into the sewer."

Shooting him a glowering grimace, Crutch slid the awkward, tarp-wrapped bundle onto the wagon bed. "The charity catacombs was full up last time I showed up with a body. Don't know what they're gonna do with this 'un." He raised the tailgate, secured it with a leather strap to the wagon's wooden side and wiped his hands on the seat of his filthy pants.

"That's not your problem." John slid a coin into the man's waiting hand and turned to Miss Charlemagne, who was in the doorway, arms folded inside her cloak. "Thank you for your help. We'll be back for rounds later. Come along, Abigail. I'll walk you back to the professor's."

As she and John rounded the front corner of the hospital, Abigail looked up at him. "Rounds are every day?"

"Yes. And lectures in the afternoons." He crossed the lawn toward the street, where carts were beginning to rattle toward the market, stirring the early morning quiet.

Abigail squinted at the rising sun, which radiated violet and gray streaks across the tops of the buildings. "You'll have a long day, then. Thank you for bringing me with you tonight."

He checked as a dray passed, then ducked across Common, heading for the dark green sward of the park. "Tell me how you came to learn a nearly dead language." Shortening his long stride, he pulled her hand through the crook of his elbow.

Wondering if he was aware of the courteous gesture, she smiled at him. "My father taught me to read, translate and speak Greek and Latin. He was a schoolmaster as a young man, then became a minister."

"But you're—" He looked down at her, perhaps unwilling to state the obvious.

Abigail sighed. "Of course I'm a female. But that doesn't mean my brain doesn't work. I had little to otherwise occupy my time—until recently, that is. Not much time to study in the sail loft."

John stared at her, still clearly perplexed.

She smiled. "I'm grateful my father had no sense of propriety regarding the education of females. And that I am an only child. Otherwise he might have concentrated his considerable talents as a teacher on my hypothetical brother."

John chuckled. "I salute your unconventional sire." He walked on in silence, then after a moment gave her a sheepish look. "I beg your pardon again for my bumbling and embarrassing questions. I asked out of pure curiosity and had no intention of insulting you. It's just that—" He paused and she felt the sudden tension in his arm under her hand. "I'm sorry, but I've simply never encountered a woman who is both gently raised and entirely without qualms regarding the more grisly aspects of the medical profession. The scientific mind is not usually associated with femininity."

"That's ridiculous."

"I'm beginning to think you're right." He smiled at her. "But if you met my sister you might understand my point of view."

"Perhaps no one has yet made the effort to enlighten and educate her."

"Undoubtedly true. But my mother would be horrified at the idea of teaching Lisette anything beyond the ability to snag a socially acceptable husband. In fact—" John's lips tightened. "I had to fight for my own education beyond the basics. My father wishes for me to continue in the family business." He drew Abigail to a stop and looked up at the imposing brick facade of the building to their left.

Abigail looked up. They had walked down this block earlier, of course, in the dark. The sign above the front door was painted in enormous block letters: "Crescent City Shipping—Offices—Warehouses located on Commerce at Joseph." On either side of the sign was a large crescent moon—a symbol that had haunted her dreams since she'd left China nearly a year ago.

She stared for a moment, incapable of speech. "Your father is—this is your family's enterprise?"

Apparently he didn't notice the strain in her voice. "Yes." He started walking again. "I suppose, like you, I have rather mixed feelings about my father. His business acumen has enabled me to afford my medical college fees and books. But it has been a source of considerable contention between us that I refuse to follow him into the transportation industry." His voice took on a bitter edge. "China this, China that. One would think that nothing of value happens on this side of the world. You should count yourself fortunate that your own father was more interested in the classical languages than the exotic ones."

Abigail swallowed, suppressing the impulse to give John Braddock a shove and run as fast and hard as she could. "Indeed," she murmured. "I am very fortunate."

"Appleton, please tell my mother I've answered her summons." Handing his hat over to the Braddock family butler, John looked around. He hadn't been home in several weeks. Fleur, the housekeeper, had placed fresh chrysanthemums in the tall crystal vase on the mahogany side table; their spicy aroma filled the entryway.

"If you want me to put it in them terms, Mister Johnny, it ain't gonna be a pleasant visit," Appleton said cheerfully, dusting the hat off by whacking it against his thigh.

John shook his head, grinning a little. "I'll trust you to interpret." Although perhaps not the personification of the well-trained servant, Mick Appleton had served as first mate on John's father's maiden voyage thirty years ago.

Upon his retirement from the sea when John was only nine years old, Appleton had landed in a position of household authority second only to Eliza Braddock. For all intents and purposes part of the family, he was in the nature of a favorite uncle to John.

Whistling, Appleton limped up the stairs while John wandered into the Chinese parlor situated just off the entryway. It was overwhelmingly red and black, the ebony furniture upholstered in crimson velvet with thick brass studs; tapestries woven of exotic silken designs hung between and on either side of the two wide French windows, clashing with a complex striped wallpaper pattern. John closed his eyes. Lack of sleep had engendered the beginnings of a migraine and his mother's hideous decor did nothing to help.

Still he couldn't regret last night's rendezvous in the morgue. Abigail Neal was easy to look at, if one overlooked the statuesque build and frequently sardonic expression. At least she didn't make fun of his struggle with Latin as the other fellows did. And she was teachable and appreciative of a fellow's talents.

He was standing at the window, smiling at the memory of Abigail's inventive imagination when he heard a rustle of skirts in the doorway. He turned. "Mother—it's good to see you."

Never one to release her self-control, Eliza Dreher Braddock extended both hands and offered John a smooth cheek to kiss. "John, my dear. It's been too long since we saw you."

"Seventeen days, I believe you mentioned in your note." He waited for her to seat herself upon a red slipper chair before he sprawled in the wing chair opposite. Her light brown hair was dressed as usual in a complicated mass of loops and curls, and her high-necked pink gown complemented her still-slim figure and unlined fair skin. "You're looking beautiful as usual. Where's Lisette?"

With a pleased smile, his mother accepted his compliment as her due and relaxed against the arm of the chair. "She is driving around the Commons with Dorothée Molyneux. They enjoy one another's company so, one would think they are already sisters."

"In this nasty weather?" John ignored the blatant insinuation in the word "already."

His mother gathered her shawl closer. "Yes, indeed, it is messy, but these young girls… Always after attracting the attention of the town beaus. Dorothée will be wed before the year is out, I am sure, and Lisette will be inconsolable to lose her best friend."

John suppressed a sigh. "Perhaps we could arrange transportation for semiannual visits at least," he said lightly.

"John, you know what I mean." His mother pouted charmingly, although a firm edge lined her soft voice. "I don't understand why you put off courting Dorothée, now that she's had her debut season. Her parents are expecting you to call."

He crossed one knee over the other. The gloves were off. "Mother, I'm far too busy with my studies to waste time sipping tea and dancing attendance on a spoiled little girl with the vocabulary of a six-year-old."

Mother stiffened. "There is no need for insult."

"I'm sorry. I've tried to hint that your hopes for a match between me and Miss Molyneux aren't likely to come to fruition."

"But John—"

He held up a hand. "And don't try foisting some other equally boring debutante on me. If you could see the stack of textbooks waiting on my nightstand, the contents of which I must absorb before Christmas—"

"John." His mother frowned, her fine hazel eyes dampening. "I do not understand why you must be so obstinate about the one thing I ask of you. If *you* could see the times I have intervened when your father wanted to refuse the funds that pay your matriculation fees…" She bit her soft lips together and looked away. "I only want to see you settled with a nice girl."

He stared at her profile, his headache now raging. His mother had indeed provided a much-needed buffer between him and his sire. *Was* he being selfish? Would it be so terrible to find himself shackled to plump, dimpled Dorothée Molyneux? At least maybe then his parents would leave him alone. He could set up his own household, take on a titular role in the shipping business and pursue his studies unmolested by social obligations.

He rubbed his temple and sighed. "Perhaps I might call on her for a drive, after I finish my anatomy examination next week."

Mother spread her fan, looking at him over its lace-edged top. "Really, John?"

He had to smile at the hopeful flutter of her lashes. "No promises of courtship, but I'll make an effort to get to know her."

She dropped the fan and exhaled a happy sigh. "I'll give a party. A ball! We'll invite the Molyneux family and the Lanieres and perhaps the Girards, if you insist. I'm sure there are others I'm not recalling at the moment, but it will be a grand occasion. You'll have *such* a lovely time, John."

He thought of the cool dark recesses of the morgue, where he'd been challenged, amused, and touched by a tall young woman in a patched dress. He sighed. "I'm sure I shall, Mother."

Abigail had been struggling to stay awake all afternoon as she helped Camilla put up squash. The second time Abigail's eyes closed while she was pouring a pot of boiling water through a sieve in the sink, Camilla took the handle of the pot from her.

"Sit down, my dear, before you drop that and scald us both." Camilla finished straining the squash.

Abigail sat down, her knees buckling. "I'm fine. Really."

Camilla glanced over her shoulder as she set the pot on the stove. "Certainly you are. Did you not sleep well last night?"

Abigail forced her eyes open again, then gave up and rubbed them with both fists. "Not particularly." She yawned. Professor Laniere had told her not to tell anyone about the autopsy. Presumably that meant his wife as well.

But Camilla was not easily deflected. She frowned as she dumped the next batch of squash into a fresh pot of water. "You stayed up all night studying, didn't you? I admire your persistence, but you can't function without sleep."

Abigail grinned at her. "Says the woman who stayed up three nights running with poxy children."

Camilla laughed as she sat down across from Abigail. "Well, I've caught up on sleep the last two nights. Thank goodness the children aren't itching so badly anymore."

"I remember when I had those. The blisters felt like fire ants crawling all over, me and every child in the village had them. It was the way my mother found out I'd been sneaking out of the compound—" She stopped herself too late.

"Compound?" Camilla's eyebrows were up. "You mean a missionary compound?"

Abigail stared at her, dismayed. If she hadn't been so tired… Finally she looked away. "Please, I don't like to talk about it."

Camilla was silent for a moment, then reached out to touch Abigail's hand. "I won't interrogate you, if you insist. But—Abigail, I confess I'm curious about your spiritual upbringing. There's nothing shameful about being the daughter of missionaries."

"It depends," Abigail said, endeavoring to keep her voice level. "There are missionaries and then there are missionaries." She risked a look at Camilla, whose lips were pursed thoughtfully.

"Are there, my dear?" Camilla said gently. "Tell me about it. Where were you?"

"China," Abigail blurted, unable to contain the burden any longer. "The Shandong Province. I was five when my parents moved there. For days on end it was just me and my mother in our little house, until I found a way to slip out." She swallowed. Her mother's depression had led to long bouts of sleeping, day and night. Abigail had found herself virtually alone while her father went into the village and taught the Chinese "heathen" about Jesus.

"And you caught chicken pox and your mother found out?" Camilla leaned her elbows on the table, her topaz eyes bright with interest. The pot of squash boiled merrily on the stove unheeded.

"Actually," Abigail said reluctantly, "it was my father who found me, scratching away, when he came home one evening." She touched her stomach. "I have scars to this day and it's miraculous the blisters hadn't yet infected my face. Papa woke my mother up and told her the infection was going around the village. Demanded to know why she'd taken me out of the compound."

"And of course she hadn't," Camilla guessed.

Abigail nodded. "Papa beat me with a strap, then Mama bathed me in some herbs the Chinese women had given her."

"He *beat* you? A seven-year-old who was ill with chicken pox?"

Abigail looked up, startled out of her memories. Camilla looked as ferocious as a gentle-eyed woman with tawny hair curling all over her head and spectacles on her nose could look. "I disobeyed him and left the compound. I suppose he thought it was dangerous." She shrugged. "After all, I did contract that infection."

"Where was your mother while you were out on your own?"

Abigail's instinctive response was to defend her mother. Mama had been fragile, physically and mentally—unlike Abigail, with her large hands and feet, her tough, boyish body, her insatiable curiosity. "She—she wasn't well. I made her nervous. So I learned to read and play by myself. Eventually I found an opening in the compound wall and kept going farther and farther until I saw the Chinese children. They laughed at me, but eventually they taught me to speak and sing in their language. That is, until Papa caught me."

"You speak Chinese?" Camilla gaped.

Abigail felt the old inner chant: *freak, freak, freak.* She had said too much. She shook her head. "Camilla, I confess, I'm exhausted. May I go to bed? Dr. Laniere promised I could join the class for early rounds in the morning, then I'll come back to help you finish the squash."

Camilla released Abigail's hands and glanced at the pot. "Of course. This is the last batch anyway." She rose, patting Abigail's shoulder as she moved to the stove. "Sleep well, my dear, and don't worry about what you've told me. I'm good at keeping secrets."

Abigail nodded. "Thank you, Camilla. Good night." She rose and staggered toward the stairs. If knowledge was power, please God she had not revealed too much to Camilla Laniere.

Chapter Ten

Rounds. There was something in the word, John thought, that aptly described some parts of his chosen profession. Repetition. Procedure. Scientific experiment.

Early on Friday morning, he and Girard, Weichmann and a couple of other fellows, tagged behind Prof, with the ever-present Abigail Neal bringing up the rear. Unlike the rest of them, her eyes were bright and alert, taking in every detail of the professor's movements—the way he gripped a patient's wrist to check a pulse, the position of the stethoscope on the chest or back, the firm but careful flexing of a limb. When the men arrived, she'd been waiting inside the hospital, perched on the bottom entryway stair, hands clasped demurely atop her knees.

Prof stopped at the bedside of the woman with the gallbladder case, who was recovering nicely from her surgery. John glanced at Abigail over his shoulder; her cheeks reddened as she met his eyes. Maybe she was thinking of the way she'd grabbed his hand during the hemorrhage scare. At the time he'd been too startled to enjoy it, but the memory of the strength and delicacy in those beautiful, long fingers returned every time he looked at her.

"How are you feeling this morning, ma'am?" asked the professor.

The woman let out a theatrical moan. "I never had so much pain." She lifted the edge of her gown, revealing a neat white four-by-six-inch gauze bandage. A faint pink stain revealed the location of the wound, a minor indication after such serious surgery, in John's opinion. "Those nurses don't pay enough attention when a body needs to take care of certain…necessary functions."

The professor smiled. "The fact that you feel the urge for those necessary functions is a good sign indeed. I'll ask one of them to tend you." He looked around at his students. "Come, gentlemen."

Abigail cleared her throat. "I'll stay and help her, Professor."

Prof looked over his shoulder. "Very well, Miss Neal. You may catch up with us as soon as Mrs. Catchot is comfortable." He walked on.

"It's a wonder he trusts her not to break open the wound," muttered Marcus, catching up to John. "She's not a trained nurse."

As late as yesterday, John might have agreed, but last night's adventure in the morgue had forever altered his view of women in general and one in particular. He scowled at Marcus. "I've observed Miss Neal to comport herself with great common sense as well as compassion."

Girard's mouth fell open. "Hey, whose side are you on?"

Prof looked around with an amused glint in his eye. "Braddock, I want to speak with you." He lengthened his stride, leaving Marcus to fall back with the other students, and addressed John without slowing down. "How did your project proceed yesterday?"

John looked back to make sure the others were still occupied in arguing over the relative benefits of carbolic acid and iodine as a disinfectant. "Cause of death was liver failure, as far as I could tell." He lowered his voice. "And she performed very well, considering…. Well, she's a dashed odd woman," he burst out. "The first time I ever autopsied, I was sick all night."

Prof chuckled. "As we wend our way into the next decade, if the Lord tarries, I suspect we fellows are going to have to abandon all preconceived notions of womanhood."

"That's exactly what I mean, sir. It's not natural for a woman to show such interest in disease and death. Isn't there some biblical injunction about women maintaining modesty in public?"

The professor stopped, raising a hand to capture his students' attention. "Gentlemen, please proceed to the next ward. I'll want reports of pulse, temperature and other indications on each patient when I join you in a moment. Mr. Braddock, a word with you."

Mutiny built on Marcus's square face. "But Prof, wouldn't we all benefit from your instruction?"

Dr. Laniere frowned. "This is a matter of a personal nature, Girard. You may serve as clerk while the others do the examinations."

Giving John a puzzled look, Marcus regrouped and hustled to the head of the line of students traversing the hallway.

With a jerk of his head the professor indicated that John should follow him, then wheeled into an open room which served as supply closet and office for the nurses. It was empty at the moment.

Prof shut the door. "What do you know about biblical instruction to women, Braddock?" The professor's tone was dry, but not unkind. "I was under the impression that you regard the spiritual implications of medical treatment rather by the way."

John scrambled for dignity. "I…confess the subject has piqued my interest of late, sir. I did a quick survey of the copy of Scripture my mother gave me when I reached my majority."

"A quick survey? May I ask what caused this sudden religious fervor?"

"Well, sir, there have been some rather peculiar events occurring lately." John tugged his cravat. "Your willingness to include a woman in our lessons here at the hospital being one. And—and I'm dreaming about things that never used to bother me."

Prof's rather flinty black eyes softened marginally. "What sorts of things are bothering you, Braddock?"

"The baby we buried on Sunday." John looked away. "I wake up, shaking it to make it cry. And the woman we autopsied, Abigail and I—she was pregnant. Did you know that, sir?"

The professor sighed. "She was a prostitute, Braddock. Are you truly surprised?"

"No. But I find myself wild to understand what it means. How to help these girls, so they won't slowly kill themselves and their babies with opium." To his horror, John's voice cracked. "Until Sunday, I never thought much about it. Medicine was a little like a—a large puzzle, but all of a sudden it's like some veil has come off my eyes, and—Professor, I really don't know if I can stand it." In his agitation he cracked his knuckles and stared at his mentor.

For a long moment the professor stood with his hands clasped behind his back, head bowed. The little room hummed on a dense silence. The odors of lye and disinfectant, the distant rattle of carts in one of the wards, reminded John that they were in a hospital.

Dr. Laniere looked up and gripped John's shoulder. "I remember the moment when something similar happened to me." The professor's deep voice was quiet, intent, his eyes searching. "I had partially finished my training as a doctor, but had given it up because—" he sighed "—a set of complicated circumstance demanded it. But I met a young woman whose faith challenged my cynicism and selfishness. It seemed everywhere I went I saw the hand of God moving in miraculous and loving ways in spite of dire and dangerous circumstances." He smiled, a slight curve of the lips. "Eventually it began to seem ridiculous to run."

"What does this have to do with allowing Abigail Neal to study medicine?" John squirmed internally at the personal twist the conversation had taken. He wasn't sure it was proper to know so much about one's teachers.

The professor lifted his brows. "Come, Braddock. Miss Neal's presence is a minor irritant. A symptom of the disease, if you will. Your real problem is spiritual."

John glowered at him. "You know the respect I have for you, sir, but I have great difficulty reconciling science and faith. Part of me *wants* to believe. But then I slam up against the fact that one simply cannot prove God."

"And that is exactly the point. God is so big that one can never prove Him—at least with human measurements. But once I took off in a leap of faith He began to prove *Himself* to me. Over and over. Surrender came surprisingly easy, once I realized what I was missing."

John lifted his hands. "And what was it you were missing?" He felt unmanned, asking these kinds of questions. But one thing he'd learned in the laboratory, one never learned anything without questions.

"Love, my dear boy," said the professor simply. "The best kind of love—not the finite love of a woman, although that came later for me—but the kind of love that looks past every conceivable fault and receives a man on the basis of unearned favor. The kind that Christ exhibited by giving His life."

If those words had come from anyone other than his esteemed professor, John would have laughed and walked away. He stared at Prof, heart thundering as if he'd run all the way from the docks. "You know my father," he said in a strangled voice. "If he thinks I've become religious, he'll assume I've caved in about joining the family business. I cannot let him roll over me."

Prof was silent for a moment. "This is not entirely about your father, John, just as it only peripherally has to do with Miss Neal. And it's not about being 'religious,' as you put it. But if you're worried about how Phillip will react, you can leave him to me. I'll be the buffer." He squeezed John's shoulder. "Make your decision on your own."

"I'll—think about it," John said with difficulty.

"Professor? Mrs. Catchot is asleep now."

John looked at the doorway and found Abigail Neal standing there, hands clasped at her waist, expression perfectly bland. He wondered how much of the conversation she had overheard.

Flushing, he stepped out from under the professor's hand and turned toward Abigail. "I'm off to make sure the other fellows haven't set the ward on fire." He stepped past her, careful not to touch her.

She murmured something to the professor, then caught up to him while the professor followed at a more measured pace. "Is everything all right, John?"

He glanced at her. "Certainly. Did you read the paper this morning?"

She blinked at the sudden shift in topic. "No, I—you know I was here early, first thing. Was there something of particular interest?"

"There was a fire in the District this morning."

He shouldn't have been so blunt. Her eyes widened in horror. "A fire? Where?"

"Not on Tchapitoulas," he said quickly. "It relates to the hospital. The board of directors had set up an infectious diseases clinic and apparently some of the neighbors resented it. They decided to take matters into their own hands."

"People set a *clinic* on fire? To burn out sick people?" Abigail looked horrified. "Was anyone hurt?"

"Two dead, three burned terribly. And there were a couple of caretakers injured as well." John cracked his knuckles, wishing he could wrap his hands around the neck of the cretin who had set the fire. "Some of us are going over there later to see what we can do to help. Thought you might like to come."

"Of course I would! If Mrs. Camilla can do without me, that is." She turned. "Professor, did you know about this— the fire? Why are we not over there right now?"

"We'll go directly after we finish rounds," said the professor. "The rest of the available hospital staff and faculty are already there."

With the conversation safely deflected from the topic of his soul, John relaxed his shoulders and joined Prof and

Abigail in planning strategy for treating second- and third-degree burns and outlining the supplies they would need.

He could think about God later, when there was not such pressing need for action.

The scene was chaos. Abigail scrambled out of the ambulance wagon behind John, then involuntarily halted to look up at the smoldering black remains of a tenement house not so different from her old home with Tess. The roof had caved in on one side; shards of glass blown out of the upper-story windows crunched underfoot as the students worked to transfer supplies from the wagons to the brick street, which had been blocked off from foot traffic. Horse-drawn fire wagons were rattling away from the scene. The air reeked of smoke and charred wood and other pungent but unidentifiable smells.

"Abigail! Come on!"

Startled, she looked around and found John standing on the sidewalk, medical bag in hand. When she caught his eye, he turned and hurried toward a huddle of fire victims in the middle of the street.

Drawing a clean handkerchief from her pocket, she folded it into a triangle and tied it over the lower half of her face, covering her nostrils. With her breathing now unhampered by contaminated air, she followed John. She had no medical instruments of her own but had managed to stuff bandages, antiseptic and rolls of cotton lint into a canvas knapsack one of the nurses had given her. She carried it by its drawstring, and it bumped against her legs as she ran.

By the time she caught up to John, he had knelt beside a man with a bleeding head wound and started rooting around in his leather case. Coughing, he looked up at Abigail. "I forgot iodine."

She flung herself onto her knees on the other side of the patient. "I brought it." She yanked open the drawstring of her bag and extracted the heavy brown bottle that had bruised her leg.

"Good. Swab this clamp, then hold the wound together while I stitch."

She wet a lint pad with the yellow-brown iodine, glad of her handkerchief which blocked its pungent odor. Capping the bottle, she took the clamp from John and used it to hold the patient's torn flesh in place. It looked like he'd been sliced by a jagged piece of wood; splinters still clung to the man's matted, bloody hair. Thank God he'd already fainted from the pain or he would undoubtedly have been writhing and therefore impossible to treat.

John plucked a pre-threaded needle from a small case inside the larger bag, swabbed it with the iodine-soaked pad, then took a breath and proceeded to sew. Because she had watched him tend to Tess, Abigail was not surprised at the neatness and thoroughness of his work. But the expression on his face made her stare at him in wonder. The cold detachment with which he generally operated had been replaced by a grim, almost feverish determination.

She wasn't sure it was a good thing. His hands shook.

"John, what's wrong?" she said quietly.

"What?" He glanced at her. A crash from inside the house accompanied the shouts of firemen and doctors, the dying crackle of the fire.

She raised her voice. "Are you all right?"

"Of course I'm all right. Don't let the clamp slide."

He was back to his normal curt self. Biting back a breath-wasting retort, she adjusted her grip and watched him sew. When he finished, he reached into the bag for a pair of scissors and cut the suture thread. He looked around. "We've got to move him to a wagon. He needs to go to the hospital."

The man began to stir. His eyelids fluttered. "Help me," he murmured. "Libby…the baby…"

"Be still." Abigail laid a hand on his shoulder. "We'll find—"

"Never mind, Abigail, get his feet." John stood up. "I'll take his shoulders." He seemed to realize she was all the help he was going to get. The other doctors and students were occupied with victims of the fire. With the rising of the sun, the stench of burned flesh had become so powerful that it was hard for Abigail to breathe, even through her handkerchief. She didn't know how John could stand it.

"Hold on," she told their patient. "We're going to carry you to the ambulance."

"No!" He tried to sit up as John grasped him under the armpits. "Where's my wife? Libby—"

"We'll find her," John grunted. "Abby—get his feet!"

It was a good thing she was a tall, sturdy woman, she thought as she and John hauled the heavy patient with as little jostling as possible toward the nearest ambulance wagon. He had fainted again before they got him there; they made him as comfortable as they could, leaving instructions for Crutch to keep him still if he should wake up and go looking for his wife.

For the next two hours Abigail accompanied John from patient to patient, soothing burns with aloe extract, bandaging or sewing up flesh wounds, once setting a broken leg with a splint made from a piece of doorpost. In an attempt to find their first patient's wife, Abigail addressed every woman they encountered as Libby. She was unsuccessful in that, but she learned more about medicine than by reading a stack of textbooks. John was swift, efficient, thorough—and she was increasingly impressed with his gentle touch.

It was nearly noon, with the sun straight overhead, when Professor Laniere called his students together. They clustered under a bare-limbed sugar maple across the street from the burned tenement, panting and sweating despite the clammy chill. The men had all removed coats and cravats and rolled up their shirtsleeves; Abigail would have given anything to be shed of her high-necked, full-skirted gown. As it was, she defied convention by unbuttoning her wristbands and rolling the sleeves as high as they would go on her forearms. She had also unfastened her detachable collar, tossing it into her supply sack. Let them call her a strumpet: at least she wouldn't faint from heat exhaustion.

"Gentlemen—and lady," the professor added with a slight smile for Abigail, "the worst cases have been cared for and sent on to the hospital for the nuns to settle into quarantine. You've all acquitted yourselves well. Lectures for this afternoon will be suspended."

A general huzzah erupted from the students as they dispersed.

Abigail detained the doctor by touching his sleeve. "Professor, there was a man we treated—Mr. Braddock and I, that is. The man was looking for his wife and baby."

The professor's calm gaze went from Abigail to John, who had hesitated when she stopped. "Where is he now?"

"We put him on the ambulance," said John. "Told him we'd look for the woman—her name is Libby."

"But neither of us saw her. Or any babies either, for that

matter." Abigail knitted her fingers together. She'd given a promise. "Do you suppose the firemen found her too late?"

"Several unrecognizable bodies were recovered and taken to the dead house before we got here," the professor conceded. "I'll inquire. The baby ought to be a giveaway."

John nodded. "Thank you, Prof. Will you let us know if you find them?"

Dr. Laniere agreed and took his leave to stride across the street, where the last of the ambulance wagons waited.

"Happy now?" John smiled at Abigail, the brilliance of his hazel eyes augmented by sweaty smudges of charcoal across his forehead and cheeks where he'd repeatedly wiped his face.

She nodded, thinking he looked like a particularly handsome and well-bred savage. Even though she'd never denied his physical beauty, for the first time she found herself attracted to the man, the doctor. She had watched him perform today like a hero in a penny novel.

Then his gaze shifted over her shoulder and he nearly crushed her hand. "Father. What are you doing in this part of town?"

Abigail turned to find a tall, heavily built gentleman bearing toward them. A stovepipe hat covered his dark, longish hair; muttonchop side-whiskers, a thick mustache and heavy eyebrows accented a pair of ice blue eyes.

Mr. Braddock reached John and laid a large hand on his son's shoulder. A broad smile revealed strong white teeth, although there was little real humor in his expression. "Seems a man has to attend a fire in the worst street of the District to have a conversation with his offspring these days. Your mother told me you were by the other day. Why did you not stay for supper, you ungrateful whelp?"

Abigail's instinct to run was forestalled by John's grip on her hand. He didn't look at her, but she knew somehow that her presence helped him. But oh, how she wanted to get away. She tried to shrink behind John's broad shoulder. *He doesn't know you. He's never seen you,* she reminded herself.

John tugged her hand through his arm. "I have afternoon rounds and examinations to study for, Father."

"Yes, we all know how busy you are these days. No time for the fellow who pays the bills." Braddock Sr.'s laughter boomed as he squeezed John's shoulder hard before releasing it. He looked around. "Just hell-bent on rescuing every pox-infected dock worker on the south side of town. Now when are you going to introduce me to your fair companion?"

Abigail wished she'd thought to roll down her sleeves and replace her collar. Desperate to evade the sneering inspection of those cunning blue eyes, she tried to pull her hand from John's elbow.

John visibly regained some of his customary aplomb. "Father, may I make you known to Miss Abigail Neal, who is a houseguest of Dr. and Mrs. Laniere? Miss Neal, I present my father, Phillip Braddock."

John's defiant gaze was on his father's face, but she detected a faint tuck in the corner of his mouth. Facing the senior Braddock, her chin went up a notch. Perhaps in her creased and stained gown, hair disheveled and falling down about her shoulders, she did look like one of the inhabitants of the red light district. But she literally was staying with the Lanieres. "How do you do, sir?" she said with all the demureness her mother had taught her when she was still a tiny child.

John's father studied her for another moment in patent disbelief, his eyes moving from her sunburnt nose to the open vee of her dress to her bare wrists. "You're a guest of Gabriel and Camilla?" He pursed his lips. "How very interesting." Dismissing her, he gave his son another jocular look. "In that case, you should invite Miss Neal to your mother's party next week. I'm sure Dorothée would delight in a new acquaintance."

If he expected John to back down, he was sorely mistaken. John inclined his head with a marked absence of respect. "As you wish, Father. It will be my pleasure to introduce Miss Neal to the finest of New Orleans society. She'll make a glittering addition to my mother's company."

Phillip Braddock stared at his son's mocking face for one pulsing moment before he smiled without warmth. "I'll see that her name is added to the invitation list. Good day, my son." He turned on his heel and swung down the street toward the docks.

Abigail wheeled, jerking her hand out from under John's arm. "That was not funny, John."

"Oh, yes it was." Chuckling, he slung an arm across her shoulders. "Worth the price of admission. I see Weichmann hailing us. Let's go see what other mischief we can get into."

Chapter Eleven

As he tangled with a declension of the word *suppurare,* John sneaked a glance across the library table at Abigail Neal. Tongue between her white teeth, she was studying one of his pharmaceuticals texts. He couldn't wait to find out what his sister would think about her. Abigail had returned to the Lanieres' for a bath before meeting him in the school library to help him with his languages. While he pored over a Latin translation, she'd wandered around, poking at the shelves until she found something to interest her.

Now that he looked at her, he noticed that her sage green gown—white collar firmly attached and sleeves buttoned from elbow to wrist—turned her eyes to a velvet moss color. The sunburn lent her skin a glowing, Raphaelesque beauty that would have made his sister, famous for her magnolia-white complexion, scream with envy.

He'd introduced Abigail to his father mostly as an irritant—and as a buffer against some of the nonsense with which the old man liked to bully him. The more he thought about it, however, the more he liked the idea of pitting the acerbic tongue of the eccentric Miss Neal against his sister's sugary steel wool charm. As he watched Abigail's fine eyes flit down the page, appreciation for his own idea grew until he felt the urge to stand on his chair and crow his brilliance.

Abigail looked up and frowned. "That was very badly done of you, you know. You embarrassed me and your father, and now your mother will have uneven numbers at her dinner table."

"And the world will fall in upon itself if one's dinner numbers do not match." Very perceptive she was. How had she ascertained the direction of his thoughts? "Tell me, Miss Neal—how many formal occasions have you attended in your short life?"

"Five," she retorted. "One of them with an emperor. So do not, if you please, make fun of me."

He stared at her. "Put that book down and tell me how you know an emperor."

"You wouldn't believe me, so I shan't bother." She lifted the forty-pound translation of *Treatise of Elemental Chemistry.* "Lavoisier lists light as an element. How is that possible?"

"It's not. Light is electromagnetic radiation. Lavoisier was a genius, but he had some blind spots—which could explain why he ultimately lost his head."

Abigail laid her book down and regarded him with amused exasperation. "Braddock, you're horrible!"

Apparently she knew the great French scientist had been beheaded at the height of the French Revolution. John grinned. "Tomorrow I'll let you borrow Maxwell's *Treatise on Electricity and Magnetism,* which explains his theory of light as waves. Fascinating stuff." That a woman should be not only interested in scientific subjects like the properties of light, but also capable of comprehending them, was astonishing.

"I should love to read it. How are you coming with the translation?"

"Suppurare comes from *sub-*, meaning 'under,' and *pur* means pus." He squinted at her. "So any word that has those derivatives will have related meanings?"

She smiled. "Now you have it."

"It's beginning to make sense. I'd begun to think things were randomly named just to give us poor English-speaking fellows a hard time."

"You did not."

"Well, I suspected there must be some kind of code, but I couldn't break it. Mathematics I can understand. The rules don't change."

She sat quietly for a moment, her eyes on the book. "I didn't get the impression you like rules so much, John."

"I do when I see the reason for them."

Her gaze lifted. "What would you do if the rules said you couldn't study what you want to study because you were born male?"

"You *are* studying." He thumped the back of her book. "Nobody's stopping you."

"That's wrong on so many levels. First of all, perhaps I borrowed a couple of textbooks, but even if I learned everything Professor Laniere knows, I couldn't hold a license to practice medicine."

John frowned. "Are you going to be one of those man-eaters like that crazy Stanton woman?"

"Who?"

"Mrs. Stanton. The one who's trying to get women the vote."

"Why shouldn't women vote?"

Because Abigail's tone was inquiring rather than aggressive, John tried to explain. "I'm not saying they shouldn't. But my father says most know nothing about the political process. And they're going to vote with their husbands anyway."

"If we were allowed to gain higher education we wouldn't be ill-informed. And the only reason I'd never heard of this Stanton women is because I've been…out of the country. That doesn't make me ignorant." Abigail frowned. "I don't dislike men in general. But I resent being treated like a child—by anyone. Don't you?"

John thought about the way his father spoke to him. "I suppose," he said slowly, studying Abigail. There was nothing remotely childlike in her broad brow and wide, intelligent eyes. "But voting is a huge responsibility."

"Raising children is an even greater responsibility. Women do that all the time."

"But you're suited to that."

"*You?* Do you mean women in general or me in particular?" Abigail was smiling now. "I assure you I would make a terrible mother."

"No, you wouldn't." He suddenly knew that as well as he knew his own name. "I've seen you with the Laniere children and the children in the hospital. In fact," he added recklessly, "you would make a stellar doctor."

"You think I would make a good mother, a good doctor, but not a responsible citizen?" She laughed. "John, that's ludicrous."

"You're twisting my words. I was trying to give you a compliment."

Her eyes still twinkled. "I'm honored, I assure you. And

I'll enjoy the Maxwell book, if you're serious about lending me it."

"I'll be happy to." John looked around the library. It was late afternoon and he and Abigail were the only ones left. "We should go. You must be exhausted after the morning we had."

Abigail slammed the Lavoisier textbook shut and rubbed her eyes. "Not really." She yawned, then laughed. "All right, I'm tired, but it's a good kind of tired. We helped people this morning."

"Yes, we did." He stood up and offered her a hand. "Come on, Doctor Abigail. I'll walk you home."

She looked away and sighed. "Home? I'm not sure where that is…" She laid her hand in his and rose.

But he stood looking into her face, her physical presence warming him like the gaslights that sent shadows flickering across her cheekbones. His gaze traced her sweetly curved lips and he laid his free hand at the back of her neck, just under the thick knot of brown hair. She flinched.

"What's wrong, Abigail?"

She took a sharp breath. "A lady doesn't allow familiarities."

"Make up your mind." He stared at her in frustration. "Are you a lady or a woman who wants to be a doctor?"

"Why can't I be both?" She stepped back, eyes clear. "I'm going to change the definition of a lady."

"Fine. Be a lady. And I'll be a gentleman…a gentleman who wants to kiss you." His lips curved as he moved to whisper in her ear. "Call it a gesture of friendship."

"Friendship," she scoffed, but this time she didn't step back. "You don't offer to kiss the other fellows you study with."

"Touché." Cupping his hand under her jaw to tilt her face, he bent his head. "You have no idea how beautiful you are."

Her lips parted and softened under his for a startled moment before she put her hands against his chest and pushed. "Don't, John."

He stared at her for a moment, then picked up the stack of textbooks he'd brought with him. "Friendship, Abigail, comes in several varieties." He tried not to show his triumph. She'd almost kissed him back.

On Saturday afternoon Abigail worked alone in the dispensary. Winona had gone home to visit her parents and Camilla had taken the children to the park.

She walked along the shelves, taking down jars of medicines one by one, dusting them, opening them to smell the contents and compare them to the list of ingredients the professor had given her. With the inventory alphabetized, it was a simple matter to memorize their efficacies and side effects. Maybe John didn't want to go to the bother—"I can always look 'em up," he'd told her brusquely—but she had to believe that an understanding of chemistry was essential to treatment. Even though she'd grounded herself in herbology as thoroughly as possible before leaving China, advances in pharmaceuticals had blossomed in both Europe and America, far outstripping her Chinese instructors. Why not prepare herself in both disciplines?

Coming to several little brown bottles of morphine and its derivative, laudanum, she hesitated before taking one down. Lying in her palm, it looked innocent enough, with its cork stopper and label printed neatly in her own fine hand. She unstoppered it and allowed the sickly sweet odor to evaporate into the narrow aisle between shelves. She squeezed it in her hand, resisting the urge to fling it down to smash against the tile floor. *Mama, oh Mama. The first taste is what destroyed you.*

Bitter truth that what could ease pain, even save a life, could also create untold heartache. Hurriedly she replaced the cork and set the bottle back on the shelf. No need to study this one. She knew it intimately.

She had reached the third row of shelves when the distant sound of the clinic door opening and closing caught her attention.

"Abigail?" Winona's voice came closer, rising in distress. "Abby, where are you?"

"In here." Abigail moved to the door of the dispensary and leaned out. "What's the matter?"

Winona, holding a small girl by the hand, stood in the kitchen doorway with her back to Abigail. She turned, an expression of relief breaking over her lovely dark face. "There you are! Thank goodness!" She tugged the sobbing child, who looked to be five or six years old, toward Abigail. "Would you mind taking a look at Essie's ears? She's in awful pain."

Abigail frowned. "You should take her to one of the doctors or a student at the very least. I'm not—"

"They're all in class or in surgery." Winona dropped the child's hand and drew her close. "Besides, you've got more kindness and common sense than all those arrogant young men put together." She brushed her hand across the little girl's tightly braided black hair. "Please, Abigail."

Abigail could see nothing but the child's coffee-colored little ear peeking from the folds of Winona's apron. The heartrending sobs sounded both congested and painful. Abigail thought quickly. She'd been left in charge of the clinic, with instructions to refer any emergency patients to Dr. Lewis, Professor of Obstetrics and Diseases of Women and Children, whose home office was two blocks over.

She opened her mouth to say so, but Winona held up a hand. "And don't tell me to take her to that whiskery Dr. Lewis," she said. "He's so deaf he roars like a lion and scares the little ones."

Unable to suppress a smile, Abigail shook her head. "I don't have a license to prescribe medicines. But perhaps I could just look and see if there's something simple I could do to temporarily relieve the pain." She smiled at Essie, who had stopped wailing long enough to peep at Abigail. Cognizant that she was the center of attention, she promptly recommenced the concert.

Winona winced. "Thank you." She led Essie into the clinic, picked her up and set her on the examination table situated next to the window. "Here, lambie, be a big girl and stop crying."

As Abigail rooted through a storage cabinet in the corner, she did her best to ignore the child's cries because they had shifted in tone from real pain to a sort of self-conscious bleating. She extracted an otoscope, a cone-shaped metal tube which she had observed Dr. Laniere using to view the inside of a patient's ear. She'd studied drawings of the ear canal in the medical texts she'd read over the last weeks and had a fair notion of what she should expect to see. A real human ear, however, was quite different from the flat black-and-white page.

A little flurry of excitement rose in her stomach as she gently grasped Essie's small ear with her left hand to stretch the canal a bit, then inserted the narrow end of the tube. Even with the strong afternoon sunlight flooding through the window and illuminating the ear canal almost to the eardrum, Abigail wondered how she would know if there were anything behind the eardrum causing the child's pain.

Essie began to hiccup, and Abigail rubbed her back as she removed the otoscope. *Lord, I don't have a clue what's wrong. Please help me.*

The prayer had flitted through her mind without her conscious volition. She glanced at Winona, who was watching her anxiously. Winona believed in prayer as Abigail used to. A rusty gate creaked open in her heart. God had seemed to fade away during the months she'd been on that vile opium-bearing ship, then disappear altogether when she was living in abject poverty with Tess in the District. And she'd turned away from Him when Tess's baby had died.

God? She closed her eyes. *Are you there?*

Suddenly she had a vivid mental picture of watching Dr. Laniere demonstrate the otoscope in the hospital a couple of days ago. He'd peered inside an old man's ear, then taken another instrument from the case.

Abigail's eyes popped open. She hurried to open the cupboard again. "Look, Essie," she said with a smile, manipulating the long, flexible snakelike tube of a Siegel's otoscope. She showed the child the silver bell at one end and the small mouthpiece at the other. "Watch this." Putting the mouthpiece between her lips, she held the bell against Essie's neck and blew gently.

Essie giggled. "That tickles!"

Abigail smiled at Winona, who watched with approval. "I'm going to blow just a bit in your ear and see if you can feel it. Can you sit very still?"

Essie stared at her, brown eyes wide. "Yes, ma'am," she whispered.

"All right. Here we go." Abigail placed the bell into Essie's ear canal, peered into it and softly blew through the tube. The child jerked, but managed to stay quiet. Abigail realized, as she had suspected it might, that the membrane of the eardrum had remained rigid. Infection had packed mucus behind the ear, rendering it immobile.

Abigail removed the otoscope. "Does your ear feel stuffy? Like you've got cotton in your ears?"

The little girl nodded. "It hurts when I lay down."

"I'm sure it does." Abigail wiped off the earpiece with alcohol, then coiled the otoscope tube around her hand and tucked the instrument back into its space in the cupboard. "Have you had a cold?"

"Yes, ma'am. But it's better…"

"Well, your ear got swollen from the cold and trapped water inside your eardrum. That's why it feels all stopped up." She looked at Winona. "I know what the problem is, but there's not much to do about it. She needs to rest, drink lots of water, eat oranges."

Winona's brow wrinkled as she cupped her hands over Essie's ears. "She lives in a orphanage in the worst part of the city. Her mother died and her father is a stevedore at the docks, a former slave. He couldn't take care of her…"

For the first time Abigail noted the threadbare state of the little girl's rough-spun dress and the broken, too-small shoes. She frowned. "Clean water is a problem, then."

Winona nodded. "And fruit's out of the question. There's more'n thirty children in that orphanage." She pulled Essie close.

"With proper care she'd get well on her own." Abigail sighed. "All right then. Go to the market and find some witch hazel for the pain. If she can sleep with her head elevated, that will help. Tell the matron to do her best to keep her quiet until the stuffiness goes away. Within a week or so the fluid should have drained away."

Winona nodded and looked down at the child, who already seemed better for the attention. She was playing with the ribbons on Winona's skirt. "I knew you'd help."

"I haven't done anything," Abigail said helplessly. "I wish Dr. Laniere—"

"Hello! Anybody home?" The clinic's outer door slammed, rattling the windowpanes.

Winona smiled. "Lectures must be done for the day. We're in here, John," she called.

Abigail squelched an unexpected leap in her midsection when John stuck his handsome head into the clinic.

"Can a fellow get a chunk of bread and cheese?"

"As a matter of fact, we all can. Come along, Essie, let's feed the ravening hordes." Winona boosted her little charge off the table, took her by the hand and curtsyed to John on her way by. Essie dimpled and copied her.

John looked at Abigail. "Who was that?"

She avoided his eyes as she latched the cupboard doors. "A case of acute otitis media with effusion."

John's eyebrows rose. "And how do you know this?"

"The eardrum doesn't move. Don't worry," she added, "I didn't presume to prescribe anything but rest and elevated sleeping couch."

"I could look at her."

Abigail put her hands on her hips. "You could. But why upset her again? She's just stopped crying."

"And crying would increase the pressure and the pain." John stared at her for a moment. "All right. Come share a bite of cheese and I'll tell you about the surgery."

"Does your boarding house mistress not feed you?" She followed him into the kitchen.

"Her bread isn't nearly as fine as Winona's." He gave her a teasing grin. "And she's not nearly as pretty as you two." He flung himself onto one of the benches at the table and rubbed his eyes. "It's been a tedious afternoon. Stuck in an amphitheater with a lot of smelly fellows watching Prof sew some poor fellow's leg back together. He'd gotten it stuck in a cotton press and nearly mangled it to the bone."

Winona, slicing bread at the counter, looked over her shoulder. She looked pained. "John. Please."

"Oh, sorry." He laughed. "I knew Abigail the Ghoul here would want full details." He glanced at Abigail, hazel eyes twinkling. "I'll tell you later."

Abigail poured a cup of milk for Essie and sat down beside her. "I'd rather have been there. It's not the same secondhand." She stroked the child's thick braids and watched her gulp the milk. "Do you men ever go into the homes of the poor?"

John accepted a basket of bread and cheese from Winona with a smile of thanks. "As often as we can. But usually it's all we can do to care for the worst cases that come to us."

Abigail absently took a slice of the fragrant bread. "It seems you'd prevent some of those worst cases coming to be. If you could treat people early, I mean. Maybe even…" She glanced at John, who was munching contentedly, oblivious to Essie staring wide-eyed at his beautiful bottle-green coat. "Maybe you could teach principles of good health in those communities where disease spreads so quickly and easily."

"I've wondered that myself." John shrugged. "But it's not practical, Abigail. The doctors' energies are needed at the hospital. Besides, the nurses go into the parishes every day, with little accomplished. People live the way they want to live and they're skeptical about medical advances. You tell 'em sickness is caused by things you can't see and they look at you like you're crazy."

"But when they come to the hospital to see a doctor, don't they go along with whatever he says? That's why it's important for the medical community to be active in public health." Abigail leaned her elbows on the table. "People mistrust the nurses because they don't know any better. Education is—"

"I like the thought, Abigail." John looked uncomfortable. "But the professors are very busy. You've seen Prof's schedule." His eyes were intent on her face. At least he was taking her seriously.

Winona cleared her throat. "I'm going to take Essie back. It's my day off, remember. I'll be spending the night at home." She paused. "Abigail, would you like to come to church with me in the morning?"

Abigail blinked, jerking her gaze from John's. She'd nearly forgotten Winona and Essie's presence in the kitchen. "I suppose I could," she answered, rather at random. "Mercy! And I promised I'd start supper for Miss Camilla." She scrambled up from the bench. "Where should I meet you, Winona?"

Winona met her gaze with a knowing twinkle in her dark eyes. "I'll be at the corner of Philippa and Poydras at ten. If it's raining, wait under the balcony of the millinery shop." She backed out of the kitchen, tugging Essie along with her.

Abigail edged around to put the table between herself and John. She wasn't exactly afraid of him. It was herself she couldn't trust. She'd almost given in to kissing him yesterday. "I have to get supper started. Did you need something else?"

He sighed. "I suppose not. I wanted to talk to Prof about the surgery, but it can wait." He tipped his head. "So you're going to church in the morning?"

"Is that so odd?" Taking a pot off its hook over the stove, she set it in the sink and began to pump water into it.

He was silent for a moment. "I suppose you don't need an escort."

His tone was so odd that she looked over her shoulder. Their gazes held for a moment. Flustered, she shifted the pot and slopped water all down her front. "Oh my." She looked down at herself. "I imagine you'd be quite out of place in Winona's church."

"And you wouldn't be?" He sounded amused.

"I'm invited." She didn't know where to look. "You'd best attend with your family. I'm sure they'd miss you."

"If I appeared for services at St. Domini's, my family would assume someone had died." His familiar sardonic expression appeared as he stood. "Never mind. Clearly my presence would make you and the lovely Winona just as uncomfortable as you seem to be now. I shall remove myself." He plopped his hat on his head and bowed. "Good day, Miss Neal."

The door shut gently behind him and Abigail fought the urge to call him back. He was gone and she was glad. What had possessed him to ask if she needed an escort? It was almost as if he wanted to come to Winona's church—but no, that wouldn't be like him at all. Still, she couldn't help imagining what it would be like to attend services in the company of a man like John Braddock.

Chapter Twelve

A damp chill enclosed in a messy fog drifted from the river to blanket the tumbledown buildings and twine around Abigail and Winona's ankles as they crossed Poydras Street the next morning. Abigail wished she'd brought a wrap. But that would presuppose she *had* one, which she didn't. Perhaps she could save a bit of what Camilla paid her in next week's wages and make something serviceable for the mild New Orleans winter—a cloak or even a shawl. The cold weather would come in fits and starts, then be gone by March. But when one needed a wrap, one needed a wrap.

She looked around. Nothing in the District had changed, of course. Same hovels with uncovered windows and broken doors, same pitted road, same reek of garbage in the gutters. Barely a week since she'd moved in with the Laniere family and already her life was so drastically different she hardly recognized herself. She'd gotten used to cleanliness and order, the fresh scents of baking bread, antiseptic and lye. As she walked along beside Winona, hugging herself, dodging mangy dogs and vacant-eyed beggars, she held her breath against the almost palpable odor of corrosion and fear.

She couldn't help thinking of the families who had been evicted from the burned tenement, particularly the man whose wife and baby had gone missing. They had never been found. *Oh, Lord, where are you when I come back here? Have you abandoned these people?*

She glanced at Winona, whose curly dark hair was twisted in a knot at the back of her head, the ends of a sober brown shawl blowing around her shoulders as she walked. Dressed in a brown-spotted cotton dress, a bit faded with washing but otherwise neat, Winona managed to look fresh and content with her circumstances. Well, and why not? Like Abigail, she had somehow escaped the clutches of the District, to hold a position with a prominent family who treated her with respect and paid her an adequate wage.

Abigail's thoughts leaped helplessly back to Friday afternoon in the library. After John had walked her home, maintaining an amused silence that set her teeth on edge, he'd bid her adieu in the clinic anteroom and sauntered into the kitchen to talk to Winona. Abigail had rushed up the stairs. Pausing at the landing, she'd listened shamelessly, but John and Winona's conversation was serious, their voices low and intense. An unexpected discomfort made Abigail hurry on to her room. She was *not* jealous. Positively not.

But why must her thoughts continually circle back to a pair of laughing hazel eyes?

To escape her circling thoughts she touched Winona's arm. "Have you lived here all your life?"

Winona glanced at her and smiled. "Since I was small. My parents were slaves over in Mississippi. We escaped here after the Union took New Orleans."

"Oh my." During the American war between the states, Abigail's family had been in China, insulated from the conflict that tore apart her place of birth. In the short time since she'd returned, she found herself jarred again and again by the ramifications of the recent struggle.

Winona sighed. "Freedom's a blessing. But you know the lives of our people—it's far from easy." Her gesture took in the buildings jockeying for place along the street, the levee at its end, which held the Mississippi River at bay. "From day to day you never know if education is gonna be extended or withheld, what jobs will be available, whether housing and property will be taken without warning…" She looked down, lifting her skirts as she stepped over a pile of refuse in the bumpy, muddy street.

"Yet you seem to be content." Abigail couldn't put her finger on the source, but it was more than happiness. It was a sort of bone-deep assurance she was loved and protected. Abigail longed to possess that sort of peace, but had no idea how to pursue it.

"The Bible says to 'count it all joy when you encounter various trials and the testing of your faith.'" Winona's smile was inward. "My family's always full of joy."

Abigail hesitated. "I've had trials, too, but I don't know that they make me happy. In fact, I rather resent them."

Winona's eyes smiled. "That's natural, unless you understand the trials are making you stronger, increasing your faith, making you more like the Master."

"Do you really believe that?" Knowing the answer, Abigail hurried on. "My father wanted to preach the gospel to the heathen, so he took me and my mother into some awful places. Strange places where we were looked upon as outsiders. Always outsiders." She'd never told another person about it and didn't feel any better to air it. If anything, her chest burned with deeper bitterness.

Winona flicked a thoughtful look at Abigail. "I also knew about being an outsider."

Shame washed over Abigail. Maybe she *had* been a tall, gawky, light-haired stranger in an Asian nation full of tiny black-haired people, but at least she had never been enslaved. "I'm sorry—"

"No, no." Winona laid a gentle hand on Abigail's arm. "I only meant I understand. But, Abigail, any of us who follow Christ gonna be outsiders in this world. Because the world wants to go its own way. And the world can't understand what only spiritual eyes can see—that we're loved by God in an all encompassing way. And He wants to love others through us with the overflow of that love, so they'll be more likely to see Him."

Abigail walked a few more paces, hardly aware of the overcast sky, the fog blanketing tin-roofed shanties with half-rotten porches on either side of the road. A window seemed to have opened inside her—a window through which light poured on the paucity of her faith. How could a woman who had grown up in a missionary compound have managed to escape the glowing truth in the words of a former slave?

"Will I find it?" She fumbled over the words. "That love…in your church today?"

"For certain. But now's a good time, too. God listens to your heart all the time."

Perhaps He *had* been listening all along—all the way from China, through the poverty of the District and into the relative comfort of life in Professor Laniere's clinic. Maybe if she continued to seek Him He would lead her into her heart's desire.

A chance to study medicine, a chance to practice her gift of healing.

Maybe God would heal *her.*

By the time John, Weichmann and Marcus exited the High Hat saloon, the morning fog had burned off, leaving a bright winter day in its wake. As they crossed the street toward yet another drinking establishment, John exchanged disgusted glances with Weichmann. High noon on a Sunday morning and already Marcus was three sheets to the wind.

John himself couldn't bring himself to drink his beer, which had sat at his elbow while they played cards and listened to the singing drift from the churches in the Quarter and the Treme neighborhood nearby. He wasn't sure why he'd agreed to come. Funny how his taste for alcohol had dried up since that conversation with Prof. And without the haze of liquor clouding his mind, he found little enjoyment in Marcus's ribald jokes nor the sugges-tive conversation of the easy women who frequented the bars. Instead he and Weichmann wound up discussing Friday's surgery.

Now the three of them marched along the side of the street, John and Weichmann bracing Marcus on either side to keep him from lurching into the gutter.

"The yeller-haired one wanted me to come home wi' 'er, I swear." Marcus hiccuped.

John steadied him. "And you'd've come home with the pox, so it's a good thing you ran out of money."

"Well, but what're we goin'a do the rest of the day?" Marcus gave John a belligerent look. "Jus' because it's Sunday, nuffin' goin' on our side of town. Boringest day of the week."

Weichmann leaned around Marcus to speak to John. "Hey, that looks like your Amazon."

John followed Weichmann's gaze to a tall figure in a dark blue dress disappearing around the side of a black-smith shop on the next corner. "She's not my Amazon," he said automatically but dropped Marcus's arm and hurried after Abigail. He rounded the corner just in time to see her enter the front door of a barnlike two-story building on the other side of the blacksmith.

He stopped, frowning. What was she doing in a colored orphanage?

"Braddock, what's got into you?" demanded Marcus from behind him.

John turned to Weichmann, who was supporting the weight of Marcus's shoulder against his arm. "She went in the orphanage. Want to come along?"

Weichmann moved away and looked around with a grin when Marcus sat abruptly in a mud puddle. "Good thing you're so close to the ground, old man." He caught up to John in two long strides, paying no attention to Marcus's yelps of indignation. "What do you suppose she's up to?"

"No idea. But I'm going to find out."

The orphanage yard was a weedy, soupy mess that ruined his boots before he got to the door. The odor of rotting vegetation was indescribable, even to a man who had exhumed and preserved bodies for dissection. He tugged his handkerchief from his pocket to cover his nose and knocked on the door.

It was yanked open by a young girl dressed in the same rough brown fabric as the child Winona had had in the clinic yesterday. This one was older, perhaps twelve, her wiry hair braided neatly and coiled around her head. She looked up at John with huge near-black eyes.

Because she appeared to be dumbstruck, John lowered the handkerchief and smiled at her. "Good afternoon. I'm looking for Miss Neal."

"She's back in the baby room," the girl whispered and stood back for John to enter. "With Miss Winona and Mammy."

He looked around to make sure Weichmann followed and found an expression of extreme discomfort on his friend's thin features. "Buck up, Weichmann." John stepped into the dark interior of the orphanage. "We've seen worse."

"I doubt we've smelled worse," muttered Weichmann. But he followed John inside, closing the front door behind him.

John stopped, appalled. He'd seen some bad places, including tenements like the one in which Abigail and Tess had lived. But that had been a palace compared to this: scrubbed wooden floor with gaps so wide he could see the mud beneath, oiled paper windows, crumbling brick walls covered here and there with sailcloth. There was not a stick of furniture in the place except for a few crates upon which fifteen or twenty children of various sizes, genders, and shades of brown sat playing with bits of wood and metal, apparently scavenged from the docks.

John could hear babies crying through a closed door at the back of the room. He looked around at Weichmann, who stood near the front door, arms folded, lower lip between his teeth.

Weichmann shrugged and came off the door. "I didn't know this was here, did you?"

"No. Come on, Weichmann." Something had shifted in

John, something irrevocable as a broken levee. While the girl who had let them in squatted to tend to a weeping toddler, John strode through the children, who looked up at him with wide, curious eyes. He lifted the latch of the interior door and it swung open with a loud creak of rusty hinges. "Abigail?"

She was sitting in a straight-backed chair facing the door with a colored infant in her arms. Winona sat on a crate nearby, holding two more in her lap, and a black woman leaned over a rickety crib in which four or five babies were tumbled together like a litter of puppies.

Abigail looked up at him, lips parted and eyes wide. "What are you doing here?"

"Following you." He stepped aside to admit Weichmann. "We saw you round the corner—"

"I told you not to—"

"We didn't come for church."

Winona laughed. "You boys out hunting up trouble on Sunday morning?"

"Who has to hunt?" John glanced at the babies gnawing on their fists in her lap. "Are they sick?"

Abigail jiggled the wailing infant. "We just got here. Did you speak to Essie on the way by?"

"Who? Oh, the little girl from yesterday. Is this where she came from?"

Winona nodded. "I suppose you should meet the matron, Mammy Jonas. Mammy, this is John Braddock, one of the students from the medical college."

Mammy, a thin, sharp-faced Creole woman, lifted one of the babies out of the crib and looked John up and down. "You the one took our cow and left her tied to the flagpole at the courthouse?"

That had been Marcus, and John had tried to talk him out of it, but explanation would be pointless. "No, ma'am," he said, mustering all the humility at his disposal.

"Humph." Mammy dismissed him with a regal turn of her head. "Young men ought to have better things to do."

John nodded absently as he walked to the crib. "Where'd these babies come from?"

"You've had advanced anatomy and you have to ask that?"

John shot Abigail a look. "You know what I mean." He leaned over to lay the back of his fingers against the cheek of one sleeping infant. "There are so many of them."

"They mamas left 'em to go wet nurse rich white mamas' babies." Mammy's voice shook. "They make good money and leave a bit in the church poor box—which we get some of."

John stared at Abigail in horror. Wet nursing was a common enough practice, but he'd never considered the implications for these abandoned babies. If anything, he'd assumed the nursing mothers had lost their infants to death. "Is this true?"

Abigail bowed her head, tracing the beautiful black wing of the baby's eyebrows with her finger.

"The practice has to be stopped." John said. "Wealthy women ought to be able to nurse their own babies."

"Of course they can. But they'd rather shop and take tea and drive around the Commons."

John could hardly blame Abigail for her cynical tone. His own mother and sister were at this moment driving home from church in a tooled leather carriage, dressed in fine cotton gauze, satin ribbons and Mechlin. They would have passed this orphanage without a second glance.

"Do they have enough to eat?" The one lying on his

back with his thumb in his mouth looked wiry and tough, but there was a rattle to his breathing that John didn't like.

"Once we got our cow back," Mammy said with an undertone of humor.

"I'll get you another one." Weichmann's sudden deep voice startled them all. He plucked one of the babies out of Winona's lap and laid him against his shoulder, eliciting a loud burp. Laughter leavened the tension in the room.

John had no idea where Weichmann would get a milk cow, but had no doubt he'd manage somehow.

By mid-afternoon John and Weichmann, assisted by Mammy, Abigail and Winona, had examined every child in the orphanage, diagnosing two cases of pleurisy, a cleft palate—which John thought could be improved with surgery—and rampant disorders of the lower intestines. He wanted to bring the little fellow with rattling breathing to the hospital for further examination.

On the way back to the Lanieres' the four of them discussed the problem. "If it's pneumonia and we don't treat it, he'll die," John argued.

Weichmann shook his head. "The nurses don't like contagious cases brought in."

"There's got to be a place to take them," Abigail said. "Those children deserve professional care." She looked at Winona. "I know Mammy's doing the best she can, but proper nutrition and hygiene would make all the difference."

"If my mother could just see..." John muttered. "She could make a difference." He stopped and grabbed Abigail's wrist. "That's it. We'll make her see."

"How are you going to do that?"

He looked around. Weichmann and Winona had walked on, leaving John and Abigail behind. "My mother is throwing a party to introduce my sister to society. You remember, my father mentioned it. I want you to come."

Her gaze flew to his. "You can't be serious. I'm no society deb, John. I'd be completely out of place. I have no pretty dresses—"

He cut her off with a slice of his hand. "I'm sure Camilla will find you something appropriate. You always look neat."

She gave him a fulminating look. "Neat is one thing. Evening dresses are quite another. Do you have any idea how much silk costs?"

"Of course I know what silk costs." He waved away the objection. "I've a bit left of my last quarter's allowance. I'll buy you a dress."

"You cannot!" she gasped. "Even I know a lady doesn't allow a man to buy her garments unless they are wed." To his astonishment, tears sprang to her eyes. "You're trying to shame me."

"And you're being unreasonable. You need a dress and I can help you get it. What's wrong with that? Nobody has to know. Abigail, please. I want you there. I..." He swallowed. Somehow the conversation had shifted from sick children to something more personal. "I need you there."

She stared at him. "What possible difference could my presence make at some family dinner party—or whatever it is."

"Dinner, drinks, dancing. You might actually enjoy it."

She turned her head, deliberately, though he could tell she was weakening. "John, I don't even know how to dance. I'd be humiliated."

He leaned close to her ear. "I'll teach you. I'm a good teacher, remember?"

She swayed toward him, then stiffened. "No. You've got

some selfish motive behind this and I'm not falling for it. Ask someone else."

He sighed. "All right. I'll come clean." He slid his hands down to cup her elbows. She stared at the top button of his waistcoat. "It's not just the children. My mother has a girl picked out for me to court. She'll be there and I don't want to get stuck with her before I have a chance to look her over. I need you for a sort of…buffer."

Abigail's mouth dropped open. Then she began to laugh. "You're absolutely mad! Nobody in their right mind would take me as a rival for some finishing school debutante. Your mother will throw me out of the house the instant she lays eyes on me."

John's eyes kindled. "She most certainly will not. As my guest you'll be afforded all proper respect. Besides, my father already invited you."

"John, I could come in with a fistful of invitations and nobody's going to take me for anything but what I am—a misfit clinic attendant from the District."

He stared at her for a moment, his lips clipped together. "If you won't take my word for it, would you believe Camilla?"

Abigail shrugged. "Camilla has more common sense than you. She'll agree with me."

John grinned and leaned down to give Abigail a loud kiss on the forehead. "We'll see about that."

Chapter Thirteen

With a creak of leather and springs, the Laniere carriage stopped in front of the Braddock mansion on Chestnut Street. Abigail waited for Camilla to move, not sure what manners dictated in these circumstances. She had never in her life been delivered to the door of a mansion via any method but her own two feet. Even the dinner with the emperor had required no transportation, as she and her father had been housed within the palace.

Before she could do more than glance at Camilla, however, the carriage door was jerked open from the outside, and the Lanieres' man-of-all-jobs slid the steps in place.

"Go ahead, Abigail," said Camilla kindly. "I'll be right behind you."

Abigail took Willie's gloved hand and stepped down. As she waited for Camilla and the professor to alight, she smoothed a hand down the side of her dress. It was the most beautiful garment she had ever owned. Made of jade shantung silk and trimmed with pale green banding, it hugged her waist and hips, bunched in a smooth bustle in the back and fell in graceful folds to her dainty slippers.

The Vandyke bodice was modest, its lace jabot tickling her chin, but the design accentuated the curves of her figure. Camilla had assured her it was appropriate for a formal occasion, so Abigail had to take her word for it.

Smiling, Professor Laniere was offering an arm each to Camilla and Abigail. "Ladies?"

Abigail slipped her hand in the crook of his elbow and looked up at the lights blazing from the enormous three-story brick house. The second level was ringed by a wrought iron balcony in the French style, supported by four tall, white columns. At least eight windows opened on each level, spilling gaslight halfway down the street.

Abigail wanted to stop and simply stare, but she meekly followed her hosts up the flaring front steps. Somehow John had managed to have her included in the invitation delivered to the Lanieres' front door by post a week ago. She'd tried to demur, but Camilla was a force to be reckoned with. Insisting on providing Abigail with a new dress, she'd accompanied her to the shops for silk, thread and trimmings. Then she provided slippers and a fan and the most luxurious silk-lined cloak.

The cloak was so soft and warm, Abigail was loath to part with it when the Braddocks' funny, Cockney-voiced butler tried to take it. Recollecting herself in the reflection of Camilla's amused eyes, she relaxed and let Appleton, as he called himself, bear it off in triumph along with the other guests' outer garments.

And then she was following the Lanieres into a ballroom dazzling with lights and music and laughter. She hung back, overwhelmed. She was going to embarrass her hosts, humiliate herself, say something in Chinese or Latin, spill something on that polished marble floor.

She'd actually picked up her skirts and turned to run when John stepped in front of her.

"Where are you going?" His eyes were bright, amused.

She'd barely seen him since the encounter in the orphanage nearly two weeks ago. And never had she seen him so elegantly and formally dressed in white shirt and stock, pristine against black dinner jacket and trousers. His hair was arranged to fall into his left eye, his side whiskers neatly trimmed to accent the strong jaw and humorous mouth. He belonged here in this beautiful home, with all these beautiful, glittering people.

"I'm going home." She tried to step around him.

He blocked her again. "Abigail, you can't cross the city by yourself at night."

"I'll take the streetcar. Let me pass." Panic surged through her stomach.

His smile faded. "It's not like you to run away. I want to introduce you to my parents." John stepped closer and took her gloved hand, letting his eyes caress her face. "You look lovely tonight. I want to dance with you."

"John!" came a sweet feminine voice behind Abigail. "There you are. Dorothée is asking for you."

"Lisette." He looked over Abigail's shoulder with a smile. "Come here and meet Miss Neal."

Abigail snatched her hand away and clutched her fan so hard she heard it crack. She turned and found a diminutive dark-haired young lady staring up at her with huge, myopic brown eyes.

"Oh! You're so very tall!" exclaimed Lisette Braddock. "I mean—How do you do?" She dropped a blushing curtsy.

"Miss Braddock," Abigail murmured, surveying the

girl's sunny yellow gown, which displayed a thin, childish figure. Lisette couldn't be more than eighteen.

Lisette dimpled. "Please excuse my staring. I'm nearsighted, and Mama insists I may not wear my spectacles during a formal occasion. Isn't that silly?"

Abigail relaxed, charmed by her young hostess's ingenuous chatter. "I'll defer to your mama." She glanced at John. "Perhaps, because you're wanted elsewhere, your sister will consent to make the introductions to your parents."

Lisette beamed. "I'd be happy to—"

"That won't be necessary. I'm sure Miss Molyneux will find her dance card quite full without my monopolizing her time." John offered his arm to Lisette and took Abigail firmly by the elbow. "You're not getting away from me that easily," he murmured into her ear. "Speaking of dance cards," he said more loudly, "where is yours, Miss Neal?"

"I don't have—"

"Oh, I have an extra!" Lisette fumbled in a tiny beaded bag dangling from her wrist and produced a small square of cardboard connected to an equally wee pencil stub. She handed it to Abigail. "Be sure to make John—"

"Thank you, Lise," he said affectionately, "but I'm capable of contracting my own engagements." He commandeered the dance card, wrote Abigail's name at the top and scrawled his name on it three times. "There." He handed it to Abigail. "Now you can't run away."

"Run away?" Lisette looked bewildered. "Why would she run away?"

"Your brother is teasing us both." Abigail sighed. She would have to make the best of this awkward situation and use it to help the women of the District. She smiled down at John's sister. "Miss Braddock, I understand you've an interest in philanthropy."

Lisette looked uncertainly at her brother, who didn't even try to hide the twinkle in his eyes. She put up her small, pointed chin and smiled at Abigail. "Yes, of course I do."

Abigail ignored John's chuckle. "Then might I share with you a need that your brother and I have encountered in a neighborhood not far from here? There is much good that could be done with just a little effort." She linked arms with her young hostess, and the two of them began to stroll toward the stairs, which presumably led down to the ballroom on the ground floor.

As they walked, John accompanied them, mercifully containing his part in the conversation to murmurs of agreement as Abigail explained the need for education in maternity and nutrition in the poor areas of the city. Lisette was a quick study, her hero worship for her big brother patent, and plied Abigail with intelligent questions. By the time they had reached the head of the stairs, where a middle-aged couple stood receiving guests, Lisette and Abigail were in perfect charity.

Lisette eagerly tugged Abigail toward her mother, a brown-haired woman in dark blue satin, who had Lisette's fragility and John's fine good looks. Her husband Abigail had already met, of course. His evening clothes did little to hide the air of ruthlessness that hung about him like the cloud of smoke emanating from the cigar between his fingers.

"Mama!" Lisette rushed to take her mother's elbow. "You must meet John's Miss Neal. She has quite opened my eyes to a way we can help our neighbors. She's the one staying with the Lanieres, and she's from—" She turned to Abigail, confusion in her nearsighted eyes. "Oh dear, I forgot to ask where you came from!"

"Lisette," Mrs. Braddock sighed, clearly exasperated by her daughter's social ineptitudes. "*Try* for a little decorum." She smiled vaguely at Abigail. "Welcome to our home, Miss Neal. I hope you will find our little party invigorating. This is my husband—"

"Miss Neal and I are already acquainted, my dear," said Phillip Braddock heartily. "She was helping John and the other fellows haul bodies out of the tenement that burned in the District a couple of weeks ago. Wasn't that enterprising of her?"

Lips parted, Mrs. Braddock gave Abigail a blank stare. "Er—quite. John, I don't believe you mentioned that to me."

Wishing she could sink through the floor, Abigail felt the muscles of John's forearm cord under her hand.

His face remained bland, however, as he laid his hand on top of hers. "Miss Neal is one of the most heroic women I've ever met, Mother. Capable of saving lives—a much more useful talent than ruining reputations, wouldn't you say?"

"I—" Eliza Braddock helplessly looked at her husband.

He executed a brief bow, as if in touché, toward his son. "It appears our guests have all arrived, so if you'll excuse me, I'll speak to the orchestra director and start the dancing."

He was gone, leaving Abigail to stare at the floor while John gave his mother more unwanted details about the aftermath of the fire. Lisette, however, seemed enthralled with the story, gasping at appropriate intervals.

"I could never be so brave," she said, looking at Abigail with wide, admiring eyes. "I'm afraid the closest I've come to such adventure is in the pages of a book. Did you read *Uncle Tom's Cabin,* Miss Neal? I found it *most* instructive."

"Indeed, I did," Abigail said. "My father had it in a shipment of books from—" She paused, noting too late the frost in John's mother's eyes. Mrs. Stowe's antislavery novel would not be a popular title with the Southern gentry. "That is, I lost my copy some time ago. Oh! I hear the music. What fine string players…".

"Indeed, they are." John gestured toward the staircase where the strains of a waltz drifted from the ballroom. "And I believe this is our dance, Miss Neal."

"Is it?" She glanced at the little dance card, blind with embarrassment.

"It is. Mother, if you'll excuse us?"

Abigail found herself stumbling down the stairs beside him, hardly aware of her surroundings except for the fine texture of John's sleeve and the strength of his arm beneath her fingers. She didn't belong here and she was a fool to have agreed to come.

They descended into a glittering gaslit room—one wall lined with mirrors, two painted with a spectacular garden mural and the fourth a bank of French windows opening onto a well-lit brick terrace. As she and John twirled round the room Abigail felt as if she were in the center of a floral kaleidoscope, the dresses of the women like colorful stained-glass petals against the reflected greenery of the walls.

She hung on to John, staring up into his unsmiling face, feeling one of his gloved hands at her waist, the other clasped around hers. They had explored death together. This mindless shuffling of feet should not have been so exalting. But she found herself moved to the point of tears by the burn of his eyes on her face. His fingers gathered hers closer, threading through hers, palm to palm. And then his lips curved, a lazy droop to his eyes.

Oh, he knew what he was doing to her.

She stiffened, jerked her gaze to his shoulder. "Stop it," she whispered.

"Stop what?" His voice was slow, amused.

"I don't know what you want from me, but you don't have to look at me that way."

"Abigail. You're a beautiful woman. How else am I supposed to look at you?"

"Is this a show for Dorothée or whatever her name is?"

He chuckled. "It'll give my mother something to think about. Quit jerking at my hand. You're ruining the rhythm. *One* two three—Which reminds me. You told me you didn't know how to dance."

"I'm a fast learner." Trembling in the circle of his arms, she turned her head away, terrified that she might have revealed her feelings. And how had this happened, anyway? How could she have any sort of affection for a man she so mistrusted? A man who was so different from her in every way? He might *say* she was beautiful, he might pretend to look at her with that tender, amused gleam in his eyes, but why on earth would a man like *him* want *her*—tall, desperately gauche, without any sort of financial or social recommendation?

"Indeed, you are," John said quietly. "In fact, I think you could learn anything you set your mind to."

She looked up at him, mutinously silent. He wanted her to bat her lashes, simper, fall at his feet in adoration. This she could not afford to do. The hard-won measure of respectability she had regained was too fragile to withstand the kind of dalliance he clearly had in mind.

He chuckled, snatched her close for a breathtaking moment, then whirled her to a halt next to several young matrons. He bowed to Camilla Laniere. "Mrs. Laniere, I return your protégée healthy and whole."

Camilla tucked her arm through Abigail's. "My dear, are you having a good time? John, you must procure a glass of lemonade for Miss Neal. She's looking quite flushed."

"I'll be happy to." He bowed again, turned and disappeared into the crowd.

Abigail flipped open the fan she'd borrowed from Camilla for the evening. "I'm having a lovely time. It's just the heat..." She plied the fan vigorously.

Camilla laughed. "Indeed. I remember it well."

Abigail gave her a doubtful look, but judging by Camilla's sly expression, pursuing her cryptic remark would not be wise. "Your husband said there was a gentleman he wanted me to meet."

"Yes, I believe he—oh, there he comes with Dr. Girard— and Drs. Pitcock and Cannon and—Gabriel, what on earth is going on?" she demanded as her husband approached at the head of a line of well-dressed gentlemen. "You aren't planning to talk shop at Eliza's party?"

Dr. Laniere smiled and tucked his arm around his wife, a quite unfashionable public sign of affection. "Only for half an hour, my dear. If one invites a bunch of physicians to the same event, a certain amount of medical conversation is inevitable."

Camilla raised her brows. "You might have given us some warning that you planned to descend on us all at once," she teased. She caught Abigail's alarmed gaze. "Miss Neal, I beg leave to present the faculty of the medical college en masse—well, as near all as makes no matter. Here is Dr. Girard, professor of chemistry and clinical medicine. You've met his son, I believe." She nodded at a bald, roosterlike man, who bore a striking resemblance to Marcus.

Abigail dipped a curtsy. "Sir." His skeptical look made her wonder what wild tales Marcus had told his father about her.

"And this," Camilla continued, "is Dr. Lewis, professor of obstetrics."

The jowly gray-haired gentleman gave her a grumpy scowl and shouted, "How'd'ye do!"

Remembering Winona's characterization of the elderly doctor as a lion, Abigail smiled but didn't try to penetrate his obvious deafness with a reply.

Camilla nodded at a suave middle-aged man who surveyed Abigail with blatant curiosity. "Dr. Pitcock is professor of physiology and pathological anatomy."

"The rumors of the autopsy cannot be true," he murmured to Dr. Laniere.

"Wait and see," Dr. Laniere replied and smiled at Abigail. "One more in the lineup, Miss Neal. Dr. Cannon is our retiring professor of anatomy and clinical surgery. We've worn him out over the last twenty-five years, poor fellow."

Abigail's gaze went to a thin, wispy old gentleman notable for a pair of thick-lensed spectacles perched on a beak of a nose. Of the four doctor-professors, he was the only one who bowed to her as if she were as much a lady as Camilla Laniere. "Miss Neal, I look forward to discovering what has triggered your interest in the medical sciences."

She looked at Dr. Laniere in alarm. "But—is my interest general knowledge, sir?"

"No, no, my dear—only among us professors. I would never have your name bandied about in the general community." He sent a cautioning look at Dr. Cannon. "But I confess we're all fascinated by the idea of a female of such exceptional talent in a field previously reserved for the male sex. In fact—" he glanced at his wife "—I would be interested to see what would happen if your wits were pitted against those of some of our best students."

Abigail's lips parted. "You cannot be serious." She looked around the ring of teachers staring at her as if she were a specimen under a microscope.

Dr. Pitcock sniffed. "Women are entirely too weak-minded to compete with men in the scientific fields, Laniere. You're wasting our time."

Adjusting his glasses, Dr. Cannon leaned toward Abigail to peer into her ear. "She's very tall, but I confess I was expecting a larger head—if she were truly as bright as you say."

Caught completely off guard, Abigail laughed. "Why would the head of an intelligent woman be larger than a man's?"

"Never mind that," growled Dr. Girard. "Is it true you're fluent in Greek, Latin and Mandarin Chinese? What happened to ladylike languages like French and Italian?"

Dr. Laniere coughed. "Er, perhaps we should dispense with personal remarks and see if Miss Neal might be willing to stand for a few questions. I believe you gentlemen will find her quite well-spoken."

"I want to ask the girl some questions!" roared Dr. Lewis.

"Good idea," Cannon shouted into his ear.

Unfortunately, at that very moment the music halted, along with the conversation, and every guest in the vicinity turned to find the source of the commotion.

Abigail wanted to be allowed to quietly study medicine and she had begun to dream of one day holding a license to practice. Finding herself the center of a gawking crowd, however, was her idea of a nightmare. Her old instinct to run kicked in.

Then she happened to see John Braddock, standing just behind Dr. Laniere's shoulder, a glass of lemonade in each hand. His expression was frankly horrified, as if a pet bear had suddenly got loose.

His patent disapproval sent a steel rod up her spine. "I'll be happy to answer your questions," she said clearly. "I studied Latin and Greek with my father because the sciences were originally documented in those languages, and I was frankly interested. I learned Mandarin out of necessity." She paused, flicking a glance at Camilla for courage. "What else, professors?"

"You *used* me to get yourself into the school!" John shoved one of the glasses of lemonade at Abigail and dragged her behind a potted palm.

"Don't be ridiculous. How could I have possibly imagined they'd ever consider admitting a female?" She waved her hands, sloshing lemonade all over his mother's ballroom floor.

"You—you stood there and answered questions as cool as a cucumber!"

"What did you imagine I would do? Go up in hysterical flames?"

He almost wished she had. As she'd defended herself quite competently, he had experienced a revolting mixture of worry, embarrassment and suicidal pride in her utter self-possession under attack. And he hadn't been able to do a thing about it. She hadn't even needed his lemonade.

Now she seemed likely to pitch the contents of the

glass in his face. To his surprise, she instead tipped it up and drained it in one long gulp. "Thank you," she said tight-lipped.

"You're welcome," he said coldly. "Do you think anything but disaster is going to come of the spectacle you made of yourself? And of me?"

"I was under the impression that you care very little what anyone else thinks, particularly your father. And what my behavior could possibly have to do with you, I fail to see."

"Everyone saw us dancing. Now they'll think—"

She uttered a short, hard laugh. "No one will suppose you anything but a benevolent host to the crazy woman who thinks she can compete intellectually with men. How Professor Laniere could do that to me in public—" She looked away, her throat working.

"Don't you see? He did it in public so that your abilities cannot be denied. Everyone saw you answer every question—brilliantly, I might add. You made Professor Pitcock look like a moron."

"Which will in no way endear me to him," she muttered.

"It doesn't matter. Now they'll be bound and determined to put you in there and prove you can't survive."

She looked at him, her green eyes burning with something that might have been rage, might have been humiliation, but was in no way tame or feminine. "And where do you stand on the issue, John? If Professor Laniere sponsors my application, do you think I can survive?"

He wanted to shout *yes!* He wanted to assure her again that she could do whatever she put her mind to. But the truth was, he was afraid for her. If she entered medical school, her reputation as a lady was gone and she would be forever lost to him.

Four bars of a minuet lilted before he shrugged. "I don't know."

For half a moment her eyes shone brilliant with unshed tears. Then she blinked and straightened her shoulders. "Well. Ultimately it doesn't matter what you think. Professor Laniere says I can do it. And he's willing to talk the others around." A hard smile pulled at her lush mouth. "Which will make me a rival for that first spot you want so badly. So you'd better learn to study, John Braddock."

Chapter Fourteen

In the quiet darkness of the enclosed carriage, Abigail huddled inside her cloak opposite Camilla, who was asleep on her husband's shoulder.

"I shouldn't keep her out so late." The professor tenderly adjusted the hood of Camilla's cloak. "The children wear her out, plus running the house and clinic… It's been good to have you for an extra pair of hands, Abigail. Winona's going to miss your help."

Abigail, who had been drowsing, head jarring against the seat's leather squabs, jerked awake. "Sir? Are you throwing me out?"

The professor chuckled. "Not at all. But when you start regular lectures and rounds you won't have time for tending babies and peeling potatoes and doing laundry. That's why you're the perfect candidate for our little experiment. No husband, no family, no other responsibilities."

"No money," she added drily and laughed with him. "I'm not naive enough to suppose the tickets to the lectures and matriculation fees come free. How can I expect the professors to teach me at no cost?"

"Hmm. That is a most excellent question." The professor's voice was smooth and quiet, but a hint of something else prickled the nerve cells along Abigail's neck. "I do have a proposition that I think might solve your dilemma… and be of some service to me at the same time."

Abigail's stomach clenched. The evening's social confrontations had worn her to the bone, rubbing all her defenses on the raw. As she tried to imagine what else would be expected of her, her mind leaped from one terrifying possibility to the next. The things she had seen in Shanghai…

But surely Dr. Laniere was the moral, upright gentleman he seemed to be. He had never said or done anything untoward; in fact, he had treated her with the utmost respect and kindness.

"What is it, sir?" she forced herself to ask. "I can't think of anything I'm qualified to do, other than the housework you've already said will be out of the question."

"No need to sound so terrified, my dear." The professor sounded amused. "Having observed your gift of observation and memory, I merely ask you to apply it in a more specific sense. However, before I divulge anything else, I require your promise to keep this conversation between the two of us."

Abigail hesitated. "Is Camilla aware of this…assignment?"

"She knows some, but not all. You are free to talk to her at any time, of course, but I should prefer that you come to me first."

The fact that the professor had not excluded his wife was reassuring. Abigail took a deep breath. "All right, then," she said recklessly. "I'll give you my promise of secrecy. And I'll help you with anything that is within the bounds of the law."

"Good." The professor nodded and settled back. "Then I should first explain a bit of my background. I don't make a practice of airing this information in our circle of acquaintance, but during the war between the states I served as an intelligence operative for Union naval forces."

"Did you, sir?" Abigail's political leanings were decidedly ambiguous due to her foreign rearing. She considered herself an American mainly because she had been born of American parents. "How very enterprising of you."

She could hear the smile in his voice. "Enterprising? Perhaps, though convincing my Southern-born bride to elope during the height of the conflict turned out to be a bit tricky. At all events, you can understand why I find it difficult to say no to serving my country when asked."

Abigail considered that. "I think I can. I still don't understand what this has to do with me."

"I'm getting there. My investigative duties after the war shifted back into the field of medicine, which, after all, was my first love. By then Camilla and I had married and started our family, so I needed a more stable and less dangerous way to earn a living. Research and teaching became my focus. But those of us on the forefront of the public health arena are increasingly convinced that regulation of licensing and control of addictive substances, at least at the state level, could be beneficial to the country as a whole. Our governor in particular is concerned about the unrestricted spread of opium use across the Deep South." He paused. "I have heard you discuss the issue with John Braddock on more than one occasion."

"We've disagreed on morphine's efficacy in pain control." She hesitated, unwilling to sound defensive, particularly with this learned and demonstrably broad-minded doctor. "American and European physicians are quite disparaging about Chinese acupuncture and herbology."

"We tend to discount what we do not understand," he agreed quietly. "Personally, I believe morphine and other opiates can be used safely and effectively when under the control of trained medical professionals. However, what concerns me is the widespread recreational misuse of these drugs."

Suddenly and quite unexpectedly Abigail was caught in knife-edged flashes of memory. She fought for breath, stuffing the shards away. "I…share your concern, sir."

After a moment, Dr. Laniere cleared his throat. "Would you care to share your story?"

"I cannot." She swallowed. "At least not now. Just…tell me what I can do. I can't imagine—"

"We think opium is being smuggled in through someone at the hospital, probably a student who needs the income to pay tuition. There are several in arrears and I've had my eye on them all, but so far have not been able to get close enough to obtain the information I need. I want to plant you inside as another set of eyes and ears."

"Me? But I'm a woman! The men will barely accept my presence, let alone talk in front of me."

"They will also view you with a certain amount of— let's face it—intellectual contempt. I'm hoping they'll be less likely to guard their tongues." He paused. "I also hope the novelty of having a women in lectures and demonstrations will distract from the questions you must ask."

"You know I'll do my best," Abigail said, trying to control her shaking voice. She assumed a man of Dr. Laniere's experience would have considered all the drawbacks, but she had to make sure. "What about one or two of the other students who...who do not seem to be in need of funds? John Braddock or Marcus Girard, for example. Wouldn't one of them be a better choice for this type of mission?"

The professor sighed. "For reasons I cannot go into, Braddock and Girard are both under suspicion themselves." He paused. "I hope you won't find it impossible to be objective where young Braddock is concerned."

Abigail's heart bounded into her throat. "I've no illusions about John Braddock's morals or lack thereof."

"It seems to me—in fact, one of the main reasons your participation in this little enterprise occurred to me—Braddock has demonstrated a rather marked affinity for you."

"You are mistaken, Professor," Abigail said in a suffocated voice.

"I rather think not," he said gently. "In any case, if you agree to the assignment, come by my office in the morning after rounds. I'll arrange to purchase your textbooks, equipment and supplies and meanwhile make you a loan of mine. You'll need to make appointments with each professor for tickets—which I'll pay for in advance—and be sure to see the dean for scheduling." He hesitated. "There's the formality of your application approval, but with myself and the four other faculty members who interviewed you tonight in your corner, you should have nothing to worry about." He laughed. "Except, of course, passing your courses! Do you think you can do that?"

"If Marcus Girard can do it, I can," Abigail said grimly. Or she would die trying.

Weichmann's breath wheezed in and out rhythmically as he and John followed Dr. Cannon around the pediatric ward Monday morning. Of course the rest of the group was back there as well, but Weichmann's debility hovered like a cloud, a reminder that there were some things even advanced medicine could not cure.

The thing about pediatrics, John reflected, wincing as Weichmann palpated the distended abdomen of a three-year-old little boy in bed four, was the noise. When children hurt, they screamed. Or whined. Or their mamas pestered the living daylights out of anybody who passed within a mile of the ward. Usually he could block it out, focus on the physical challenge. But this morning he found himself easily distracted. Wondering, for example, whether Abigail Neal had had the nerve to act on Prof's preposterous offer of admitting her into the medical college.

John hadn't minded helping her, loaning her books, teaching her to autopsy, accepting her help with the languages. There'd been no reason not to. After all, who was going to let a woman into medical college?

And then it happened. Dr. Laniere had lost his mind and decided it would be a good idea for *this* woman to invade the sacrosanct halls of medical academia.

Weichmann licked his lips and glanced at Dr. Cannon. "Professor, it feels like a lump—a ball of something—just under the skin."

"Really." Cannon brushed Weichmann aside and put his hands on the little boy's stomach. The child squealed. "Shush, bubba," said Cannon sternly, "the doctor's just checking on your tummy."

John exchanged glances with Weichmann. "The little guy's scared," John whispered.

"That knot's a bad one," Weichmann muttered. He looked at his hands, which were still trembling. Weichmann loved science, but was rather frightened of real people. "So, Braddock," he whispered with a sidelong look, "you run into any more burning bushes lately?"

John shrugged. "Breakfast was a bit lively this morning. Clem caught the toast on fire."

Weichmann laughed. "You know what I mean. I've been thinking about what you said. You think God cares what we do?" He glanced at the little boy, who suffered the professor's examination with tears leaking from the corners of his eyes. "Patients get well, patients die. We cut 'em up to find the cause, but by that time they're beyond help…" He sighed. "I'm losing focus, Braddock. I thought I knew why I wanted to do this, but sometimes it all seems…pointless."

Professor Laniere's words drifted through John's head. *Your real problem is spiritual, Braddock….Once I took off in a leap of faith, God began to prove Himself to me.*

It had been acceptable for John to discuss such matters with his professional mentor, a man of Prof's stature and experience. But a man did not admit confusion and weakness to his peers.

Evidently Weichmann hadn't the usual compunction.

And Dr. Cannon had frowned over his shoulder at them. Twice.

John shook his head at Weichmann. "I know what you mean," he whispered, "but we'll talk about it later." He crowded closer to the attending doctor. "Will you operate, sir?"

Dr. Cannon pulled at his mustache, covering a pleased smile. "I most certainly will. This is a most unusual case, gentlemen, a malignant tumor rarely seen in a child of this age, probably a *fungus hematodes*. Notice the unusual size of the obstruction." He patted the child's thin shoulder. "Lie still, laddie, the doctors want to examine you. One at a time, gentlemen, slide your hands slowly, firmly across the abdomen, stopping at the tumor." He stepped back to allow the six students to gather closer. "Notice its firm, perfectly round contour. We will arrange for the surgical theater tomorrow morning and you may observe as I remove it."

John, who had waited with his hands warming against his body as he had seen Abigail do, took his turn to examine the presentation of the tumor's exterior. He gently pressed, expecting to feel something in the nature of a rock under muscle, but found less resistance—more of a jellylike texture. The little boy gave an involuntary yelp of pain, quickly swallowed when John smiled an apology at him. "Sir—" John looked around and found the professor engaged in making notes on a sheaf of papers. "If this is a tumor, shouldn't it come out now?"

Dr. Cannon looked up and frowned. "There is no immediate danger, Braddock. The thing's been growing for some time, and one more day won't matter. I wish to give my colleagues the opportunity to observe as I remove the mass—in the morning, when there are less distractions."

John made way for Girard to move in. Of course surgeries were in the nature of performances. The bigger the audience the better. If he were in Cannon's place he would have done the same thing.

He glanced at Weichmann. Or perhaps he wouldn't.

On Monday morning, due to unexpected complications in getting Abigail's supplies and textbooks settled, it was nearly nine o'clock before Dr. Laniere strode into the first ward with Abigail and six other first-year students in tow. Because the professor considered tardiness a sin punishable by hanging, his mood this morning was, in the words of young Ramage, a baby-faced cotton farmer's son from Booneville, Mississippi, "acid on persimmons."

The group finished its round of the ward in record time, and all would have been well had not a well-dressed woman of some thirty summers planted herself in Prof's path as they passed the pediatric ward. "Here, you!" She pointed, bosom heaving. "I've been waiting for someone to come for thirty minutes. I want you to look in on my son."

The doctor's countenance darkened at the woman's presumptuous tone, and Abigail tensed. She had discovered that the medical school's seven faculty members retained full attending privileges as physicians of Charity Hospital and divided the students among them for daily rounds, rotating them in and out of the various wards. The surgery wards were generally assigned to either Dr. Laniere or Dr. Cannon, depending on the severity of the injury or illness and Sister Charlemagne's mood at the time of admittance. The doctors' attitudes tended toward territorialism.

"This is Dr. Cannon's ward," Prof said reasonably enough. "Has his group not already completed rounds?"

"Yes, but I'm not satisfied with the diagnosis." The woman's face reddened. "What, if you please, is a *fungus hoematodes*?"

Abigail watched Dr. Laniere's expression go still. "How old is your son?"

"He is six." The woman swallowed. "He's in a great deal of pain and they won't operate until tomorrow morning."

"Hmm." Dr. Laniere's black eyes scanned his group of cowering first-years and fixed on Abigail, towering over the lot of them in the back. "Miss Neal. Is your Latin up to this one? *Fungus hoematodes.*"

Terrified, Abigail cleared her throat. "*Fungus*—dating

from 1529, parasitic spore-producing organism. *Hoema-todes*—gathering of blood. It would be a cancerous growth which attaches to an organ and…" Faltering as the woman's face went ashen, she swiftly transferred her gaze to her teacher. "It can be removed with surgery."

Dr. Laniere nodded. "Yes, and those kinds of growths are exceedingly rare in small children. Perhaps it would be instructive for us to take a look. Mrs…?"

"DeFord," the woman supplied, looking relieved. "My boy's name is Roddy."

"All right, then. Gentlemen and lady—" he smiled at Abigail "—follow me."

At least she hadn't made a complete fool of herself, Abigail thought as she trailed behind the men into the pediatric ward. The sounds and smells here were unlike those in the adult wards or the Lanieres' home clinic. The nurses had done a good job of making the six little white iron beds clean and orderly, and straight-backed wooden chairs provided a place to rest for the few mothers in the room. But the fretful crying of the babies and the listlessness of the older children in all this spartan whiteness struck Abigail as nothing sort of depressing.

The professor seemed not to notice. He followed Mrs. DeFord to a bed in the center of the east wall, where a small blond-haired boy lay on his side. Tears slowly leaked from beneath his closed eyelids and dripped on the pillow.

"Roddy," said his mother, touching his hair gently, "this other doctor is going to look at you. Can you lie on your back?"

"It hurts, Mama." But he obeyed, drawing down the sheet himself to expose his midsection. There was a perfectly round egg-sized bulge on his right hip.

Dr. Laniere leaned over to palpate the affected area. "Did you injure yourself somehow, son?"

The little boy blinked. "I don't know. Me and my brother was playing in the hayloft one day, and the next this big bubble popped up."

The doctor glanced at his students. "Does anyone know what would be characteristic of a fungal mass? Texture, shape, color?"

The six male students looked at one another, avoiding the eyes of both the professor and Abigail. Several of them shrugged.

Abigail tipped her head, meeting the professor's eyes. "I don't know for sure, but common sense says such a mass would be lumpy, asymmetrical, hard to the touch."

Dr. Laniere nodded. "Correct. Touch this lump, Miss Neal." He moved aside to allow her space next to the bed.

Insecurity turned to curiosity as Abigail did a quick visual scan of the little boy's hip, then slid her hand over the protrusion. She looked at Dr. Laniere. "It has a jelly-like interior. That's pus—it's not lobulated like a fungus hematode would be." She paused, shaken by doubt. "Is that right, professor?"

His eyes lit briefly, although he did not smile—perhaps to avoid offending the boy's mother. "That's right," he said softly. "Good work."

A ridiculous burst of pride shot through Abigail, quickly squelched as she imagined the pain this poor little boy must be enduring. "So what will you do, Professor?"

"*You* tell me what we will do."

Her gaze went inward as she pulled up her meager store of information on abscesses. "Anesthetize him and open the hip. Depending on the location of the abscess, we'll lance and drain the affected area, then close him up, inserting a tube to release any remaining mucus that collects."

Dr. Laniere looked around at the young men listening to Abigail, mouths ajar. "Do you fellows see any reason to postpone the operation?"

"Actually, sir," said Ramage timidly, "if we wait, the abscess could burst and poison the boy within minutes."

"Then we'd better hurry," said Dr. Laniere. He touched Mrs. DeFord's elbow. "Do you understand the danger your son is in? I presume you have no objection to going through with the procedure."

"No—I mean, yes, I understand the danger, and of course you must proceed as you see fit." The woman bent to kiss her son's sweaty brow. "Mama will be right with you, Roddy, praying for you. Be a brave boy for the doctors." She backed away from the bed, glancing at Abigail with reluctant respect. "Thank you, miss."

Abigail nodded. "He'll be in very good hands."

"All right, then." Dr. Laniere patted Roddy's arm. "Miss Neal and Mr. Ramage, because you two have been brave enough to admit to having studied the affliction, you may both scrub up and attend me in the main operating theater." He turned to a nurse who had appeared in the doorway. "Our patient will need to be prepared for surgery. Be so good as to send Crutch to prepare the theater and then bring a wheelchair to transport young Mr. DeFord."

Abigail and Ramage stared at one another for a moment; then, galvanized, they rushed after Dr. Laniere, who was already halfway to the door.

Abigail could hardly restrain her exultation. She was going to assist in a surgery—because she had corrected the diagnosis of a tenured surgical and clinical professor. She had no notion how she had come into this situation—but suspected that it should be attributed to the intervention of the Almighty.

"Thank You, God, oh thank You," she whispered as she slipped into the washroom behind Ramage.

Chapter Fifteen

"**W**hat I want to know is how she managed this." John, lined up against the back wall of the peds ward with Girard and the other second-years, shot an envious look at Abigail. She stood quietly at Dr. Laniere's side as Dr. Cannon vented his feelings about his patient being co-opted by another professor.

"No explaining Prof's reasons for anything he does." Girard shook his head. "Thought old Loose Cannon was going to have an apoplexy right there in the ward. Still might." He glanced at Dr. Cannon's flushed cheeks, then Dr. Laniere's notably unrepentant countenance. "But Prof was right to go in immediately. Even *you* knew that lump didn't look or feel like a tumor."

"I'd have looked like an idiot, contradicting my professor. Still—glad the little boy's recovering, even if I didn't get to attend the surgery."

"You don't think they're really going to let her come to lectures, do you?" Girard's broad brow wrinkled. "I mean, a *woman* in the classroom—just ain't right. Might as well serve tea and put up curtains. She'll be fainting at the first sight of—"

"Girard, this is no maudlin wilting lily. You haven't seen her—" John stopped. He wasn't going to mention the autopsy. "—do an examination," he ended lamely.

Marcus made a rude noise. "Yes, I have. She's a pervert, if she can examine an unclothed body without losing countenance."

"It's not like that and you know it. After all, *we're* not perverts, are we?"

"Well, no, of course not. But it's different for women." Marcus was looking at him as if he'd gone round the bend.

Perhaps he had. Abigail Neal had turned John's life wrongside out on so many levels there was no going back to normal. Whatever "normal" was. One minute she was all soft and feminine and confused—as she'd been when they danced together—the next she was taking over territory that had previously belonged to him. *You'd better study, Braddock.* What was a fellow to think about a woman like that?

The argument between the two professors sharpened into focus, with Abigail's serene face in the background. John looked at her more closely. There was a tiny crease between her eyebrows. And her knuckles were white where her fingers clasped one another at her waist.

John pushed away from the wall.

"Cannon told us to stay put, you moron," Girard whispered stringently.

Ignoring him, John moved next to Abigail, allowing his shoulder to briefly touch hers. She looked up at him, her expression shifting from that faint anxiety to annoyance. When he winked at her, her mouth pruned slightly.

Professor Laniere turned. "Ah, Braddock. Now that Dr.

Cannon and I have gotten this situation sorted out, I believe we'll move on toward the schedule for the latter part of the day. You fellows may go for lunch, then report to my classroom for this afternoon's lectures." He turned to Dr. Cannon. "I trust this plan meets with your approval, Professor?"

Dr. Cannon visibly struggled not to argue. "Fine. But I insist on a faculty meeting no later than tomorrow. I wish to present my objections to the rest of the board."

Dr. Laniere bowed as John snagged Abigail's elbow and towed her along with him toward the door. "Come on," he muttered out of the side of his mouth. "Let's get out of here before you start something else."

"It wasn't my fault!" Abigail balked as he hustled her quickly down the stairs behind the rest of the students. "I could tell by Professor Laniere's face there was something wrong with that diagnosis."

"I'm sure you could. But Dr. Cannon is the *last* person you want on your list of enemies."

She shot him a look. "John, they're *all* my enemies— except Professor Laniere, of course. Nobody wants me here, not the doctors, not the students." Unexpectedly, her eyes glistened. "Don't pretend you like having a woman in the school."

"Of course I don't," he said, surprising her into a snort of laughter. "But Prof has made up his mind and until he boots you out I know what side my bread's buttered on." To his relief, her incipient tears had vanished. "If you want to stay, you'd better not let the other fellows see any sign of weakness."

"Weakness?" She marched ahead of him down the stairs. "Is it a weakness to wish for one single friend?"

John clattered after her. "I'm your friend."

"Don't let the *other fellows* hear you say that."

"I think my reputation can stand it." They reached the landing and John moved to open the heavy front door. "Besides, it's time I quit spending all my free time cutting up with the boys."

"Indeed?" She gave him an amused glance as she passed him.

"Yes. My mother keeps telling me so, anyway." He looked up at the iron-colored clouds painting the afternoon sky. "It's going to rain. We'd better hurry."

She nodded, picking up her pace. "Supposing you suddenly reform—what are you going to do with this sudden massive quantity of free time?"

"I like experimenting. I thought I might invent something." It was the first thought out of his head, a random comment intended to make her laugh.

She rewarded him with her infectious chuckle. "That's a splendid idea. What are you going to invent?"

Clasping his hands behind his back as they crossed Common Street and headed toward Canal, John gave Abigail a sidelong look. She was taking him seriously. "A folding wheelchair," he blurted. "With an interior push wheel so the patient can push himself and not get his hands dirty."

"That's magnificent! You should really do it."

He hunched his shoulders, plowing his hands into the pockets of his trousers. "It's absurd. I don't know anything about engineering."

"But you could find someone who does. You understand the needs of the sick and injured." She beamed up at him. "You're bright enough to figure it out—"

"John! Johnny! What are you doing here?"

John turned at the sound of his sister's voice and found

her leaning out of the family carriage as it rolled down Canal Street. He waved.

"Stop, Appleton!" Lisette called to the driver. "I want to speak to my brother. Stop, I say."

As the carriage came to a halt with a creak of springs and rattle of harness, John leaned close to Abigail's ear. "Rescue me, I beg you."

She shook her head and smiled, but accompanied him across the muddy brick street.

Lisette's bonnet had disappeared inside the carriage, but the door suddenly popped open, exposing small slippered feet and a froth of petticoats. His sister beckoned imperiously. "Hurry, John! It's starting to rain and we want your company!"

"We?" He approached the carriage with no intention of obeying his sister's ridiculous commands. Making sure Abigail was behind him, he rested his forearm on the side of the carriage "Is Mother with you? Where are you going?"

"Not Mother!" Lisette bubbled with giggles. "It's Dorothée. We're on an expedition for new gloves and ribbons." She turned to speak to her companion. "Move to the other side of the carriage, Dorothée. We have to make room for John."

The carriage lurched as, presumably, Dorothée shifted to the other seat. Sighing, John met Abigail's eyes. "I suppose we could ride with them as far as Bienville. I didn't bring an umbrella."

Abigail, clearly reluctant, stepped back. The rain was coming down in earnest now, soaking her hair and clothes. "Go ahead, I'll catch up to the others."

"Don't be ridiculous." He leaned into the carriage.

"Move over, Lisette. Miss Neal will need space, too." As Abigail climbed in, he gave Appleton instructions to drive to Descartes's Oyster Bar, then got in after her.

If Dorothée Molyneux was less than enthused about sharing the carriage with a strange female—and an exceedingly damp one at that—she covered her chagrin by batting her eyelashes at John as he sank onto the leather seat beside her. He watched Abigail pull her skirts close, making herself as small as possible next to Lisette. Raindrops trembled at the ends of her black lashes, the long spikes accenting the green of her eyes, and her dress clung to her figure. John made himself look at his sister.

Despite Abigail's drenched aspect, Lisette seemed to have no trouble recognizing her. "Dorothée, I don't think you met Miss Neal at our party—it seemed every time I tried to introduce you, John whisked her off somewhere else. She is a fellow bibliophile and has done amazing and heroic things with John and his medical friends. And then of course, she answered the questions of the professors quite brilliantly. I promise I should have been absolutely *stricken* to have been so put on the spot."

Blond Dorothée, whose voice reminded John of a squeaky door, simpered. "What a positively ferocious brain you must have, Miss Neal."

Since Miss Molyneux's brain rarely contended with anything more taxing than deciding which ribbon to add to a bonnet, John didn't waste time arguing with her. Besides, he thought, letting his gaze skate back to Abigail's amused face, Abigail did indeed possess a rather razor-like mind. It was one of the things he most admired and feared in her.

Abigail ignored the implied insult. "Thank you for

taking us up, Miss Braddock. Your brother and I have to be back for a lecture in less than an hour."

Lisette's expression quickened. "What kind of lecture? John never tells me anything he's learning."

"Lise, you know you're ill at the sight or even the description of blood." John flicked a glance at Abigail. "Be careful what you tell her."

"I'd be faint at the very idea of touching sick people." Dorothée shuddered. "Indeed, Miss Neal, I can't comprehend how you can stand being with all those cadavers and…skeletons…and naked body parts!"

"I don't really think about it in those terms," said Abigail. "I'm interested in what makes people well. The body is so intricately put together that the slightest flaw sends it into imbalance. Yet most of us walk around healthy and whole. That's quite miraculous, I think."

John studied her. For a long time he'd denied the handiwork of Almighty God in designing the human body. Lately it had begun to seem only natural to believe.

"When John becomes a real doctor I suppose we shall hardly see him," Lisette sighed. "There are truly a great many sick and injured people in this city! Mama says she feels very sorry for Camilla Laniere because her husband is always at the hospital and bringing home one disease or another to the children. I could never marry a doctor!"

"If I married a doctor," said Dorothée with a thread of grit in her shrill little voice, "I should make him stay home in the evenings. How selfish—to endanger one's own family for the sake of strangers."

"That's quite a novel view of the responsibilities of the medical profession, Miss Molyneux," John drawled. "Not to mention those of a wife."

"My brother is the most unselfish person imaginable." Lisette frowned at her friend. "Why, he saved the lives of thousands and thousands of people after that fire."

John laughed. "That's a bit of an exaggeration."

Dorothée's blue eyes widened. "Of course I believe in charitable works," she said, flirting a look at John. "I only meant that the love between a husband and wife should take precedence over one's ideals."

"You are going to have quite a search to find a gentleman who will entertain such romantical notions, Miss Molyneux," said Abigail.

Though John agreed, the deep cynicism of her tone made him wonder. Her hands were clenched around her reticule, her lips tight.

But before he could question her, Lisette touched Abigail's hand. "I didn't say I agree with my mama. In fact, we had quite an argument with Papa last night." She looked at John. "That's why I'm so glad to see you today. I want you to ask him to allow me to go to college." Lisette set her little chin. "I want to learn how to do something that will help other people. If Miss Neal can do it, why can't I?"

"Because you're—" He stopped. *The daughter of a gentleman. My giddy little sister.* His gaze caught Abigail's, and the ironical look there shamed him. "What sorts of things would you do to help people?" he asked Lisette gently.

She shrugged. "I'm not smart enough for medical school, but I might like to be a teacher. I like children."

"You're going to have children of your own." Dorothée rolled her eyes. "You don't have to go to college for that."

Dorothée interference put John's back up. "I'll speak to Father next chance I get," he said but felt compelled to add, "just don't get your hopes up, Lise. You know how he feels about educating women." Just then the carriage drew to a stop in front of Descartes'. John looked out. The rain had dwindled to a fine sprinkle. "Here we are, Miss Neal," he said, opening the door. He stepped out and extended a hand to help Abigail alight. "Lisette, give my love to Mother. Miss Molyneux, your servant."

John and Abigail ducked into the oyster bar, a dark, smoky establishment patronized by law and medical students, as well as denizens of the docks. The decor was plain and rough, but the food cheap, hardy and freshly prepared. Abigail didn't seem to notice the overwhelmingly male company as she plunked herself on a stool beside John at the bar. In fact, she was so abstracted that John ordered two dozen oysters on the half shell and a couple of chicory coffees without her so much as opening her mouth.

He studied her tense profile for several moments after their drinks came—she simply held her cup in both hands, staring blankly at the mirror over the bar.

"Tell me, Abigail, why it is you don't subscribe to Miss Molyneux's penchant for romantic love between marriage partners."

She blinked and cut a glance at him. "What?"

"I'm curious to know if you're one of those women looking for all-consuming passion in a marriage partner."

"I shall never marry."

He laughed, assuming she was joking. But when she simply stared at him, his amusement faded. "You cannot be serious."

She shrugged. "Who would marry me?" A faint smile tipped her lips. "According to Dr. Pitcock, my head is too big."

"No—what he said is that you are surprisingly normal

for such a bright woman. I suppose you think there isn't a man capable of keeping up with you."

She sipped her coffee, made a face, and pushed it away. "That's bitter." She shook her head. "I'm not so arrogant. But I've too much to accomplish to tie myself down to household and children." She gave him a wry smile. "Which generally accompanies marriage. Miss Molyneux is right in a sense—there are responsibilities that go along with committing to such a lifelong partnership. And when one party or the other is consumed with some outside passion, what you have is tantamount to adultery." Her lips tightened. "It's a difficult tightrope to walk and I will not place myself in the situation of making a choice between medicine and marriage."

"I think you're very cynical."

"No. I'm *realistic*." Her eyes glinted. "Don't tell me you're actually thinking of marrying that little twit. She'd drive you mad inside a week."

"Of course I'm not thinking of…I'm not thinking of marrying anybody. It's just that I hate to see you cut yourself off from the possibility of… Never mind," he said hastily, catching the tray of oysters as the cook slid it down the bar. "Eat up and let's get back to class. I don't want to be late."

She picked up an oyster and slipped in a knife to expertly pop it open. "Your sister is surprisingly broadminded and educated. I like her."

John shrugged. "She's spoiled, of course, but she has a good heart. My father has several charitable enterprises that Lise dabbles in."

"Your father doesn't strike me as the charitable sort."

"He's been spending considerable political coin to bring better sewage to the poor sections of the city near the levees—which was largely his idea, by the way. He knows he's got to protect the homes of the dock workers for the benefit of his own livelihood." John rapidly put away his lunch as he tried to explain. "So his city improvements aren't entirely altruistic—but he's not as bad as some people paint him."

Abigail glanced at him, her expression unreadable. "How much of your father's business activity are you aware of?"

"Not much. Frankly, I'm not interested. As long as he pays my medical college expenses…" That sounded both selfish and ungrateful. "I mean, the old man's absolutely rabid about shipping, trading and building. At first he couldn't conceive that I was serious about studying medicine." John slid an oyster down his throat, remembering those months of icy silence between him and his family. "Went so far as to cut me off last summer."

Abigail's eyes flew to his face. "What about school? Did you have to drop out?"

John shook his head. "For a while I managed—I'd been putting aside my allowance, when I could. Finally swallowed my pride and asked Prof to see about having my tuition deferred."

"The faculty would do that?"

"Happens all the time. The professors are good about lending a hand to fellows who fall into arrears."

Abigail was silent for a moment. "I don't know how I'm going to manage," she said slowly. "I certainly have no money."

"It's an expensive education, Abigail." He wondered how far she'd actually go, what she'd give up to obtain her medical license. He'd never met a woman with more guts and determination.

"Yes. It is." She moistened her lips. "I hear there are ways of making money…under the table."

"Under the table? What do you mean?"

"This is a huge port, John, and smuggling opium is big business. Is that what you did?"

He stared at her open-mouthed. "I may not be the righteous specimen you think I ought to be, but I don't cheat or steal. Or smuggle drugs. And you'd better not try it either!" he added, for good measure.

"You know how I feel about opiates." Her expression was an odd combination of relief and curiosity. "I take it you eventually made up with your father."

He nodded. "Prof went to my father and talked him around somehow. The Lanieres have influence with the governor, and the pater's got political ambitions."

"Your father sounds like a ruthless man."

"I suppose." He glanced at her half-empty plate. "We need to finish and get back to class. If you don't want those, hand 'em over."

Looking troubled, she shoved her plate toward him.

He ate the oysters, sliding them down one after the other in rapid succession. Yes, his father was ruthless, but how else would a man make his way from bayou fisherman's son to the owner of the largest shipping line on the Gulf Coast? Since when was John appointed to be his father's conscience? And what was Abigail implying anyway?

Over the next few days, Abigail kept her eyes and ears open as she followed Dr. Laniere around the hospital. Pending a meeting of the entire faculty, the other professors tolerated her presence in the lecture rooms, but only reluctantly answered her questions. Dr. Cannon in particular, as John had predicted, remained cold and contemptuous. The male students, except for John, treated her more or less as a joke..

One afternoon she arrived in dissection lab to find that her cadaver had a suggestive note attached with a string to the toe. Swallowing her furious embarrassment, she'd removed the note without comment, slid it into her pocket and proceeded with the lesson. At the first opportunity she'd given it to Professor Laniere. He seemed to think he'd be able to analyze the handwriting to discover the prankster's identity. Leaving it at that, she'd tried to dismiss her humiliation. If that was the best the "boys" could do in their desire to be rid of her, she had little to worry about.

But on the Monday of the second week of December, she sat at breakfast in the Lanieres' kitchen, reading with dismay—and mounting indignation—the morning edition of the *Times Picayune*. A second-page editorial wondered in derisive language what the medical school board members were thinking, to consider attempting the higher education of a woman, "thereby opening the doors to a most shameful liberality of morals which would ultimately result in the demeaning of pure femininity."

"What rubbish!" she muttered, folding the paper and handing it back to Camilla, who sat across from her feeding the baby. "Why must my morals always be called into question?"

Camilla slipped the spoon into Meg's mouth. "People attack when they feel threatened."

"Threatened? By what?"

"Some men worry that their control over their households will be upset. If you complete a professional degree, other upper-class women will follow suit." Camilla thumped the spoon comically against the table. "No more dependence on husbands and fathers. Complete anarchy will ensue!"

"But—I'm hardly upper-class." She thought about John's aborted response to Lisette's question in the carriage the day they had lunch at Descartes'.

"Perhaps that's the point. If women can give themselves independence with an education, social lines will inevitably blur. Think about it. One element of a man's power status is his ability to keep a wife in indolence." Camilla shook her head. "Personally, I think the women of my class would benefit from greater mental and physical exercise. My husband agrees, which is why he has taken you on as a sort of project." Her smile was warm and a bit anxious. "Don't let him down, Abigail. He's risking his reputation to champion you."

"I have no intention of backing down, I assure you." Much more than Dr. Laniere's reputation was at stake here.

Chapter Sixteen

Friday evening John handed his hat and overcoat over to Appleton, who gave him a bluff "Family's in the Chinese parlor, mate" and waddled off toward the coat room like a cheery little tugboat.

John strode into the parlor to find his mother, dressed in plum-colored velvet, at the pianoforte twiddling over Mozart. His sister sat on the fainting couch yanking at the knots in a sampler held close to her eyes, her yellow skirts spread decoratively around her.

Looking relieved at the interruption, Lisette dropped the fabric and hoop. "Johnny! You're late."

"There was a jam-up on the street car line. A wagon full of cordwood spilled across the rails at Esplanade." He crossed to the fireplace and picked up the poker. "Where's Father?"

His mother turned on the piano stool, her mouth drawn into a moue. "He sent a note around an hour or so ago, saying not to wait dinner for him. Business delay."

Business. Nothing unusual about that, but John couldn't help thinking of Abigail's questions about his father's shipping enterprises—enterprises that had been the family income since John had been in short pants. There was no reason to think there was anything "under the table" involved. Smuggling opium, for instance.

John returned the poker to its stand with a clatter. "If you don't mind, Mother, there's a book I remember seeing in Father's study that I'd like to borrow. Perhaps we could delay the meal after all, while I look for it."

His mother rolled her eyes. "You men can't leave your pursuits and relax for more than ten minutes at a time." She sighed. "Very well. I'll tell Cook to keep everything in the warming oven for a bit. But don't get distracted and forget about us!"

Already at the door, he turned to wink at Lisette. "Me? Distracted?"

In the study he shut the door, then walked around the perimeter of the room, running his hand along the spines of hundreds of books his father had collected during his travels. Two of the walls were lined, floor to ceiling, with leatherbound copies of the classics as well as modern-day bestsellers. More than likely Father had actually read few of them. Phillip Braddock was a man of action, a man of business. Sitting for hours with his nose in a book would not have appealed.

Why, then, had he amassed this collection that would have made Abigail Neal stare with envy? Was it purely to make a gentlemanly impression on visitors?

John stopped at a long, narrow table on the inside wall upon which a teakwood humidor rested beside a tray containing a set of snifters and a corked bottle of fine brandy. Here were his father's true pleasures, tastes John used to associate with manhood and cosmopolitan polish. Because of the influence of a professor and a beautiful young woman, he now found more value in the knowledge contained in books.

And best of all, he'd come to know God in an intimate, life-changing way.

So what would his Lord expect him to do about his father's misdeeds—if indeed there were any?

He looked around, trying to pin down what it was that made him so sure Father was hiding something in here. Little things. The fact that, despite his father's complaints of his absence, John was never invited to spend time with him in this room. The odd comment about "concerns" in China. Nothing concrete enough to draw undue attention. But puzzling nonetheless.

John touched the humidor's latch and it swung open. He spun the carousel and let the dense odor of fine tobacco permeate the air. John had smoked his first cigar at the age of sixteen, but it wasn't a taste he'd cultivated for long. Conscious of his bodily health, he didn't like the way the smoke hampered his breathing, even though he knew many physicians who smoked. Tobacco wasn't for him.

Still, it was a minor vice, certainly not illegal and it didn't warrant any particular concern for his father.

No, there was something else. He was about to move to the big mahogany desk when the door jerked open.

His father stood in the doorway and stared at him for a moment, then advanced into the room, shutting the door gently behind him. "What are you doing in here?"

"Looking for this book." John pulled a copy of *The History of China* off the shelf. "Is Mother ready to serve dinner?"

"She sent me to find you." His father dropped awkwardly into his desk chair. His face was pasty, John noticed, except for the red veins in his nose. "But stay a moment—I want to talk to you without the women listening."

"What is it?" John tucked the book under his arm and sat down in front of the desk.

Maybe he could broach Lisette's desire to attend college. Abigail had already asked if he'd followed through, and a man should keep his word.

His father pulled a cheroot from his pocket and lit it. "It's that woman," he said. "The one stirring up trouble about the medical college."

John sat up straight. "You mean Miss Neal."

"Yes. As a trustee, I felt I should intervene before the reputation of the entire college is damaged."

"Wait. Father, you're not getting embroiled in that, are you? I assumed the faculty would be the ones making the decision whether to admit her or not."

"The faculty can be influenced. They should listen to reasonable minds, especially those of us with a financial investment in the college."

John stared at him. "What financial investment? Why, you've sabotaged my every ambition of graduating."

"Well, it's more in the nature of a loan." Father smiled sourly. "I'll have to credit you with determination, son. I decided that if my heir was going to be associated with the institution, I had best make sure it succeeds."

"Father, what have you done?"

"Only what was necessary." His father looked at the glowing tip of the cigar. "As you know, Gabriel Laniere's proposition to admit Miss Neal had found favor with some of the faculty. I have simply argued that the students whose diplomas will be affected should have some say in the matter."

"What do you mean?"

"Next week the matter will be taken to a vote of the student body. The faculty—even Dr. Laniere—agreed that if the students balk at Miss Neal's presence, she will be refused admittance." His father's shoulders lifted. "It's fair and reasonable."

If there was anything Phillip Braddock failed to control, John had yet to encounter it. He shouldn't be surprised at this interference. The students would vote Abigail down, of course. And having come so close to achieving her dream, she would be devastated.

"How much?" John asked quietly. "What did it take to buy that much influence?"

"There's no need to be crude." His father leaned forward to tip the ash into a granite tray on the corner of the desk. "But because you asked, I've loaned just under seven million dollars to the college."

All the air left John's lungs and his voice came out in a hoarse croak. "Seven million—Father, where did you get that kind of money?"

"Tea. Silk. And other necessary substances." His father's eyes narrowed. "I've worked hard to build my fortune and have something of value to pass on to you and your family. Which is why it's critical that you marry for political power."

John stared at him grimly, thinking of Abigail's questions about opium smuggling. Would his father consider the drug to be a "necessary substance"? "I thought I'd convinced you I want to make my own way. Neither your fortune nor your political advances mean anything to me."

His father slammed his big, meaty hands on the desk. "And I keep telling you, your precious medical college depends on it."

"We shall see." John rose and made his father a stiff bow.

There was no possibility of him being open to Lisette's interest in college. "Mother and Lisette are waiting. Perhaps we'd better join them."

For a long moment they stared at one another. Finally, his father nodded and rose. The two of them left the room and walked side-by-side into the dining room as if they were casual acquaintances, rather than father and son. John didn't know how he was going to help Abigail, but he knew he had to do something.

And he was going to start with prayer.

Abigail had never heard such music in her life. Standing beside Winona in the third pew on the left-hand side of the little clapboard church building on Basin Street, she let it move her to tears and laughter. There were hymns, of course, like the ones she'd learned as a child at her mother's knee—like the one she'd heard Winona sing when she first came to live with the Laniere family. But the preaching was also interspersed with loud, emotional bursts of extemporaneous chants and choruses, echoes of an almost wordless energy that was foreign to her in every sense of the word. Still, she found herself stamping her feet, swaying and shouting "amen!" with the rest of the congregation. God seemed a real personality who hovered and yet infused, who was pleased and honored by His people's exuberant adulation.

When it was over and the congregation started filing out to shake the sweating preacher's hand, Abigail followed in the wake of Winona's family, almost in a stupor of joy. She felt electrified all over, as if she'd experienced the Scriptural text firsthand. *Enter into His gates with thanksgiving and unto his courts with praise.*

This was the fourth Sunday she'd attended church with

Winona since that first time—the day they'd visited the Colored Orphans Asylum. The day she'd first seen real compassion in John Braddock. As she shook the pastor's hand, accepting his blessing on her week, she wondered if John had a place like this to belong to. Only recently had she become aware of the absolute necessity of surrounding oneself with likeminded believers. Faith without support became vulnerable to discouragement. She should have encouraged John to come with her when he asked. Selfish and self-protective of her to put him off.

Come to think of it, she thought as she walked home with the Caldwell family for lunch, she didn't know for sure the level of John's faith. He'd admitted never attending church with his family, but he'd solicited his mother's help with the orphans. The last time Abigail and Winona went back to check on them, they had found conditions much improved.

"Take care, Miss Abigail," cautioned Winona, dropping back from a conversation with her younger sister to hook arms with Abigail, "or you gonna be falling in one of these big old potholes and we'll never find you." She steered Abigail around a rut in the road. "What's that weighing so heavy on your mind?"

Abigail hesitated. "I was thinking about John Braddock."

"Ohhhh." Winona's beautiful black brows went up. "Now there's a subject that'll keep a girl up all night. I told you he could charm the birds out of the trees if he halfway tried."

Abigail fought her embarrassment. "He seems to like you a lot—confide in you maybe—I was just wondering if you'd talked to him about—about God or church or—" She swallowed. "You know what I mean."

"He asks me questions sometimes, but I don't know that

John Braddock opens up to anybody." Winona shook her head. "He's pretty sure of himself on most subjects." She slanted a look at Abigail. "Why don't you ask him yourself?"

"I rarely see him, now that I'm busy with classes. He's a year ahead of me, you know. It was just—being in church today, feeling so happy and accepted, I worry about John. He seems so lonely—well, except for those young men he runs around with. They hardly seem like elevating company."

"I dunno." Winona looked thoughtful. "That curly-haired boy seems all right. The one who came with him into the orphanage."

Abigail nodded. "Tanner Weichmann. He is nice, although he's a bit shy."

"Tanner," Winona repeated with a smile. "I didn't hear his name that day. They said they were going to get some help for the little ones, but they never did."

"I was just thinking about the orphanage. Mrs. Braddock has helped some, but perhaps she could think of some ways to get some more wealthy people interested in helping out down here in the District. Some of these folks work so hard in the cotton presses and sail lofts and at the docks." Abigail continued thinking out loud as she blindly followed Winona into her parents' home. "I worry about the children most. If we could just open up a free clinic for the women and children, maybe staff it with medical students under the supervision of a rotating doctor…. Not to compete with the hospital, but to bring the most basic care here where people live."

She looked up and found Winona grinning at her. "You sure are a dreamer, Abigail Neal. Wouldn't have known that about you at first."

* * *

As she passed the saloon on Franklin, Abigail scanned the row of horses and carriages tied to their hitching post. She hoped she wouldn't encounter anyone from either the medical school or the hospital here. Not that she had anything to be ashamed of, returning just to make sure Tess was all right. Still, explanations could be tedious.

She'd been planning to make the trip down to her old habitation eventually, but it was Winona who encouraged her to do it today. "You're a strong woman, Abigail," Winona had assured her as they parted ways at the corner of St. Louis and Marias. That big warm smile had lit the colored girl's dark eyes. "You don't got to be afraid of losing your place now. Besides," she added mischievously, "those Laniere children got so used to having their personal storyteller around, they'd send their daddy after you in a heartbeat if you decided not to come back."

Losing her place was the least of Abigail's worries now. She was more afraid of getting sidetracked by the desperate needs here in her old neighborhood. Certainly, she knew, there was immediate good she could do—even with the limited training she'd received so far. But she could best serve her friends by finishing.

Press on, she reminded herself as she knocked on the warped, peeling outer door of the tenement where she'd spent six months with Tess. *Don't look back.*

She was just about to give up and go home when the door opened under her hand. Tess stood there for a moment, her face a blank of surprise, before she flung her arms around Abigail with a glad shriek. "You came back! Oh, I missed you!"

Abigail returned the hug, strongly, laughing. "I missed you, too. But I've been so busy—"

"Come in, come in." Tess let go of her and backed up to admit Abigail into the little square entryway. The floor looked like it had recently been mopped, which was a good sign. Tess was a fanatical housekeeper when she wasn't plagued by depression. "I was just having a Sunday afternoon splurge, making tea." Tess bumped open the apartment door with her shoulder. "Have you had lunch?"

"Yes, do you remember the black girl we met in the Lanieres' kitchen? The housekeeper, Winona? I came down to attend her church and had a meal with her family." Abigail stopped just inside the door, taken off guard by an odd queasiness. It was almost as if the person she'd been when she lived here wanted to reinhabit her body. Which was nonsense.

"I remember. Sit down, sit down." Tess moved to the cookstove in a flurry of motion, waving at two wobbly chairs, new since Abigail had left. Other than that, Tess hadn't moved anything. Her old roommate might profess to be a rebel, but in practice, she didn't like change. "Della Tackwood has moved in. She's a singer at the Mermaid—she's gone to rehearsal and won't be back until late. You'd like her."

Tess continued to chatter as Abigail gingerly took a seat at the three-legged table and laced her fingers together in her lap. Apparently the loss of her baby hadn't affected Tess in the way Abigail had imagined it would. Abigail studied her friend as she poured tea into a couple of cracked mugs and stirred in a few grains of sugar. On second thought, maybe there was a brittle edge to her bright conversation.

When Tess set the mugs on the table and bounced into the other chair, Abigail laid her hand on Tess's wrist to still her frenetic motion. "Tess, this is me," she said quietly. "You don't have to pretend."

Tess's fingers tightened around the handle of her mug. Her eyes flashed to Abigail's face, stricken. "I don't know what you mean."

"It's been five weeks. Not a very long time for such a great loss."

"Oh. The baby, you mean." Tess sat back, looking away. "I didn't want a baby, remember? No husband. No way to feed an extra mouth. It's much better this way."

Abigail saw the start of tears. "I'm sorry, if you don't want to talk about it."

"No, I—it feels good to get it out." Tess pulled in a breath and held it a moment, clearly trying to gain control. "All right, I would've loved to have a baby, but I wasn't ready for the responsibility. And I learned my mother was right about men." She laughed. "You can't trust them to stick around, so it's best to avoid them."

Abigail thought of Dr. Laniere and John Braddock and other men she'd encountered in the last five weeks. Winona's father and brothers. There *were* good men, if one looked for them in the right place.

Then something in Tess's acerbic comment struck her. "Tess, where is your mother? Is she still alive?"

Tess's mouth tightened. "I don't know. I suspect she is. But she's got my sister and doesn't need me."

Abigail stared at her. "Why on earth would you say that?"

Tess shrugged. "I've been right here, half a day's train ride away and they've never come looking for me."

"Half a day in which direction? In Mobile?"

Tess's eyes widened—apparently Abigail's guess had been correct or close to the mark. "I'm not going back there.

They didn't want me. Let's talk about something else. Tell me what you've been doing. You look so beautiful…so healthy and well-fed." With patent envy she examined Abigail's plain but neat dress of navy blue worsted. "The rich doctor's family must be treating you well."

Abigail smiled. "Tess, you won't believe it, but they've let me stay, and—and there's a possibility I may be allowed to study medicine. Maybe even earn a license to practice." She paused, then blurted, "God has been truly good to me."

Tess looked skeptical. "I hope you're not banking on that overmuch. You're the one who always said people will take advantage of you if you let them. There's got to be some catch."

"No, I was wrong." Abigail leaned forward, intent on making Tess listen. She'd always been so bullheaded, it was miraculous the two of them had stayed friends. "I've seen people who live their faith in Jesus—not like my father and that awful man he wanted me to marry."

Tess's gaze sharpened. "So that's it! I always wondered what you were running away from. Was it some missionary?"

Abigail almost laughed the question away. Once she'd gotten out of China, she'd refused to speak of Stephen Lawton. But if she expected Tess to trust her, perhaps she should return the favor.

She nodded reluctantly. "Mr. Lawton was my father's friend, a younger missionary from England." She spoke slowly, awkwardly. How strange to tell the story aloud after carrying it inside her head for so long. Once begun, the words poured out quickly. "After his wife died on the field, he and my father decided it would be convenient for me to marry him. Papa was terrified I'd meet and fall in love with a Chinese national and there were no other single white men within hundreds of miles."

Tess stared at her, lips parted. "I have to confess, my life as a spoiled rich girl doesn't seem so bad. How did you get away?"

This was the part that was so difficult to tell. Abigail swallowed. "There was another man who—who traded with the Chinese. Not a good man. He bought silk and tea in the bigger cities like Shanghai, but the villages like the one my family lived in were encouraged to become opium farms. My parents didn't see the harm because it seemed like a way for them to keep from starvation. But then my—my mother tried it and she…"

"Oh, Abby."

Wretchedly, Abigail met Tess's eyes. "She became addicted. Eventually she just…drifted off one day and never woke up. After she died, my father pressured me harder—" Tears overtook her, flooding down her cheeks and dripping from her chin to her bodice. "Papa wanted to be able to go out farther into remote areas and didn't want me to come, so he—he insisted Mr. Lawton would take care of me."

Tess jumped to her feet and flung her arms around Abigail's shaking shoulders. "The miserable villain! I told you men are no good! Especially religious men."

Abigail pressed her wet face into Tess's shoulder. "Tess, that's not always true—"

"Well, I haven't seen one. Anyway, what happened next? Obviously you're here and not in China."

Drawing back, Abigail wiped her face on her sleeve. "The opium trader came to the compound one day when my father had gone into the village. I'd thought and thought about what to do. You have to understand that by that point my faith in God had almost died. I had certain morals ingrained in me—I was not going to sell my body, not to Stephen Lawton, not even to buy passage on a ship back to America—but I had no compunction about lying. I told the trader I was an heiress. That my grandfather—my mother's father—would welcome me back to the States, if I could only find a way to get there, and that he'd reward the man who brought me."

"Abigail!" Tess's mouth fell open as she sat down again abruptly. "That's ingenious. But how did you convince him to believe you?"

"I'm such a liar," Abigail said, inwardly writhing in shame. "I don't know how God will forgive me. But I showed him my mother's journal. I had copied her handwriting and added enough details to make it sound like she was indeed a runaway heiress. I can be…very convincing when I try."

Tess laughed. "I'm sure you can. You talked that stuck-up doctor into making a house call on a girl he thought of as a prostitute." She shook her head. "So you sneaked away from the missionary compound and then what happened?"

"My protector took me to Shanghai and left me in a bordello for nearly a week while he transacted business. He was an agent for the same New Orleans company that had been transporting opium from China to the United States. He threatened to kill anyone who touched me, but Tess, you cannot comprehend the evil of the men who run those places. Even the places here in the District aren't…" She shuddered, remembering the dead eyes of the women who lived in that house in Shanghai—drugged, abused, hopeless. "Some of the younger ones, as young as ten or eleven, were brought to the States with the opium on the ship. I don't know where they went once we got here—I was too intent on saving my own skin." She paused, twisting her fingers. "I can't let the Toad find me. He'll find out I lied to him about the inheritance…and he knows I saw all the terrible dealings the company was into—the drugs, the prostitute trafficking. He'll kill me."

Tess gasped. "How did you get away?"

"When the ship docked, one of the sailors, a Creole, felt sorry for me and promised to help me. He hid me in a tea chest and delivered it to an out-of-the-way warehouse, but he just…left. I suppose he was afraid of the Toad. I got away from the docks and—"

"—and met me in front of the sail loft," Tess finished. "You've had enough adventures to last a lifetime, my friend." She shook her head. "What are the chances of this toad-man looking for you in the hospital?"

Abigail wet her lips. "Slim, I would have thought. Except for one thing. I'm almost sure it's John Braddock's father who owns the shipping line that brought me from China. He's the one who makes the Toad jump."

"Abigail! You're sitting right in the adder's nest!"

"I know. But I have the chance to earn a medical license! I can learn to treat the diseases and handle the injuries that affect so many helpless women and children. I've even thought about going back to China one day—"

"Are you crazy? After what it took to get out of there?"

"I know it sounds insane. But my life is so different now. *I'm* different. I have a gift for healing. There are so many people without hope…" She and Tess stared at one another, at an impasse, for several moments. Finally she sighed, gripped Tess's hands. She felt almost lightheaded. "I've told you all my sordid stories. You'll have to tell me yours."

"My little story is a nursery rhyme compared to that," Tess said drily.

Abigail smiled. "Well, one reason I came back today was to retrieve my mother's journal. I left it in my hiding place in the bed."

Tess spread her hands. "Help yourself. I'm sure Della hasn't disturbed it."

While Tess cleared away the tea things, Abigail got up and knelt on the floor at the foot of her old pallet. From the beginning she and Tess had kept their meager store of valuables tucked away here. Her and Tess's ideas of what was valuable couldn't have been more different.

Reaching into the straw ticking, Abigail pushed aside Tess's little walnut box full of jewelry. Her fingers closed on the journal. Extracting it carefully, she sat back cross-legged and stroked the book's creased leather cover. Her thumb fanned the worn gilded edges, opening the book to a page near the front. She stared at her mother's lacy, feminine script.

It was Mama who had awakened Abigail's interest in Chinese herbs and acupuncture by recording what she learned from the village women early in their lonely isolation. Abigail had memorized the list long ago, the words as beautiful and strange as the plants they represented. Flipping another page, she studied the diagrams her mother had sketched, ink drawings of the supine human form, arrows and lines indicating acupuncture points. Tears blurred her eyes. Mama had willingly joined her husband in spreading the gospel. In the end her obsession with science had cost her her life and forced Abigail to run.

Now perhaps both those things—faith and medicine— would save Abigail's life.

Chapter Seventeen

Two major topics dominated conversation among faculty and students during Monday morning rounds. The medical professors were all in a tizzy over the proposed takeover of several classrooms in the east wing by the newly reestablished academic department of the University of Louisiana. The medical department claimed that, as they had invested significant personal funds in the medical school, they had a right to exclusive use of the buildings. There was to be a faculty meeting that afternoon to decide what course of action would best protect the interests of the medical school.

Normally such administrative controversies would not have been bandied about in front of the students. But the professors were distracted into indiscretion by a second issue of major debate, namely the admission of Miss Abigail Neal as a candidate for the MD degree.

After afternoon lectures, John sat in the back of the west wing auditorium, with Weichmann on one side and Girard on the other, occupying himself with his notes from Dr. Harrison's morning lecture and demonstration on ophthalmic diseases. Admittedly, however, his concentration was broken by the general buzz of humorous conversation which blanketed the room. The students had been summoned for a special convocation regarding Miss Neal's application. They were, in short, to vote yea or nay.

By the time Professor Pitcock, dean of the school, banged his gavel on the lectern at the front of the room to call the meeting to order, John's conscience was letting out a full-blown wolf howl. His fellow students were never going to vote for Abigail's admission. A similar situation had faced Dr. Elizabeth Blackwell, the first woman to be admitted to Geneva Medical College in New York, but she had only prevailed because someone had convinced the students Mrs. Blackwell's application was a joke and they all voted yea. No such prank would intervene here. John's classmates were, to a man, adamantly opposed to a woman in their midst.

For most of his life John had been encouraged to take the morally easy way out. If you wanted something, you either turned on your charm or used whatever stratagems or influence was at your disposal. Competition, however, was something else. In John's personal code of behavior, whatever was most difficult to obtain was the very thing he was determined to win. And the stronger his opponent, the sweeter the victory.

Therefore when Abigail Neal entered his life, with her rigid sense of justice and lockjaw determination to learn, he instantly recognized in her exactly what he needed to make him the man he ought to be. The only problem: her sex. On so many levels. She was his intellectual equal, but she was unqualified to compete as a student. She was beautiful and unbendably upright, and he wanted her as more than a classmate: he wanted her for his wife. But she was off-limits not only because of her class—his parents would never accept a bluestocking from the District as a suitable bride for the Braddock heir—but also because she would never give up her education to become a society matron. And beyond that, she deserved a man who would stand up to his friends on her behalf.

He wanted Abigail to have the chance to study and earn a license to practice medicine. But he was not at all sure he was capable of setting sail in a one-man boat bound to crash on the rocks of humiliation.

So while Dr. Pitcock opened the meeting with prayer and presented the agenda, John found himself literally sweating with conflicting desires. Thank goodness Abigail herself was not in attendance. He wouldn't be forced to watch her face as the male students ripped her character to shreds, laughing at her as a roaring good joke.

Weichmann nudged him. "Braddock, you all right?"

John opened his eyes, realizing he'd had them squeezed shut in prayer. "Yes, I'm—good night, it's hot in here." He yanked out his handkerchief and wiped his face.

"You look awful. Clem have one of her dinner parties yesterday?"

John seized the excuse. "You should have seen the gravy." He shuddered. "You think this vote on Miss Neal's application is on the up-and-up?"

Weichmann shook his curly head. "Dunno. Pitcock's not much for practical jokes, though Dr. Laniere might—" He straightened, elbowing John again. "Heads up. Prof's up to speak."

John realized Pitcock had taken a seat in the row of professors behind the lectern, clearing the way for Professor Laniere to step forward.

With his calm smile Prof surveyed the student body scattered around the amphitheater like ants on a hill. "Gentlemen," he began, "I trust you've all had a successful day in rounds and lectures. As Dr. Pitcock mentioned, the faculty has decided to broach the groundbreaking issue of allowing a female to enter the hallowed halls of medical education by bringing it to you, the student body, for a vote. We all recognize that the value of your own diplomas hinges directly and indirectly upon the standards to which the entire college is held. In previous years it has been deemed wise to restrict medical licenses in the State of Louisiana to those who are able to meet a rigid course of scientific requirements. Because those requirements are of a necessarily graphic and sometimes violent nature, the courses and practice of medicine have been assumed to be inappropriate for the gentle female constitution."

The rattling and whispering of the students had ceased the moment Prof took the dais. When he paused to scan the first two rows of students, face by face, John could have heard a pin drop in the silence. Someone coughed and received a scalding look from every pair of eyes in the room.

"But having lived with a particularly strong-minded woman myself for some fifteen years—" Prof smiled faintly when several people snickered— "I find myself perhaps more open to the idea of women in medical practice than others. Then, when I met Miss Neal and witnessed her intellectual capabilities, coupled with a gift for mercy and an unusually strong stomach for the harsher realities of the healing arts, I began to suspect we have found the first appropriate test case for admitting a woman to our college."

John's stomach had been sinking as the professor talked. He looked around at his fellow students and found on their faces a variety of expressions from outright contempt to amusement to rage. These young men might respect their favorite professor, but they were not going to allow a woman into their medical school.

He stood up. "Professor, I'd like to speak to the subject before we vote."

Prof stared at him, eyebrows aloft. "Braddock, I don't remember asking for comments. This is a very straightforward yes or no."

"I know, sir." John could feel a hundred twenty or so pairs of eyes scorching his face, but he kept his own gaze on the professor. *Dear Lord, help me, please.* "But there are some things my classmates don't know about Miss Neal—things *you* might not have thought of, in defense of her application." He took a deep breath. "I'll admit that at first I was resentful that you'd invited her to attend rounds with us who'd properly undergone the application process, paid tuition, met the qualifications. Maybe this was because, as you said, I'd yet to meet a female with the analytical turn of mind necessary for absorbing and processing scientific information."

An audible rustle of tension passed through the student body, all of whom were craning their necks to see the fool willing to admit the possibility of equality of intellect between the sexes. Several started to mumble to one another, an undertone that gradually became a muted roar.

Professor Laniere lifted his hand to call the meeting back to order, but John wasn't about to lose this chance to finish what he'd started.

"Gentlemen!" he shouted, and the roar reluctantly faded. "I beg your indulgence for just a few more moments. This may be the most significant decision you will be privileged to make in your lifetime. Because I fear that if we make the wrong choice now, we may not only forfeit our right to make medical history—we may become as a body the laughingstock of future generations."

A startled silence fell as he paused. Prof gave him a faint smile. "Go ahead, Braddock. But keep it short."

"Yes, sir. I only want to say that if we fail to give Abigail Neal the chance she deserves—indeed that she has earned—we'll be missing out on association with one of the finest medical talents to come along in our lifetime. Most of you have not known her as I have—" He endured a general snicker in icy silence, then continued with all the dignity he could muster. "I have watched her teach principles of good health to the underprivileged, with a clarity and simplicity only available to the truly learned. She routinely displays creative insight as to cause and effect and the ability to apply what she knows in diagnosis and treatment. Assuredly she has much to learn about the makeup and function of the human body, but I have observed an almost palpable craving to replace ignorance with wisdom. Such a tenacious and truly teachable nature, whether it be male or female, can only be an example and inspiration to the rest of us."

He looked down at Girard, whose embarrassed posture had begun to straighten as John barreled on. Weichmann gave him a soft "Hear, hear, old man."

Encouraged, he boldly looked around at the rest of his visibly confused and intrigued fellow students. "So I, for one, will be voting to allow—no, to *invite*—Miss Neal to become one of us. And I encourage you all to consider the fact that, because women will inevitably make their way into professional realms, we would be well-advised to choose to make the transition as smooth and painless as possible for all. Thank you, Professor. I return the floor to you."

John sat down amidst crashing silence, withdrew his handkerchief and mopped his face. In obedience he'd done all he could do. The results were up to God Almighty.

Abigail had stayed away from the medical college grounds all day, knowing that her fate would be decided late that afternoon. She had arrived at the fork in the road: Either she would be permitted to stay as a full-time student, officially allowed to matriculate with the men, or she would never go back.

It was an odd feeling, this abandonment to whatever might happen. For most of her life she had either run from threats or scrapped for what she felt she deserved. Not by chance, she knew, had her morning devotions included the beautiful reminder from Isaiah: "They that wait upon the Lord shall renew their strength; they shall mount up with wings as eagles. They shall run and not be weary, they shall walk and not faint."

Wait, wait, she reminded herself again as she helped change bed linens in the "unrespectable" women's ward. "The least of these" was what these women were, at least according to the people who funded the hospital. Not the nurses. They served each one, providing food and bandages and a listening ear to prostitutes and bar maids, exactly as they did in the other women's ward.

Abigail tried to follow their example, patiently ministering when she was so tired she could have fallen asleep on her feet. She had stayed awake until the wee hours, rereading her mother's journal. Parts of it made more sense now that she had a rudimentary knowledge of chemistry and bodily makeup. Mama had possessed an amazing knack for absorbing and analyzing the properties of plants and herbs. Abigail was longing to ask questions of short-tempered Dr. Girard to confirm or refute some of her guesswork.

But she knew she'd never be allowed to do so, should the students in that amphitheater vote to exclude her.

"Please, Father," she whispered as she struggled to change the sheets of a heavily pregnant woman with a gash on her forehead from falling down a set of stairs. The woman was not cooperating. "Please let them say yes."

"What's that, dearie?" asked Nurse Wilhelmina, who was expertly slipping a bedpan beneath a woman ill with syphilis.

Abigail dodged her patient's attempts to whack her on the arm. "Nothing, ma'am. I'm just praying as I go."

"A lovely habit to practice." She placidly went on with her task. But at a commotion in the hallway she looked up frowning. "Those boys don't know how to approach a ward quietly."

"Abigail!" John Braddock skidded into view, panting, cheeks ruddy from the cold. His overcoat hung open, his stock was askew and his hat had apparently fallen off somewhere along the way. The longish wavy hair fell into his wide, sparkling eyes. "Drop that right now and come with me!"

"For goodness sake." She stood between the huge exposed belly of her patient and the door. "Can't you wait just a minute or two?"

"Abigail, this is important."

Abigail shook her head. "Wait for me in the hallway. I'll be with you in a moment." She turned to finish her task— and the woman's fist hit her in the side of the head.

Sighing, John hurried over to help her. "Here now, settle down." On the opposite side of the bed from Abigail, he reached over the patient and grabbed the loosened sheet, neatly lifting her toward him. Trussed in the sheet, she couldn't wave her arms. "Abigail, spread the clean sheet on that side. Then we'll swap sides."

To Abigail's astonishment, the woman relaxed at the sound of John's deep, calm voice. Perhaps having a doctor perform such a menial task had stunned her into submission. Whatever the case, the bed was clean, fresh and unwrinkled, the patient tucked in asleep, in half the time it would have take Abigail to do it alone.

She looked up at John as he whisked her out to the hallway. "Thank you—"

"You're welcome." He snatched her up in a hug and whirled her around and around. "You're in! It was close, but they voted yes!"

Laughing, Abigail caught his shoulders for balance. "Are you sure? Put me down!"

"No. I mean—yes, I'm sure, but I'm not putting you down until you kiss me." He whirled her around again until she was dizzy, dancing her down the hall.

Her heart was pumping like a locomotive engine and she felt a ridiculous smile taking over her face. "When did it happen? How?" Her arms involuntarily slid behind his neck to keep from being slung into the wall with his wild waltz. "I don't think I believe you."

"I'm to bring you back to meet with the faculty. They'll tell you." He finally stopped spinning, staggering to a halt at the end of the hall. He dipped his knees to reach the doorknob without letting go of her and opened the door. Ducking inside, he backed against the door and shut it. "Here we go."

Abigail found herself locked in a most improper

embrace in an empty room with a tall, strong, overexcited young man. A small frisson of…something shook her. Anxiety? Excitement? She looked him in the eyes and halfheartedly pushed at his chest. "John, we shouldn't be here like this. People will think—"

"They'll think I'm going to kiss you. Which I am." He grinned at her.

Her fear dissipated. "You're incorrigible," she said, squelching laughter. "I suppose you think you had something to do with my happy news."

"Of course I did," he boasted. "Prof was about to ruin the whole thing, being all truth, justice and the American way in his presentation of your case. Those boys weren't going to fall for that—they're entirely too selfish." He laughed and shoved a stack of papers out of the way, then set Abigail on the desk. He planted his hands on either side of her hips and leaned in close to her ear. "But I," he whispered, "convinced them of the *benefits* of having a woman in our class."

"Oh, really?" She turned her head and found his mouth half an inch from hers. "And what would those benefits be?"

"I'll tell you…" He kissed her cheek. "After…" He kissed her nose. "You kiss me." He kissed her chin.

Abigail felt like a puddle of warm butter. She had never been this close to a man who was not her father, particularly one with gold-flecked hazel eyes and golden skin and a gravelly whispered voice. She knew she was in deep trouble because her reputation was paper thin as it was. He could walk out of here and tell everyone that the stories about women brazen enough to apply for medical college were absolutely true. They were women who could be coaxed into kissing men they weren't married to, in closets.

"John." She swallowed, looking at his chin instead of his warm, inviting mouth. There was a small shaving cut in its shallow cleft. "Please think of my reputation."

Slowly he straightened. He sighed as he put his hands in his pockets. "Double drat. I keep forgetting."

Ashamed that she was sorry he'd backed off, Abigail twisted her hands together in her lap. "Thank you. What do you keep forgetting?"

"That it's no longer I who live but Christ who lives in me, and the life I now live, I live by faith in the son of God who loved me and gave Himself for me." He sounded so glum that Abigail laughed. "It's not funny." He wheeled to look at the door. "It's going to be dashed hard to keep my hands to myself when you're at school and the hospital every day."

"John, are you telling me you've given your heart to the Lord?"

Joy soared inside her breast again when he nodded and looked over his shoulder. "I suppose it was inevitable, with Prof preaching at me all the time and you looking so beautiful and passionate and prim." He turned toward her again, his gaze fixed on her face. "Just look at you! Who could see that and not believe in God?"

Tears suddenly blinded Abigail. No one had ever, in her entire life, called her beautiful. "Come here," she said huskily, holding out her hands.

He stared at her for a moment. "What about your reputation?"

"I won't tell if you won't." She tipped her head. "Will you kiss me, John?"

A slow grin took over his face. He bent his head, smiling lips capturing hers softly. A moment later he jerked away and backed against the door. "That's enough," he said hurriedly. "I have to take you back to the college and I don't want there to be any question—" He picked her up by the waist and lifted her to her feet. "You're right. No more sliding into offices until—Never mind." He yanked open the door. "I have to take you back."

Abigail suffered herself to be hustled down the hallway toward the stairs and then unceremoniously bundled into the carriage he'd left waiting on the street. She kept staring at John as he drove them the two blocks over to the college. He seemed preoccupied and a little embarrassed and wholly unlike himself. Changes in him—changes in her. She could hardly comprehend the magnitude.

She'd made it into medical school, an amazing feat by any standards. An answer from God bigger than she'd dared to dream. But…she had to keep reminding herself that the last hurdle had not been passed.

She still had to deal with the consequences of her flight from China.

Chapter Eighteen

Freedom. John was as happy as he'd been in his life. But he still had to deal with his father. He'd considered asking Abigail to come with him or Professor Laniere. A bit of moral support would have made the coming confrontation easier to contemplate.

But something about hiding behind a woman's skirts, or even asking his mentor to step in to speak for him, seemed cowardly. So he'd dropped Abigail off at the college, leaving the carriage he'd borrowed from one of the professors, and walked the three blocks to his father's office. Alone.

But not alone, he remembered as he waited for the street car to rattle pass, then crossed Common. The Lord had promised to be with him. He smiled to himself, turning north toward Rampart Street.

He said the word to himself again, relishing its new meaning. *Freedom.* Freedom from that restless feeling of always reaching for something beyond his grasp. Freedom from the pressure to perform. Freedom from looking over his shoulder to see who was catching up.

He slowed as the row of offices where his father leased space came into view, well-kept brick buildings with the trademark French wrought iron gracing their balconies.

John had heard the story a thousand times, how the old man built Crescent City Shipping from the ground up, starting as barely more than a teenager with a couple of dray carts and three mules. He'd delivered supplies for storekeepers and bricklayers, iron foundries and printing companies, running back and forth between the docks and the business district until he'd earned enough to invest in a couple of small boats which could make the run out to ships at the mouth of the Gulf of Mexico. Eventually the boats had turned into ships of his own and Phillip Braddock opened the office on Common near Basin.

John had spent hours here as a child, climbing under and around the big mahogany sea chest that served as his father's desk; picking up the spyglass on the table under the window to look out over the city; begging exotic treats from the businessmen who came to visit. As a teenager he'd lost interest in the shipping side of the family income, preferring to experiment with his chemistry set. Unaware of the obsession he was about to release, his father had given the apparatus to John for his fourteenth birthday and had a workshop built for him off the kitchen.

He opened the front door, setting its bell jingling. Nowadays he and the old man were as different as night and day—except, perhaps, for that characteristic streak of obstinacy. He smiled at old Mr. Starkey, who sat on his stool with a ledger open on the counter in front of him, his spectacles propped on top of his shiny head. The lack of hair on top was more than made up for by the luxuriant gray side whiskers framing his full face.

"Johnny-boy!" The Scotsman slammed the ledger shut and came from around the counter to shake John's hand. "Hain't seen ye in a coon's age. How goes yer experimenting these days? Blown up yer ma's kitchen lately?"

John shook his head. "The last time I did that, she told me she'd put me out to sleep in the stable if I ever brought chemicals into the house again."

The old man cackled. "You was always an enterprising young pup. Hear yer growing up to be a fine medical man, top of yer class, right? Yer da talks about you all the time."

It was the first John had heard of any interest of his father in his studies. "Well, I'm working hard. I like what I'm doing." He looked around the otherwise empty office. "Is my father here? I wanted to speak to him."

Starkey's smile faded as he glanced at the stairs leading to the upper floor—his father's lair. "Crapaud's in with him. I was just about to leave for the day, but you can wait if you want, they should be done soon. They been locked in there for nearly two hours."

John frowned. He'd met his father's new agent, a non-descript roustabout with an ugly, smashed-in face, once or twice over the last couple of years and was not impressed. A man of little education and no refinement, he was not a man one wanted to engage in conversation. John supposed Crapaud must serve some redeeming purpose in his father's business.

"I'll wait." No sense putting off a bad job.

Fifteen minutes later he was still cooling his heels staring out the window at foot traffic, battling rising impatience. A clatter of boots on the stairs brought his head around. It was the agent, followed closely by John's father.

"Follow up on the problem," Father was saying. He

stopped two steps from the bottom when he saw John. "Johnny! Why didn't you let me know you were here?"

Distracted by Crapaud's quickly masked expression of contempt, John yanked his thoughts back to the subject at hand. "I needed to speak to you about something that has just come up." He wiped a sweaty hand down the side of his trousers. "Something important."

A frown darkened his father's heavy brow. "It must be important to interrupt your studies on a Monday afternoon." He reached the foot of the stairs and turned to Crapaud, who hovered, clearly interested in the exchange. "Crapaud, I'll release you to take care of your errand." He paused, a peculiar weight lending force to his words. "To this point you've not failed me. I rely on your discretion—understand?"

Crapaud dipped his squashed chin, a sardonic acknowledgment of authority. "I understand more than you think."

Dismissing his underling with a curt nod, John's father beckoned him toward the stairs. "Let's have this burning conversation, then."

John followed his father to the upstairs office, noting the fine wainscoting of the walls, the new carpet on the stairs. How could Father afford upgrades to the office and a seven million-dollar donation to the medical college as well? The business must be going very well. He trailed his hand along a fine ebony side table in the upstairs landing, new since he'd last been here nearly three months ago.

Their last conversation had been that head-on confrontation over Abigail's admission into medical school.

Breaking free wasn't going to be easy. He might resent his old man, but there was a deeply seated respect that had always kept him from permanently severing their relationship. And then, there was the need for his money, even though he'd insisted he wanted to make his own way. Praying for wisdom, John firmed his backbone. With God's help he'd stood up to his fellow students on Abigail's behalf. He could buck his father as well.

Freedom.

Leaving the door open behind him, symbolic of his intentions, he ignored the chair in front of his father's desk. Looking down at him might give him an advantage.

Father sat down heavily behind the desk. "Where are your manners, boy?"

"I'm not going to be here long." John tapped his hat against his leg. "Considering your unusual interest in the results of the vote regarding Miss Neal's application to the medical college, I thought I should be the first to inform you of its outcome. The students voted to endorse her application."

There was a frozen pause as his father stared at him. "And how did *you* vote, may I ask?"

John shrugged. "I may as well tell you—you'll hear it eventually—that I felt compelled to come to Miss Neal's public defense. I'm proud to say—I hope, I mean, that the results of the vote can be directly attributed to my remarks to the student body."

"Are you telling me," John's father's voice was ominously quiet, "that you publicly flouted my wishes?"

"Father, your interference has gone too far. Abigail Neal is more than qualified to pursue a medical degree, whatever the inconvenience to myself and my fellow students. And what is more, it's because of her influence that I've come to my senses and realized my need to surrender my life to Christ. I probably don't deserve her—and I have no idea how this is going to work out in practicality—but I plan to ask her to be my wife."

He'd almost said that out loud to Abigail, barely restraining himself with the realization that his proposal would be better offered somewhere besides an empty office. But articulating his desires to his father seemed necessary. His personal declaration of independence.

He had no idea how he was going to fund the remainder of his education. But if he had to give up his room at Clem's, move into the hospital and eat off the dole from the Church so be it. He braced himself for the explosion.

He should have known his father would never play by the rules of normal human discourse. His father began to chuckle. "Well, well, well. My own fire-breathing preacher, taking the pulpit under my very nose. I suppose I have Gabriel Laniere to thank for this. He's been trying to convert me for years. Now he's got hold of my boy."

"I made my own decision," John said with dignity. "But I wish you'd helped steer me toward God a little sooner."

The laughter on his father's face disappeared. He had that *look* in his eyes. The one that had taken him from a straw-tick bed in a boilermaker's shed to a desk at the helm of the wealthiest shipping empire on the Gulf Coast. "All right, you hardheaded young whelp. Propose to her if you insist. But you'll end by thanking me for my *interference*." He stood, leaning over the desk, knuckles planted. "Now get out. I'm busy."

John opened his mouth to argue, but his gaze fell on the shipping manifest beneath his father's hand. It contained some odd items, which he promptly memorized. Abigail was right, but the answers had been here, rather than in the office at home.

Cold apprehension settled in his gut. Clearly his father was in no mood to listen to reason and threats would do no good. He'd said what he came to say and broken with his father. There was nothing else to be gained by staying. He clapped his hat on his head and wheeled for the door.

Abigail's skirts blew around her legs as she walked along the darkening levee toward Tess's room. The street was deserted, as businesses had closed for the day and most folk were inside preparing for supper. They were smart enough to get out of the cold.

She pulled the shawl Camilla had loaned her tighter around her shoulders. The erratic December climate had finally tilted toward winter, replacing the damp chill of November with a bone-deep icy wind that blew off the river and shoved its way into every pore of a person's skin. Abigail was remembering with something akin to fondness the suffocating heat of summer. When she got to Tess's, they'd pull close to the little cookstove for a bit of warmth. She couldn't wait to tell Tess what had happened. Maybe this enormous miracle would be the tipping point to convince Tess that God did indeed have good plans for His daughters.

The meeting with the medical college faculty had been awkward in the extreme. By the time she'd arrived, the eight professors had been apprised of the outcome of the vote. Judging by the generally acidic expressions, there had ensued some kind of battle over their promise to honor the students' wishes. When she'd taken her seat at the table in the first-floor conference room, only Professor Laniere had greeted her with his usual smile. Girard, Pitcock and Cannon clearly wished her at the devil.

"What's she doing here?" Dr. Lewis had demanded in his trumpeting voice.

"The students voted her in," explained Dr. Harrison, looking as if he'd swallowed embalming fluid.

"Nonsense." Dr. Lewis looked confused. "We don't have girls in medical school."

"We do now," said Dr. Harrison glumly.

In the end, they'd made her acceptance official— perhaps only because Dr. Laniere reminded them all of their word as gentlemen. In any case, Abigail was presented with a stack of matriculation tickets permitting her to finish out the remainder of the term with six courses of lectures, and including the right to accompany any of the eight attending physicians on their daily rounds at the hospital. She was to have full privileges in the chemistry and dissection laboratories. All eight professors agreed that if she refused to fully participate in what was expected of any student, she would be expelled.

Dr. Laniere had looked at her apologetically when that pronouncement was made by Dr. Girard. "I'm afraid that's a nonnegotiable, my dear."

Putting up her chin, she'd stared them down. "And it's a reasonable rule. I see no reason I cannot comply with all requirements of the degree."

Afterward, when they'd dismissed her, so they might continue arguing over the particulars of the practical dilemmas created by their new student, she'd rushed outside and cast up her lunch in the bushes.

Now, attacked by doubts, she wondered if she hadn't been overly ambitious. How on earth was she going to anticipate every stumbling block put in her way by a hundred fifty resentful male students? And though Dr. Laniere had assured her that fellowships for worthy students were already in place, the financial aspect of the venture was frightening.

Lost in her tumbling thoughts, she barely had time to register the scuffling step behind her before a hand was clapped over her mouth, jerking her against a rough woolen coat and scarf. The impulse to scream burst against her throat, but the callused hand tightened, forcing her to gag instead. Before she could do more than awkwardly jerk her heel backward into her attacker's shin, she was hauled into a waiting closed carriage and thrown onto the seat.

"If you say a word I will kill you," growled her attacker and slammed the door.

Immediately she lunged for the door. It was locked from the outside, a cloth covering the window. The carriage lurched into motion, throwing her to the floor.

Her throat was so constricted with fear she couldn't have screamed if she'd wanted to. Shuddering like a boat in a hurricane, she hugged herself. Her worst nightmare had just caught up with her.

Chapter Nineteen

John ran all the way from his father's office and found the Lanieres' house lit from top to bottom. He pelted up the front steps and pounded on the door.

Winona yanked it open. "John! What you doing at the front door?"

"I'm in a hurry. Where's Abigail?" He peered over Winona's shoulder. He could hear the sounds of the children playing somewhere upstairs. It was nearly nine o'clock. He'd have thought they would already be abed.

Winona stepped back, eyes wide. "You haven't see her? Doc Laniere hoped—"

"No—she said she was coming here after her interview with the faculty. I wanted to know what happened."

Winona bit her lip, then pulled him into the foyer. "Come in. Miss Camilla will want to talk to you."

"Why?" He didn't want to talk to Camilla Laniere. He wanted to talk to Abigail. He wanted to tell her she was right about his father. That shipping manifest on his father's desk had contained more than cotton and tea and silk.

Winona just shook her head. "I've got to help with the

children. They're wild and it's time to get 'em in bed." She gestured down the central breezeway toward the back of the house. "Wait here. I'll go get her." She turned and darted upstairs.

John shifted from one foot to the other, turning his hat in his hands, wondering what was going on. He could hear Camilla's low, husky voice underneath a child crying and Winona shushing somebody. He wondered what had happened to Prof.

And where was Abigail?

It seemed like an eternity, although it was probably only two or three minutes, before Camilla hurried down the stairs. "John!" She grabbed his hand. "Are you sure you haven't seen Abigail?"

"No. Where do you suppose she is? When's the last time you saw her?" His stomach started to knot.

"I haven't seen her since she left the house this morning." Camilla went to the window beside the front door and twitched aside the curtain. "It's been dark for an hour. I don't like her walking by herself this late, I told her—" She wheeled to face John, her gentle face tight with worry. "Gabriel went back to the hospital to see if someone there knows where she went."

"But—wasn't he with her? There was a faculty meeting. They were to sanction the student vote, provide her tickets—"

Camilla was shaking her head. "Gabriel was going to bring her back home, but she wanted to talk to someone first, said she'd walk to the hospital, then take the street car home. John, when did you see her last?"

"Just before the faculty meeting. I picked her up from the hospital and…and…" He swallowed, thinking about their delirious dance down the hall to the supply closet, where he'd kissed her. "And then took her to the college. I've been at my father's shipping office." He and Camilla stared at one another in mutual dismay. "I'm going to the hospital. Prof may not know where to look."

"If she's there, he'll find her, John. Be patient and let's see if—"

The door opened. Professor Laniere came in, sweeping off his hat. He stopped abruptly when his startled gaze met John's. He looked at his wife. "Has she returned?"

Camilla's face crumpled. "No. Oh, Gabriel, John hasn't seen her either!"

John crushed his hat between his hands. "Prof, we've got to find her. Do you suppose she went back to the District? She's awfully fond of those orphans."

Dr. Laniere frowned. "I suppose we could look there. What about her friend Tess? Would she have gone there?"

"That's possible." Relief lifted the weight off John's chest. "I've been there—when I delivered the baby. It's beside the saloon on—Look, Prof, let's split up to make this faster. You go to the orphanage and I'll try Tess. We'll meet back here when one of us finds her."

The professor nodded. "That's a logical plan." He addressed his wife. "Camilla, I'm afraid I'll have to leave you here with Winona and the children. But Willie's here if you need anything. I'll be back as soon as I can." He leaned down to kiss her briefly, then gripped John's shoulder. "Be careful, son."

John nodded. A toxic combination of fear and anger fought for control of his gut. Abigail Neal had no business endangering herself and worrying all the people who cared about her. When he found her he was going to shake her—right after he kissed her senseless.

Sitting on a straw pallet in a warehouse storeroom, tied hand and foot with her back against a wall, Abigail stared at the Toad. He sat in a stout wooden chair cocked back against the wall, picking his teeth with his knife.

She hadn't seen many physically uglier men, but it was not his squashed-in face or the thin scar that ran from his right eyebrow across his cheek to his jaw that repelled her. It was the knowledge that he had contributed to her mother's death and her father's abandonment.

Then she reminded herself that Phillip Braddock was behind this despicable man. John's father. Impossible to reconcile. If his behavior earlier that day was any indicator, John loved her. How could he not know what his father had done? Dealing in thousands of dollars worth of illegal narcotics was one thing, but trading little innocent girls into prostitution.... Her mind recoiled.

And why had it taken her eight months to take action? Perhaps, at first she had been too numbed, too traumatized, to do more than change her name and bury herself in the District—until Tess's crisis jolted her to life again.

Now it appeared her fears had been justified. Phillip Braddock had finally connected her to Abigail Nieland. She'd waited too long to take the notes in her mother's journal about Crescent City Enterprises, not to mention her own experiences, to Dr. Lanière. She couldn't imagine why the Toad hadn't already killed her. Perhaps he thought she'd already talked. Perhaps they wanted to know what she'd told the authorities before they got rid of her.

She swallowed the nasty taste of fear that coated her

tongue and froze her throat. She'd cut open a dead body and examined its inward parts. *Through Christ who strengthens you, you can do all things.*

The fear did not instantly go away, but remembering what God had already brought her through and remembering the lives she had touched, whose lives had touched hers, gave her courage. She forced herself to look at her captor, who sat flipping and playing with the knife. What had caused that awful scar? The eye that it crossed was white and dead.

Perhaps sensing her regard, the Toad grunted. "He'll be here soon." His accent was Cajun, the timbre deep and thick.

"Who?"

He didn't bother to answer the question, just flipped the knife again, a thick, brutal blade without shine. The steel haft came down in his palm. "You been here before."

"No, I—"

"Yes. Courregé say so." The Toad suddenly smiled. "He be very dead now."

Abigail had no idea who Courregé was, but the name made her think of courage. She looked away from the Toad's dark, smiling face. *He* was coming. Did that mean John's father? What would he do to her? Involuntarily her eyes closed. Her imagination, fueled by a week in a Shanghai brothel and eight months in the District, took her places she didn't want to revisit. *Oh, God. Are You with me now? You must be.*

At the sharp creak of hinges Abigail opened her eyes. The door slid open to reveal a well-dressed gentleman in a dark green overcoat and elegant hat which made him seem taller. John had towered over his father at Lisette's party. Now she could hardly believe she'd stood in the same room with Phillip Braddock, knowing the evil dormant under that polished exterior. She'd been completely brazen to breach the wall around John's privileged world.

Having never seen her himself, Braddock hadn't known who she was then. He'd stared right at her, contemptuous of her poverty and the lack of gentility that led her to seek an equal place in a man's world.

She should have screamed his corruption to the rooftops, but fear had strangled her. As it did now.

He spoke first to the Toad. "Well done, Crapaud. You've taken care of the sailor's body?"

"Aye." The front legs of the chair crashed to the floor and the Toad bent to slide the knife into a scabbard on his boot.

"Then you may go. But hold," Braddock added as Crapaud lurched to his feet. "What about the woman from the sail loft? Does she know what her friend knows?"

Crapaud shrugged his massive shoulders as he glanced at Abigail. "Mebbe. Don't know what our girl told her."

Braddock turned to Abigail, walked toward her with his hands behind his back. "So, Miss Nieland. What exactly *have* you said to your former roommate?"

All the blood seemed to leech from Abigail's head, and a strange buzzing infected her ears. Tess was in danger because she'd told her too much. She shook her head, unable to speak past the sudden thickness of her tongue.

"Now why do I not believe you?" Braddock sighed. "Women. Always lying to manipulate us poor fellows. Fabricating that story about your mother. Did you spin the same web for my son?"

"Of c-course not," Abigail managed to stammer. "I would never—it was the only way I could think of to set out of China."

Braddock sat down, crossing his legs as if he were in someone's parlor, rather than a warehouse stuffed with bales of cotton. He addressed Crapaud over his shoulder. "Perhaps you should take care of the Montgomery woman, just to be safe. Miss Nieland seems to have trouble remembering what she said to whom."

The four-block square area just north of the hospital and medical college, generally referred to as the District, had been one of John's favored haunts since he was old enough to slip out of the house without getting caught. But with his stomach in a knot over Abigail's disappearance, carousing was the last thing on his mind.

It took him fifteen minutes to run the short distance to Tess's apartment. He arrived out of breath, his heart hammering in his chest. He banged on the rickety door, hardly aware of the blazing lights and jangling music emanating from the saloon next door. *Dear God, please let her be here. Please let her be safe.* A desperate, perhaps childish prayer. But he meant it with all his heart.

He'd set his shoulder against the door to force it, when it opened suddenly, revealing Tess's irritated face. Staggering, John righted himself. "Is Abigail here?"

Her expression shifted to surprise. "Dr. Braddock? What are you doing here?"

"Didn't you hear me? I'm looking for Abigail."

"She isn't—" His dismay must have registered. She looked around, then yanked him inside the tiny entryway. "What's the matter?"

He just stared at her. He'd been so sure he would find Abigail here. "We can't find her. I was with her around six, left her at the college. She never went home. Dr. Laniere's gone to look there and the orphanage. I thought she might have come here to tell you—"

"It's that man! He's found her."

John took Tess by the shoulders. "What man? If you know where she is—"

She jerked away from him. "*You* should know. He works for your father."

"*Who?* I don't know what you're talking about."

"Some man she called 'the Toad.'" Tess wrung her hands. "I should have convinced her to go to Dr. Laniere immediately." Tears began to pour down her cheeks.

John was even more bewildered than ever. "I don't know of anyone my father employs called 'the Toad.' And why would he be looking for her? Is she in danger?"

Tess backed away from him. "I don't trust you. I shouldn't have said anything. Get out of here."

John wanted to shake her, but instead plowed his hands into his hair. He forced his voice to remain steady. "Listen to me. I *love* Abigail. I'm going to ask her to marry me. But I've known all along there was something about her past she wasn't telling me. If you know something about it, perhaps between the two of us we can find her."

"You're not listening to *me!* Your father has something to do with her disappearance, I know it. She was afraid of him. Even if I knew anything, I wouldn't tell you—"

"Tess!" he roared, frustrated beyond control. "I saved your life! I broke with my father this very day. I've known for some time his business transactions aren't always aboveboard, but as of today I'm willing to do something about it. And if he's behind Abigail's troubles, I swear to you I'll make him pay." He lowered his voice, aware that he sounded like a madman. "Please, Tess." He reached for her hands, gripped them. "Please, if you know where she is…."

She stared up at him, clearly torn between belief and fear. "All right," she said at last, returning the pressure of his hands. "All right, I've got to trust somebody. But I think we're going to need more than just me and you. Take me to Dr. Laniere and I'll tell you Abigail's story on the way. Maybe you'll pick up on something that will shed some light on what happened to her."

Relief weakened John's knees. "Good. Get your cloak, it's cold outside."

She shook her head. "I don't have one."

John shrugged out of his overcoat and dropped it around Tess's slender shoulders. "Come on, then. It's a long walk."

All Abigail could do was pray that Tess would be able to get away. *Father, it's not her fault she befriended such a dangerous woman as me.*

"So you used my agent for your own purposes," Braddock continued silkily as Crapaud slipped through the door into the night without a sound, "then disappeared the moment you landed in New Orleans. Crapaud investigated and found that there was no such family as Neiland in New Orleans. When he informed me of how he'd been duped—and exposed our company's unsanctioned enterprises in the process—my first impulse was to do away with him." Braddock sighed. "But my anger cooled as I realized he'd been acting in my best interests. Besides, why should I cheat myself out of a valuable employee?"

Abigail just stared at him.

Braddock uncrossed his legs and leaned forward, elbows on his knees. He steepled his fingers under his chin. "We have been looking for you for six months, Miss Nieland," he said softly. "And here you have been all along, right under my nose, seducing my hardheaded son. I wonder that he thinks you so brilliant. Appearing at a party in my home, exposing yourself to public ridicule by seeking a medical degree? These are not the actions of a smart woman."

"I did not seduce John," she repeated doggedly.

"But he is completely enamored with you." Braddock shook his head. "Which is why I have brought you here for this little chat. Despite what you may think, I am not a murderer. I simply have a proposition to make."

"You'd best let me go," Abigail said in a suffocated voice. "The Lanieres will be looking for me. John will be looking for me."

Braddock raised his heavy brows. "I suppose he will. My son has never listened to wisdom. But if you'll listen to reason, he'll forget about you soon enough."

"He's going to destroy you," she said with certainty. She would have to enlist the help of Dr. Laniere to keep volatile, possessive John Braddock from sabotaging his career by exacting premature and violent justice against his father.

"No. No, I think not." Braddock tapped his fingertips against his lips. "Because you are going to accept my generous offer and disappear. I don't care where you go, as long as you keep your mouth shut and never again approach my son."

"Why on earth would I do that?" Abigail hissed. "You're insane."

"Oh, no, I'm in perfect command of my faculties." He smiled again. "And you'd best consider your response. As I told John, I've recently made a rather large loan to the medical school which would be jeopardized by any hint of scandal attached to my name."

"Your money is foul!" Abigail spat. "You made it in the course of farming and trading a narcotic that destroys people's lives. It ruined my mother! And you're shipping little girls overseas like cattle, trading them to brothels where they're exploited as prostitutes." She struggled against the ropes that bound her hands behind her back.

"There is no need to insult me." He sat back. "I made my money to take care of my family. I don't want them to endure the privations I did as a young man. And I certainly don't want my daughter soiling herself by associating with the likes of you. Which is another reason you must leave New Orleans. Lisette has become entirely too strong-minded since she met you."

"You cannot seriously expect me to just walk away from John and my chance to graduate from medical school." Abigail stared at him, panting. Should she tell him Dr. Laniere was onto him? Her skin felt like it was on fire. "No amount of money is worth—"

"I certainly do expect it. I cannot afford to lose such a valuable source of income as my opium trade." His voice had hardened, as if he'd suddenly tired of playing the paternal game. "And if you feel you cannot comply, you'll be sorry. I know where to find your father, and Crapaud would be most happy to bring his pathetic missionary efforts to a merciful close."

Chapter Twenty

John's body shook as he and Tess turned onto Canal Street, but he couldn't have said whether his tremors resulted from the cold wind whistling down the narrow deserted street or rather from his internal shock and anxiety for Abigail. Tess walked beside him, head bent, swallowed in John's great-coat. She'd been silent for several minutes, letting him absorb the story of Abigail's escape from China.

Escape? A violent shudder gripped him as he imagined the degradation, the privation his love had endured since she'd landed in the great United States of America. Forced to lie to a criminal, she'd buried herself in the seamy under-belly of New Orleans to escape whatever vengeance he would exact when he discovered she had no rich grandfa-ther. Six months of ten- to twelve-hour workdays, six days a week, to keep body and soul together, barely able to afford the paper-thin walls of a tenement room.

He glanced at Tess. God had indeed blessed Abigail with such a friend. There was something oddly refined in Tess's carriage; even her speech sometimes slipped into a cultured drawl not unlike John's own mother and sister.

He'd paid little attention to these details when she'd been a patient in the Laniere clinic; now he wondered that he'd managed to miss her beautiful white teeth—indicative of a healthy diet for most of her life—and the luxuriant reddish hair expertly twisted into a fashionable knot. The typical lifelong prostitute who worked in the District rarely took such pains with her appearance.

No wonder the two young women had been drawn to one another. When it came down to it, they were peas in a pod: resourceful, strong, loyal. It crossed his mind to wonder about Tess's faith in God. Had it survived hardship and persecution as had Abigail's? What about the father of her baby? Who was he and why had he abandoned her?

The questions flitted across his mind, but bled away in his concern for the woman he'd come to love more than life.

"Tess, do you think Doc Laniere will know what to do with this information? He knows my father about as well as anyone. Why do you suppose he hasn't noticed or confronted him about it?"

She shrugged without looking up. "You know the great doctor, John. Rich people like him—like you—don't always react the way you'd think they would."

What did she mean by that? He grabbed the sleeve of the coat dangling past her hands. "You said Abigail had come back for a journal that day. Did she take it home with her?"

"I don't remember—" Tess's gaze flicked over his shoulder, her eyes widened. "Look out! Run!" She took off.

A heavy body shoved John from behind and hurtled after Tess. Recovering his balance, John ran after the man, dove and tackled him. They fell heavily, John landing painfully on his left shoulder, but the other man quickly lurched to his feet. Rolling, John dodged a kick aimed at his kidney and jackknifed upright. He whirled to find his attacker plowing his round, bullfrog-shaped head straight for John's midsection. His father's agent, Crapaud.

John danced out of the way just in time. Too late to stop his forward momentum, the man staggered to his knees. John shoved him hard with a foot to the backside, but his opponent was more lithe than his stocky build would indicate. Grunting with pain, Crapaud flipped to his back, grabbed John's foot and threw him to the ground.

The breath knocked out of him, John lay unable to move, absorbing kick after kick aimed at ribs, face, groin. He could feel the warmth of blood pouring from his nose and mouth, pain taking over his body. The man was a bull, relentless.

But at least Tess was out of the way. Suddenly the beating stopped. John heard Crapaud's heaving breaths, even louder than his own, and a moment later, the snick of a knife coming out of a sheath. John was going to die here on the street, within blocks of the hospital. And Abigail was still in his father's hands.

He could not let that happen. Groaning, he tried to rise and protect himself. But before he could do more than shove himself to his knees, a blood-curdling rebel yell echoed along the street and running footsteps pounded toward him. He saw Crapaud's one good eye widen as he turned to look. Crapaud lunged with the knife, managing a swipe at John's upper arm before the new arrivals tackled him. John was crushed beneath the pile.

There was a confusing tangle of limbs and fists, cries of "Kill him!" "My turn!" and grunts of pain before John finally felt the melee roll off him into the gutter. Ears ringing, absorbed in pain, steadily losing blood, he simply let the battle rage. His vision went black around the edges until it overtook him, and still his thoughts, when he could grasp them, were on Abigail.

The blackness won.

She should have known John's father would be no weak pushover. Abigail had stared at Phillip Braddock long and hard, considering the consequences of each possible decision. She couldn't simply leave and overlook the things she knew about John's father. Besides, she had dropped enough hints to John about his father that there was every likelihood he'd already begun investigating. Once he discovered the truth, he would not keep quiet. On top of that, there were Dr. Laniere's suspicions to consider. He was not a man one could easily deceive.

On the other hand, telling what she knew would result in her father's execution. Papa might have been a less-than-stellar example of fatherhood; still she loved him too much to sign his death warrant.

The only thing left to do was to simply wait for rescue. So she remained stoically silent in the face of Phillip Braddock's blatant sneer.

Wait. The word now seemed to be the mantra of her life, when everything in her screamed for action. But the kind of waiting Scripture mandated involved the action of prayer: *Wait upon the Lord.* This she could do even while being gagged, rolled into a rug and unceremoniously hauled onto a man's shoulder. She could wait upon the Lord while being bundled into the frightening darkness of a closed carriage, tied hand and foot and barely able to breathe. While being tossed into a cart and transported, blinded and bruised, bumping along what smelled like the river levee, up and up a ramp onto the deck of a ship.

To be left utterly alone.

"Abigail," John muttered as a white canopy swam into his blurry vision. He blinked. The canopy shifted to reveal the creased forehead and crooked eyebrows of Miss Charlemagne. "I mean, Miss C."

She smiled and patted his shoulder. "Shush now." She dabbed a gauze pad soaked in iodine against his cheek. It stung like crazy and stank.

As he pushed to his elbows, pain radiated from his ribs throughout the length of his body. He looked around at the emergency ward at the back of the hospital. "How'd I get here?" Beyond the closed door, male voices clashed against the moderated tones of a nurse. That sounded like Weichmann and Girard.

Before she could answer, the door burst open and Girard's sandy head poked through the opening.

"Braddock—you're alive!" Girard, apparently wrestling with someone trying to restrain his entrance, spoke over his shoulder. "I'll be quiet. Mercy, what a fidget! We've got to find out what that rough-and-tumble was all about." He pushed into the room and shut the door behind him, obliterating nurse Wilhelmina's irate face. He hurried over to John and lifted his eyelid to examine the pupil. "Concussion. Lie down, old man, before you barf on my new waistcoat."

John ignored him, though he did indeed feel queasy. "I've got to go find Prof. Can you send Crutch to bring around a carriage? It'll be faster."

The nurse tsked. "I've already sent him after Dr.

Laniere. Someone responsible needs to know what's going on around here."

Girard shook his head. "You're not going anywhere with cracked ribs and your mouth split like the Grand Canyon. I had to stitch you back together once already. I'm not doing it again." He studied John's face critically. "Neat job, if I say so myself—fixed your pretty mug good as new. Maybe I'll start a whole practice, redoing people's faces."

John touched the stitches on his aching upper lip. He didn't care what he looked like as long as he found Abigail. "What happened to Crapaud—the man who attacked me?"

"With a name like that, no wonder he's so ugly. His ancestors must've worked long and hard to come up with a handle that means 'toad' and begins with—"

"What did you say?"

"I said it begins with—"

"No, the part about what it means."

Girard looked gleeful at the idea of one-upping John. "You and your languages. *Crapaud* is French for 'toad,' moron."

"No wonder—" More pieces fell into place. John's head reeled and not just from getting beaten to a bloody pulp. "My father's agent was Abigail's liaison getting out of China. Tess must have known that. That's why he went after her and beat me when I got in the way."

Girard planted a hand on John's chest and pushed him flat on the examining table. "You're raving. What's your father's agent got to do with Abigail? She hasn't been in China, she's been right here shoving her way into medical school. And who's Tess?"

"Never mind that." John knocked Girard's hand away and rolled to the side. Panting, he sat up. The room spun like a whirligig. "I've got to get to the professor and tell him…" The rest of his sentence split into shards of pain exploding through his head.

Girard grabbed his shoulders and kept him from falling off the table. "Idiot—"

"I'm here." The professor's authoritative voice cut through John's agony. "Tess said she and John were set upon." A pair of strong hands cupped John's head gently. "Let's get him back down, Girard. We've got to keep him awake."

John felt himself eased to his back again. "No, Professor, we have to look for Abigail," he mumbled. "I think my father took her somewhere. Crapaud will know where—"

"Crapaud's the scum who beat him up," said Girard. "Locked in the storage shed off the stable. Didn't know what else to do with him."

"All right, you boys get him, bring him here. We can't move John yet and I need to talk to both of them," Prof said. "Charlemagne, I've got the situation under control. Will you keep the other nurses out of the room and deal with any emergencies that arise?"

"Of course, sir."

A confusing series of footsteps ensued, the door opened and closed a couple of times and then John was alone with the professor.

"Braddock, are you lucid enough to listen to me for a moment?"

Thankfully, John's head had stopped its gyrations. He cracked one eye open and found Dr. Laniere staring at him, concern in every line of his face. "Yes, sir. What's going on, sir? I'm worried about Abigail. We can't wait around any longer—"

"Of course you're right. I had just gone home to tell you Abigail was nowhere to be found, when Tess barreled in, raving about an attacker. She's waiting outside the room in case we need her. Having heard her part of the·tale, I think I understand what's going on. But you'll be more helpful to me if you know a few more details of my part in this mess." Prof paused. "If you can follow me. Are you all right?"

John swallowed his nausea. "Yes, sir," he said through his teeth. "I'm fine."

"Good. Keep your eyes open and listen. My background is a little more complex than the typical medical professional. Since my youth I've been…assigned to government service. Although semiretired, I'd recently agreed to assist the governor with uncovering the source of shiploads of opium entering New Orleans illegally. You'll probably not be surprised to know your father was under suspicion—"

"No, sir. I'm not surprised."

"—which made you suspect as well. I'd set Abigail the task of watching for signs that you were involved." The professor sighed. "I didn't anticipate such violent results because I was not aware Abigail already had ties to your father's Chinese enterprises."

"I hope you know, Professor, I have nothing to do with my father's criminal activities." John anxiously surveyed his mentor's face.

Prof smiled faintly. "No, I don't suppose you'd be lying here on this table if you did. But I need to know anything that will help us find Abigail and stop your father's determined efforts to spread the scourge of drug addiction in America. It's already destroying China, and the empress is ready to declare war on anyone involved."

John pulled his whirling thoughts together. Prof was a

government agent. Abigail had been set to spy on him. He let out the breath he had been holding. "My father has a fleet of six ships that ply back and forth between New Orleans, Asia and Europe. I know he doesn't always report what he imports, which is how he avoids some of the heavier taxes. Until recently, I never saw the reason to report any of this—it really seemed to have nothing to do with me." He met Prof's eyes. "But now that I know the Lord, I seem to have a new set of eyes…or something. I can't just stand by and let him steamroll over everyone. I can't let him ruin innocent people's lives." Painful, embarrassing tears warmed his eyes, and he blinked hard. "I'm sorry he's my father."

Prof laid a hand on his shoulder. "We'll sort out all those feelings later, son. Right now, I'm grateful for your corroboration of what I'd suspected but couldn't prove."

The door opened, admitting Girard and Ramage, one on either side of Crapaud. The agent's hands were bound with a length of rope, his puffy face nearly unrecognizable. He had clearly been patched back together with less than the students' usual precision. The bandage which covered the top half of his head appeared to have been fashioned from his cravat and he winced every time one of his captors jerked on his arms. There was a large rip in the knee of his pants and most of his shirt buttons were missing.

John suddenly felt much better. This time he sat up slowly to avoid upsetting his head or his stomach. He still felt as if his brains might explode at any moment, but at least the room no longer spun. "What have you done with Abigail Neal?" He stared at Crapaud with loathing as John's friends shoved the man into a chair.

"You mean the Nieland girl?" The man sneered. "Ask your pa."

John glanced at Professor Laniere. "Do you know what he's talking about?"

Prof's expression stilled. "I hadn't considered that she might be under an assumed name." He walked around to stand behind Crapaud. "Is there something going on here besides smuggling?"

"I ain't telling you anything else until I know what's in it for me."

John had always thought of Crapaud as inarticulate and therefore not quite bright. Now he realized his father would never hire an agent who didn't possess a certain amount of diabolical cunning. "I'll make sure you're rewarded," he said, trying to prevent his tension from bleeding into his voice. One had to maintain a position of strength to influence this sort of man.

Crapaud didn't look impressed. "I happen to know every dime you possess depends on your pa's income. If he goes down, you go down." He shrugged. "You'll have to do better than that."

Professor Laniere suddenly clamped the muscle at the side of Crapaud's neck, near the collar bone. Crapaud yelped and Prof said silkily, "*You'll* have to do better than that if you want to avoid life in prison for kidnapping, extortion and slave trading. I imagine we can unearth a conviction for murder as well, if we look a little harder."

"Ow! Let go—All right, I'll talk. But I don't know where the girl is by now. When I left, Braddock—the elder one," he added with a contemptuous glance at John "—was trying to get out of her what she'd said to the red-headed gal."

Prof sent a warning look at John, who was getting ready

to launch himself off the table at the scoundrel. "The red-headed girl would be Tess?"

"Yeah."

"Where were you having this fascinating conversation?" Prof wandered around to Crapaud's side, his hands clasped behind his back as if they had all day. But John could see the tension tightening the corners of the doctor's mouth.

"The company owns a warehouse on the New Levee. We took her there."

"I see. I'm sure they're gone by now, but—Girard, take Ramage with you and see what you can find. Come back here to report." The two young men rushed out, leaving Weichmann protesting that he "wanted in on the fun," but Prof gestured for him to be quiet. "I may need you here. Patience. Crapaud, I want to know where Braddock is likely to have taken Miss Neal—Nieland."

Crapaud's ugly face scrunched. He paused. "Maybe a pardon?"

There was a thick, waiting silence in the examination room. John could literally feel every beat of his heart in the pulse of blood through his battered face. He watched Crapaud's still, crafty expression. *Please, Lord, give the professor wisdom. I want Abigail back. I want her safe.* He didn't give a flip whether she was an heiress or a seamstress in a sail loft. He just wanted another chance to tell her he loved her and wanted to spend his life with her.

"I don't have the authority to issue pardons," Prof said finally.

"I know where she is, Prof!" John slid off the table, heedless of bruised ribs and aching head. The mental picture of Abigail seated at a window overlooking the New

Orleans harbor, stitching grommets into a sail across her lap, had lit up his brain with sudden insight into his father's likely actions. When Phillip Braddock was cornered, he'd take to the sea. Appleton had told him tale after tale of his father as a young man, sailing off to the far corners of the world whenever the responsibilities of being husband and father got to be too much.

There were signs of it all over the house. John's chemistry set brought from Paris. The furniture from Egypt. The dining room chandelier from Germany. The Chinese silks for Lisette's dresses and the teas his mother loved so much. Only recently had he begun to slow down, when he'd taken on Crapaud as his agent.

John stalked toward the prisoner. "He took her to one of the ships, didn't he? That's the only place he could put her where no one could find her. We'd have searched all over the city and she'd be halfway to China." He snatched Crapaud by the front of his shirt and hauled him to his feet, heedless of his own screaming muscles. "Which one? Which ship is she on?"

"Hey!" Crapaud tried to wriggle free. "That's no way to treat a man who's just trying to help."

"I'll help you!" John shook him.

"Braddock." Prof set a hand on his shoulder. "Gently. I don't want you to hurt yourself."

Through a red haze John looked up at the professor, blinked and slowly released Crapaud, who sank back into his chair. Clenching his fists John scowled at the prisoner. "Where is she?"

"All right." Crapaud gulped. "The *China Doll*. That's the one he had ready to sail in the morning."

John looked at the professor, triumphant. "Can we send

Weichmann and the Sears boys to search the others in port? Just in case he's lying?"

Prof nodded. "That's an excellent suggestion."

John looked at the other three students. "That would be the *White Pearl* and the *Dancing Dutchman*." He jerked his head toward the door. "Go."

Weichmann ran, leaving John and Dr. Laniere to haul Crapaud back to his storage room prison. They locked him in, instructed Crutch to guard the door, and headed for the levee. John limped along beside the professor, thinking it was high time he started carrying a gun or at least a walking stick. A man never knew when he was going have to play knight-errant.

Chapter Twenty-One

Abigail had no idea how long she had been left bound and gagged in the hold of the ship as it rocked gently at its moorings. Perhaps hours. She slept for a while and woke up astonished at her body's ability to relax when fear had her mind in a vise. She lay encased in the warmth of the rug—at least she could be grateful not to be cold and wet. She had managed to wriggle to the edge, so that the top of her head was in the open and she could breathe freely through her nose, but could go no farther. The buckle of her shoe had caught on a strand of the rug and because her hands were tied, she could not free herself.

Realizing the discomfort of her stomach was actually hunger, she listened for activity in other parts of the ship. She hoped someone would bring her something to eat soon. Random screeches of chains and the bangs of hatches opening and closing alternated with the voices of sailors preparing to set sail. The growl of hunger turned to the acid of terror. Phillip Braddock wasn't going to be interested in feeding a woman who refused to cave in to his demands. He was more likely to make shark bait out of her.

But the fact that he'd stuffed her down here, hiding her even from the sailors, told her he had some use for her. Where was he planning to take her? His ships went all over the world. Once they sailed into the Gulf of Mexico, John would never find her.

Sudden despair overcame the optimism with which she'd forced herself to pray since the Toad had thrown her into that carriage. Had God abandoned her after all?

A few minutes of helpless and perfectly useless tears, which served only to clog her head and make her eyes puffy, left her spent. And determined not to give up. The ship's hold was darker than she'd imagined a place could be, but she closed her eyes anyway. She might be alone, but in her helplessness she knew God's presence in a powerful and sustaining way.

She didn't know how much longer she lay there before a shaft of light pierced the darkness. Her eyes flew open, and she tried to scream against the gag but only succeeded in straining her throat muscles. Ineffectually she struggled in the suffocating binding of the rug. Footsteps descended the ladder behind her head. Was someone coming to release her? Or was it one of Braddock's men?

Oh, Lord Jesus, please, please, please. I'm here…

"Abigail?"

John! she screamed inside her head. *I'm here!*

"I can't see anything below the stairs, Prof. I'm going on down."

"I'll take the other deck," answered Professor Laniere. "She could be anywhere. Look inside every barrel, every chest. There's no telling where he put her."

"Maybe we should've looked for him first. Made him tell us what he did with her." John sounded anxious, frustrated.

The very fact that he'd come looking for her sent waves of joy coursing through Abigail in spite of her discomfort. Again she screamed against the rag between her teeth. Maybe a slight sound had issued from her sore throat.

Facing upward, Abigail couldn't see John, but his footsteps had stopped near the bottom of the ladder. The lamplight swayed wildly back and forth across Abigail's forehead, making her eyes water.

"Abigail? Are you down here somewhere? Sweetheart, can you make some kind of noise so I'll know where you are?"

Sobbing silently, she gave a great sniff through her nose.

And the light poured across her face as John lunged toward her. "The rug! Oh, God, thank You!" He set the lamp down and laid his hands on the top of her head, petting her hair and laying his cheek against her forehead. "Be still, beloved, I'm going to get you out of here. Hold on, I love you, don't cry…"

It seemed to take him forever to untie the ropes around the rug—his hands shook so he couldn't manage the knots at first—and unroll her from her soft, warm prison. When she finally saw his face, her eyes widened in horror. He looked as if he'd been in a bar brawl. His nose was swollen and slightly off-center, and a series of stitches held his upper lip together. But as he regained his composure, he managed to unknot the gag.

"Are you hurt?" He worked on the ropes around her wrists. "What did he do to you?"

"I'm all right, just scared and hungry." The cotton texture of her lips and tongue made the words awkward. "John, I love you." She began to cry again. The tears seemed to proceed from a bottomless well of relief and terror. "I love you so much."

"Shh. Shh." He kissed her gently in deference to his broken mouth, and some of his natural humor asserted itself. "Jiminy, you're salty." When she laughed, he kissed her again and went back to work on her wrists. "Never mind, I'll have you free in just a minute."

"I'm already free." She threw her arms around his neck. "Praise God, we're both free."

"I think you should definitely go home to Mobile." Abigail held Tess's eyes steadily across the Lanieres' breakfast table. "You've waited far too long."

It was Tuesday morning, and the two of them lingered over coffee while Camilla hustled the children together for school. Baby Meg sat in Abigail's lap, sucking her thumb and shaking a rattle made of spools strung on a length of yarn.

Tess looked away from the baby's sweet face. She had only consented to stay overnight because John had convinced her Abigail shouldn't sleep alone last night—trauma and all that. But Abigail suspected that deep down, Tess wanted someone to convince her that she was done with life in the District, as Abigail was. It had just taken her a little longer to come to the sticking point.

"Abby, not everybody deserves a happy ending like you." Tess's voice was low, embarrassed. "They're not going to welcome me with open arms, you know. I was a selfish brat and took everything my father would give me before I left. I offended everybody who loved me, and—and I'd had another baby before the one who died in October. He's growing up with another family."

Abigail brushed her hand across the top of the baby's soft head. "Well, you won't know unless you go find out. You start by apologizing and asking forgiveness."

Tess's eyes flashed to Abigail's face. "Who forgives like that? It's too much to ask!"

"God forgives like that!" Abigail insisted. "You remind me a lot of the prodigal in Jesus's story. His father was waiting for him to come back. Saw him from a long way off and *ran* to get him!" She smiled. "That's you and me. We were both a long way off and needed to come home."

Tess didn't look convinced. "You never did what I've done. People did evil things to you, and you stayed pure."

Abigail sighed. "Oh, Tess. If you just knew how bitter and angry I was for so long. How I hated John Braddock for having everything I wanted."

"That didn't last long," Tess said wryly. "You were drooling over him the minute he took off that fancy coat and flexed his muscles."

"I was not!" Abigail hid her face in Meg's neck, blowing against her skin to make the baby giggle. She peeked and met Tess's laughing eyes. "But I admit he makes my knees weak now. Even with ten stitches holding his face together."

Tess laughed. "Looks like the stitches got him the day off from school. I see a couple of black-and-blue eyes peering through the window." She rose and went through the clinic to open the back door. "Come in, Sir Lancelot. Guinevere's dying to see you."

John followed Tess back into the kitchen. He pulled off his hat and coat and tossed them at a coat rack in the corner. His bruised eyes were on Abigail. "Tess, Meg looks like she needs her nappy changed."

Tess rolled her eyes. "I've never seen two people more in need of a chaperone than you. But I won't tell if you won't." She took the baby from Abigail's lap. "Come on, sweetums, let's go see what your mama's doing." She sashayed toward the hallway leading to the stairs, calling over her shoulder, "I'll be back in five minutes!"

Abigail smiled but instantly lost track of anything but John, who lifted her to her feet and gathered her close. She nestled her cheek against his wool coat, relishing the feel of his arms around her, the masculine smell of outdoors and strong soap. "Good morning," she murmured. "I was hoping you would come by."

"Prof told me I could sleep in this morning—in fact, he told me he'd suspend me if I showed my face before Wednesday— said I'd scare the patients if I came in the wards looking like this." He tipped up her chin and studied her face as if she were a rare and precious treasure. "Do I scare you?"

She couldn't help laughing. Besides the stitched lip and the shiner, his handsome nose now had a distinct sideways bend at the arch. "You make me want to stand on the table and dance."

"The dignified Miss Neal? I'd like to see it."

"Miss Nieland," she reminded him, sobering. She looked down at the waistcoat button she was twisting. "I'm sorry I lied to you."

John stilled her hand, covering it with his. "I understand why you did. And I'm sorry for all the tragedy my father's actions caused you." He hesitated. "In a lot of ways, we're going to have to start over getting to know one another."

Abigail pressed closer to him. "What's going to happen to your father?"

"He's been arrested and charged with trafficking in illegal narcotics. There's no telling what else they'll find in the investigation. My mother—" He swallowed. "My mother's taking it very hard. No matter what, she loves him. Abigail, I hate this for her and for Lisette."

"I know," Abigail whispered. "I'm so sorry."

"And I don't know how I'm going to finish school, with this hanging over my head. I suppose I shouldn't worry, but I…"

When he didn't finish, she looked up at him. "What?"

He looked a bit sheepish. "I don't have any business even thinking about it. But there's this beautiful woman I would like to court…and I'm afraid she won't even look at the penniless son of a convicted felon."

"Well…" Abigail's already-racing heart began to gallop. "Perhaps if you reminded her that you have a most out-standing academic record at the most prestigious medical college in the South, and that you stand to become a very rich and sought-after surgeon, she might consent to listen to your suit."

"Perhaps." A smile tugged at John's ruined mouth. "Do you think it would help to offer my services as a dissec-tion lab assistant? I mean, supposing she decides to continue with her own medical degree?"

"I can think of nothing more romantic than a midnight tryst in the morgue." Abigail giggled. "And I'm fairly positive she means to continue her medical school adven-ture. What a waste to throw away all that effort!"

John pounced and kissed her, letting out a small yelp of pain at the pressure on his lip. He let her go reluctantly. "Drat." He fingered the cut. "How long does it take for these things to heal?"

"Probably longer if you keep opening it like that." She pushed at his chest. "Tess will be back in a minute. You sit there—" she pointed at the bench on the opposite side of the table—"and I'll sit here." Slipping out of his arms, she seated herself, primly clasping her hands in her lap.

For a moment he stared at her, smiling, eyes on fire. "Oh, all right. If you're going to be all proper." He reached across the table, palms up, and she laid her hands in his. "What about your father? Are you going to try to contact him?"

Abigail looked away. "I don't know. He wounded me terribly. I don't know that I need a father anymore."

"Abigail." John's voice was tender. "Family matters."

She stared at him fiercely. "*You'll* be my family. Tess is my family. Even Camilla and Prof. Not a man who tried to get rid of me for his own convenience."

"We're both going to have to practice forgiveness." John kissed her hand. "I will if you will."

She smiled at him, a fresh wave of tenderness and gratitude washing over her. "That's a bargain, Dr. Braddock."

Epilogue

❧

"Dr. Braddock, you're wanted in the children's ward."

Abigail, seated at the desk in the second-floor nurse's office, looked up from her task of recording the injuries and subsequent treatment of a young woman admitted to the hospital this morning after a riding accident. John's handsome head peered around the half-open door. She gave her husband a vague smile. "Is it an emergency? I need to finish this report while it's fresh in my mind."

John slipped inside and shut the door behind him. "Of sorts. The McLachlin boy hid my otoscope and won't tell where he put it unless the *pretty doctor* comes to listen in his ears." He shoved her papers aside and sat on the corner of the desk near her elbow. "And I can hardly blame him," he whispered, leaning down to kiss the corner of her mouth.

"John! Anybody could come in here!" But she briefly yielded to his warm mouth, thrilled all over again at the knowledge she and John belonged to each other in every sense of the word. She pulled back and touched her thumb to the white scar across his upper lip, a testament to his devotion. "Oh, Dr. Braddock. You are a serious distraction."

Six months of marriage had not erased her wonder at God's provision for their every need. Even after John's graduation last May, which made him a fully licensed surgeon, they'd both had to work and sacrifice to afford Abigail's tuition. But somehow they'd made it, and Abigail herself would graduate tonight.

"I love you, Abigail," he murmured, cupping her face, "and I don't care if the whole world knows." He grinned. "But would you please come help me find my otoscope?"

Author's Note

This book required extensive research into the history of medical education in the latter half of the nineteenth century, particularly that of the Tulane University Medical Center, which in 1879 was the medical department of the University of Louisiana. I wanted to take advantage of the exciting advances being made in the medical profession during that year, so for the purposes of the story I veered from actual history by predating the entrance of the first woman into the medical school in New Orleans by sixteen years. Mrs. Elizabeth Rudolph was the first woman conferred the degree of Master of Pharmacy from Tulane University in 1895 (she had actually completed the two-year course in 1890 but was not allowed to graduate). Not until the 1915-16 school year were women admitted to all classes on an equal basis with men. Linda Hill Coleman of Houston, Texas, was the first woman to graduate from Tulane with a medical degree (John Duffy, *The Tulane University Medical Center*, Baton Rouge: LSU Press, 1984. 84-85, 136).

The New Orleans red light district was a real place

known simply as "the District." Early in the next century, it temporarily became a legally sanctioned region of prostitution known as "Storyville" (Duffy). I have tried to stay true to historic names of streets and streetcar lines. Because maps from that era are a bit blurry, it's possible that I've misspelled some names. For that I apologize in advance. On another note: to avoid defamation-of-character issues, I changed the names of all the professors at the medical college and created my own. There are no real historical figures used as characters, except those mentioned in the context of medical backstory (for example, when the students recount the development of surgical techniques and disease theory, and the mention of Elizabeth Blackwell's admission to medical school in New York). Charity Hospital was the university's teaching hospital and was fully staffed by Catholic nuns.

With regard to historical details, besides the Duffy book, I relied heavily on *New Orleans' Charity Hospital* by John Salvaggio, M.D. (Baton Rouge: LSU Press, 1993); *Antique Medical Instruments* by C. Keith Wilbur, M.D. (Atglen, PA: Schiffer Publishing Ltd., 1987); and *Bring Us a Lady Physician*, by Ruth Abram (New York: W. W. Norton & Co., 1985). I am also indebted to a December 2000 interview with Dr. Sam Eichold of Mobile. Dr. Eichold founded the medical museum associated with the University of South Alabama Medical School. He was most generous with his time, experience and resources.

For early critique help I would like to thank my usual partners in crime, Tammy T. and Sheri. Because it was the thesis for my creative writing master's program, this book also underwent the rigors of a most talented group of fellow graduate students. Alyson, Marylyn, Jeannie and

Tammy S—you challenged and encouraged me, and I'm looking forward to seeing your work in print one day. I'd also like to mention my University of South Alabama thesis committee, whose feedback strengthened the manuscript immeasurably: Dr. Sue Walker, Dr. James Aucoin and the inimitable Carolyn Haines, thesis director extraordinaire. Finally, kudos to my editor, Emily Rodmell. You're the best!

Dear Reader,

Crescent City Courtship was conceived as a sequel to *Redeeming Gabriel*, but the protagonists, John and Abigail, quickly endeared themselves to me in their own right. Abigail's determination to overcome her bizarre and painful childhood has challenged me to look for God's work even in difficult circumstances. Creating a young man like John, who begins as a privileged and single-minded scientist and develops into a man of compassion and tenderness, was an adventure in self-discovery. Sometimes, like John, I get so focused on the task at hand that I can overlook the basic human needs of people around me. Praise God that He pursues us and draws us to himself, not allowing us to stay the same!

I pray that you, my friend, will listen for the Father's voice as well, and that you will find ever-present help in times of trouble.

In God's grace,

Beth White

QUESTIONS FOR DISCUSSION

1. At what point does John begin to pay attention to God's voice? What holds him back from complete surrender to God?

2. What about Abigail? What was at the root of her resentment toward God?

3. Discuss things in your own life that keep you from trusting God.

4. Think about Abigail's yearning for a medical education in a time when women were not allowed to attend medical school. Is there something in your life that doesn't seem fair? What steps would you take to get what you want?

5. John's greatest lesson was humility. Discuss some scenes in the story that show him struggling with it. Do you think he was successful in learning it? Why or why not?

6. The story takes place in 1879, several years after the Civil War. What evidence do you find in the story that racial conditions had improved or deteriorated? Do you find Abigail's friendship with Winona believable? Why or why not?

7. Abigail took a big risk by fleeing China. Was she smart to do that? What would you have done in her shoes?

8. Discuss the conversation between John and Abigail in Chapter Three. Why do you think God allows doctors to heal some patients and not others?

9. What do you think about John's friends, Weichmann and Girard? Of the two, who has the greater influence on John? What does the Bible say about the company we keep?

10. Why did Abigail feel like a "freak"? In what ways do you identify with her? How did her experiences in medical school change her?

11. What do you think about Dr. Laniere's teaching techniques? Did he come on too strong about his faith? Did he hold back more than he should have?

12. John and Professor Laniere have several conversations about the relationship between medicine and faith. Discuss how the two elements intertwine in the story.

13. In marriage relationships, men and women often compromise for each other. How do John and Abigail change one another in the course of the story?

14. Have you ever been misjudged by someone? How did you feel about that? What did you do to correct the person's impression of you?

15. In the end, John and Abigail were working at the same hospital. Do you think it's good for a husband and wife to work together? Why or why not?

When a tornado strikes a small Kansas town, Maya
Logan sees a new, tender side of her serious boss.
Could a family man be lurking beneath Greg
Garrison's gruff exterior?

Turn the page for a sneak preview of their story in
HEALING THE BOSS'S HEART
by Valerie Hansen,
Book 1 in the new six-book
AFTER THE STORM *miniseries*
available beginning July 2009 from Love Inspired®.

Maya Logan had been watching the skies with growing concern and already had her car keys in hand when she jerked open the door to the office to admit her boss. He held a young boy in his arms. "Get inside. Quick!"

Gregory Garrison thrust the squirming child at her. "Here. Take him. I'm going back after his dog. He refused to come in out of the storm without Charlie."

"Don't be ridiculous." She clutched his arm and pointed. "You'll never catch him. Look." Tommy's dog had taken off running the minute the hail had started.

Debris was swirling through the air in ever-increasing amounts and the hail had begun to pile in lumpy drifts along the curb. It had flattened the flowers she'd so lovingly placed in the planters and buried their stubbly remnants under inches of white, icy crystals.

In the distance, the dog had its tail between its legs and was disappearing into the maelstrom. Unless the frightened animal responded to commands to return, there was no chance of anyone catching up to it.

Gregory took a deep breath and hollered, "Char-lie," but

Maya could tell he was wasting his breath. The soggy mongrel didn't even slow.

"Take the boy and head for the basement," Gregory yelled at her. Ducking inside, he had to put his shoulder to the heavy door and use his full weight to close and latch it.

She shoved Tommy back at him. "No. I have to go get Layla."

"In this weather? Don't be an idiot."

"She's my daughter. She's only three. She'll be scared to death if I'm not there."

"She's in the preschool at the church, right? They'll take care of the kids."

"No. I'm going after her."

"Use your head. You can't help Layla if you get yourself killed." He grasped her wrist, holding tight.

Maya struggled, twisting her arm till it hurt. "Let me go. I'm going to my baby. She's all I've got."

"That's crazy! A tornado is coming. If the hail doesn't knock you out cold, the tornado's likely to bury you."

"I don't care."

"Yes, you do."

"No, I don't! Let go of me." To her amazement, he held fast. No one, especially a man, was going to treat her this way and get away with it. No one.

"Stop. Think," he shouted, staring at her as if she were deranged.

She continued to struggle, to refuse to give in to his will, his greater strength. "No. *You* think. I'm going to my little girl. That's all there is to it."

"How? Driving?" He indicated the street, which now looked distorted due to the vibrations of the front window.

"It's too late. Look at those cars. Your head isn't half as hard as that metal is and it's already full of dents."

"But…"

She knew in her mind that he was right, yet her heart kept insisting she must do something. Anything. *Please, God, help me. Tell me what to do!*

Her heart was still pounding, her breath shallow and rapid, yet part of her seemed to suddenly accept that her boss was right. That couldn't be. She belonged with Layla. She was her mother.

"We're going to take shelter," Gregory ordered, giving her arm a tug. "Now."

That strong command was enough to renew Maya's resolve and wipe away the calm assurances she had so briefly embraced. She didn't go easily or quietly. Screeching, "No, no, no," she dragged her feet, stumbling along as he pulled and half dragged her toward the basement access.

Staring into the storm moments ago, she had felt as if the fury of the weather was sucking her into a bottomless black hole. Her emotions were still trapped in those murky, imaginary depths, still floundering, sinking, spinning out of control. She pictured Layla, with her silky, long dark hair and beautiful brown eyes.

"If anything happens to my daughter I'll never forgive you!" she screamed at him.

"I'll take my chances."

Maya knew without a doubt that she'd meant exactly what she'd said. If her precious little girl was hurt she'd never forgive herself for not trying to reach her. To protect her. And she'd never forgive Gregory Garrison for preventing her from making the attempt. *Never.*

She had to blink to adjust to the dimness of the basement

as he shoved her in front of him and forced her down the wooden stairs.

She gasped, coughed. The place smelled musty and sour, totally in character with the advanced age of the building. How long could that bank of brick and stone stores and offices stand against a storm like this? If these walls ever started to topple, nothing would stop their total collapse. Then it wouldn't matter whether they were outside or down here. They'd be just as dead.

That realization sapped her strength and left her almost without sensation. When her boss let go of her wrist and slipped his arm around her shoulders to guide her into a corner next to an abandoned elevator shaft, she was too emotionally numb to continue to fight him. All she could do was pray and continue to repeat, "Layla, Layla," over and over again.

"We'll wait it out here," he said. "This has to be the strongest part of the building."

Maya didn't believe a word he said.

Tommy's quiet sobbing, coupled with her soul-deep concern for her little girl, brought tears to her eyes. She blinked them back, hoping she could control her emotions enough to fool the boy into believing they were all going to come through the tornado unhurt.

As for her, she wasn't sure. Not even the tiniest bit. All she could think about was her daughter. *Dear Lord, are You watching out for Layla? Please, please, please! Take care of my precious little girl.*

* * * * *

See the rest of Maya and Greg's story when
HEALING THE BOSS'S HEART
hits the shelves in July 2009.
And be sure to look for all six of the books
in the AFTER THE STORM series,
where you can follow the residents of High Plains,
Kansas, as they rebuild their town—
and find love in the process.

Love Inspired

Maya Logan has always thought of her boss, Greg Garrison, as a hard-nosed type of guy. But when a tornado strikes their small Kansas town, Greg is quick to help however he can, including rebuilding her home. Maya soon discovers that he's building a home for them to share.

Look for

Healing the Boss's Heart

by

Valerie Hansen

Available July wherever books are sold.

www.SteepleHill.com

Steeple Hill®

Love Inspired.
HISTORICAL
INSPIRATIONAL HISTORICAL ROMANCE

Actress Hannah Southerland's work is unseemly, but her loyalties are strong. When her sister Rachel foolishly elopes, Hannah is determined to bring her home—even joining forces with Reverend Beau O'Toole, brother of Rachel's paramour. Beau wants a traditional wife, which Hannah is not. But this unconventional woman could be his ideal partner—in life and in faith.

Look for

Hannah's Beau

by

RENEE RYAN

Available July wherever books are sold.

Steeple Hill®

LIH82816

REQUEST YOUR FREE BOOKS!

2 FREE INSPIRATIONAL NOVELS
PLUS 2
FREE
MYSTERY GIFTS

Love Inspired.
HISTORICAL
INSPIRATIONAL HISTORICAL ROMANCE

YES! Please send me 2 FREE Love Inspired® Historical novels and my 2 FREE mystery gifts (gifts are worth about $10). After receiving them, if I don't wish to receive any more books, I can return the shipping statement marked "cancel". If I don't cancel, I will receive 4 brand-new novels every other month and be billed just $4.24 per book in the U.S. or $4.74 per book in Canada. That's a savings of over 20% off the cover price. It's quite a bargain! Shipping and handling is just 50¢ per book.* I understand that accepting the 2 free books and gifts places me under no obligation to buy anything. I can always return a shipment and cancel at any time. Even if I never buy another book, the two free books and gifts are mine to keep forever. 102 IDN EYPS 302 IDN EYP4

Name   (PLEASE PRINT)

Address   Apt. #

City   State/Prov.   Zip/Postal Code

Signature (if under 18, a parent or guardian must sign)

Mail to Steeple Hill Reader Service:
IN U.S.A.: P.O. Box 1867, Buffalo, NY 14240-1867
IN CANADA: P.O. Box 609, Fort Erie, Ontario L2A 5X3
Not valid to current subscribers of Love Inspired Historical books.

Want to try two free books from another series?
Call 1-800-873-8635 or visit www.morefreebooks.com

* Terms and prices subject to change without notice. Prices do not include applicable taxes. Sales tax applicable in N.Y. Canadian residents will be charged applicable provincial taxes and GST. Offer not valid in Quebec. This offer is limited to one order per household. All orders subject to approval. Credit or debit balances in a customer's account(s) may be offset by any other outstanding balance owed by or to the customer. Please allow 4 to 6 weeks for delivery. Offer available while quantities last.

Your Privacy: Steeple Hill Books is committed to protecting your privacy. Our Privacy Policy is available online at www.SteepleHill.com or upon request from the Reader Service. From time to time we make our lists of customers available to reputable third parties who may have a product or service of interest to you. If you would prefer we not share your name and address, please check here. ☐

LIH09

Love Inspired.
HISTORICAL

TITLES AVAILABLE NEXT MONTH
Available July 14, 2009

LOVE THINE ENEMY by Louise Gouge
The tropics of colonial Florida are far from America's revolution. Still, Rachel Folger is loyal to Boston's patriots while handsome plantation owner Frederick Moberly is faithful to the Crown. For the sake of harmony, he hides his sympathies until a betrayal divides the pair, leaving Frederick to harness his faith and courage to claim the woman he loves.

HANNAH'S BEAU by Renee Ryan
Actress Hannah Southerland's work is unseemly, but her loyalties are strong. When her sister Rachel foolishly elopes, Hannah's determined to bring her home—even joining forces with Reverend Beau O'Toole, brother of Rachel's paramour. Beau wants a traditional wife, which Hannah is not. But this unconventional woman could be his ideal partner—in life and in faith.